A Mansion for the Spirits of the Just

A Mansion for the Spirits of the Just

A MEMOIR OF LOVE, COURAGE AND LOSS IN THE GREAT WAR

J C Alexander

with the letters, writings and Field Diary of

Capt Francis H Lawless D.S.O.

The Kings Liverpool Regiment 1914-1919

Publication Information
Copyright © 2017 J C Alexander & Capt Francis H Lawless D.S.O.
All rights reserved.
Cocidius Books

ISBN: 0995701709
ISBN 13: 9780995701700

About this book

A MANSION FOR THE SPIRITS of the Just is a work of creative non-fiction. It follows the true story of the life of a single soldier from the Liverpool Pals Battalions during the Great War and beyond. Letters from the Front and an adjutant's field diary, recording one week of war during the German advances in the spring of 1918, written by Captain Francis Henry Lawless D.S.O. survive and are given verbatim here. I have set Frank's words within the context of a novel, based on incidences of his and his wife Hillie's life, which have been handed down and reimagined by me. Historical notes are interleaved between episodes of their life together, as are my own thoughts and feelings as I followed Frank and Hillie's footsteps from Liverpool, London, Flanders and the Western Front, Scotland, Shropshire and finally to Naples.

Frank, as was common to soldiers, tried to shield his loved ones from the horrors of the war and I have followed his lead here. Many others have attempted to record the disgusting brutality of the conflict better than I could. What I have tried to convey is the courage and personal and emotional sacrifice of one young couple, amongst so many of their time.

Any historical errors are my own but my sincere thanks are due to the following;

Nicky Melville for his early encouragement and editorial help; Ann Coburn for her wise mentoring and support; My sisters, Sarah for reading and commenting on the text and Sue for being the custodian of Frank's letters and plays in recent years; My cousin Carmel, who shared the letters and photographs sent by Frank to his brother Charlie in Canada; My cousin

Alan Stopani for help with genealogy research; Dr Janet Hollinshead for researching the War Memorial bearing Frank's name at the Church of The Annunciation, Bishop Eaton Liverpool

Finally and most importantly my loving thanks to my husband Jim, for his support of all my writing projects and going with me to Naples, helping me find Frank's grave and visiting Posillipo.

J C A

A Mansion for the Spirits of the Just

J C Alexander

With the letters, writing and Field Diary of

Capt Francis H Lawless D.S.O.

The King's Liverpool Regiment 1914-1919

Prologue

A Mansion for the Spirits of the Just

IF THERE IS ANY MANSION for the spirits of the just, if, as philosophers hold, great souls do not perish with the body, may you rest in peace! May you call us, your family, from feeble regrets and unmanly mourning to contemplate your virtues, for which it were a sin to mourn or lament! May we honour you in better ways —by our admiration and our praise, and, if our powers permit, by following your example. That is the true honour, the true affection, of souls knit close to yours. To your daughter and widow I would suggest that they revere the memory of a father and husband by continually pondering his deeds and sayings, and by treasuring in their hearts the form and features of his mind, rather than those of his body. Representations of the human face, like that face itself, are subject to decay and dissolution, whereas the essence of a man's mind is something everlasting. All that we loved and admired in Agricola abides and shall abide in the hearts of men through endless procession of the ages: for his achievements are of great renown. With many it will be as with men who had no name or fame; they will be buried in oblivion. But Agricola's story is set on record for posterity, and he will live.

Tacitus, The Agricola

Finding Frank

Edinburgh 2014

Dear Frank

I hope you won't mind my calling you Frank and not Grandfather. I never knew you as Grandfather and you sign yourself Frank so that is the person I have come to know. This is my second letter; I wrote the first at your graveside in Italy, tears streaming, for an unknown man whose life ended, like so many of his generation, prematurely. I tried to tell you about your child, who became my mother, your grandchildren, great grandchildren and now even great-great grandchildren.

Now I want to tell them about you. I want to tell them more than the brief description of a man documented in your Service Records;

Age at enlistment 23 years and 7 months
Height Five foot eleven and three quarter inches
Hair Brown
Eyes Grey
Complexion Clear
Distinguishing marks or scars None
Occupation Shipping clerk

I want them to know of your talents, achievements, joys and sorrows, what kind of man you really were.

I hope you will not mind that I have read your letters. I know you wanted your other writings published, and the written record you left, of part of your war, is short but intense. Each man's experience of war is his own within the greater theatre. His battles, wounds, friends and comrades, acts of courage and moments of fear are personal to him

I think it is the same with love. Each couple experience their own level of romance and intensity of feeling. They share hopes and ambitions for the future and communicate in intimate and deeply personal ways. In war perhaps that intensity becomes almost unbearable.

I have tried to get to know you both through your writings and make a record of your valour and also your love. I will use your own voice where ever I can, but when I can't, forgive me if I use my own instead.

I honour your bravery but I wish that I had had the chance to know you. You believed in freedom and honour and died for your beliefs.

I would like yours and Hillie's sacrifice to be remembered, even after all these years.

J

LONDON JULY 1913

There are days, unexpected days, that creep up and something about them changes the course of lives. Frank Lawless had no idea that this day was one of those as he idled away his time on the quay, waiting for the letters, packages and small items of valuable cargo he had been sent to collect, to be unloaded. There was no point going back up to town, he thought, just to come back later in the day, he would have to wait it out here at the docks until the bag entrusted to him was handed over. He would use the time to watch the world, hone his writer's eye, and make mental notes for use in some yet to be written play or story.

The day was warm and he preferred to keep back from the water's edge because of the smell. Dead rats, their attendant cats, litter, and bilge water rose to the surface on a summer's day producing a noxious and unappetising soup. He sauntered along, scuffing small stones and poking occasional bits of paper with his toe to while away the time. There were porters to watch, heaving trunks and heavy leather suitcases, expertly balancing them on handcarts and trollies. There were stevedores climbing and shouting, dogs sniffing the crates and boxes stacked up on the quayside waiting to be carted away. Seagulls wheeled and called above the noise of the dockyard. The scene was lively enough but generally, he liked to look at the ships.

Shipping was in his blood. His company, The White Star Line, had ships on the Atlantic run and Frank was beginning to long to travel further afield or talk to those whose travel he considered more exotic. Nonetheless he remained deeply grateful that he hadn't asked for a passage on *Titanic* the previous year, despite the temptation of visiting New York.

Today the docks were busy, and he walked around to look at a Japanese steamer, the *SS Miyazaki Maru*, newly arrived from the Far East. He calculated her tonnage, the number of passengers she might carry, considered her ports of call. Yokohama certainly, then maybe Shanghai, Hong Kong, Macau, Singapore before heading to London, perhaps with a stop in Bombay.

The passengers from the *SS Miyazaki Maru* were beginning to disembark and his eye was caught by a family group heading down the first class gangway. There was a mother, seemingly the only adult, with three children, two girls and a small boy.

Frank watched with amusement as the little lad hopped and sprung his way down the gangway, swinging on the guard rails, tipping perilously close to the water. As he reached the quay he was like a spring uncoiled, waiting to bounce into action. Frank wondered how he would have felt at the age of seven if he had been confined to a ship for six or seven weeks, no wonder the child had cabin fever.

As the group descended and porters arrived with boxes and cabin baggage and clustered around the mother and girls, the small boy took the very first opportunity he could to stretch his legs and began to run, back and forth, between two stacks of crates piled up on the dockside. His legs were unsteady on first hitting land after weeks at sea and he wobbled slightly as he ran. The boy's mother was completely occupied dealing with porters and luggage but Frank suddenly heard the older girl yell,

'Alan, get down from there this second!'

The little fellow was clambering up onto the stacked crates, each crate a step in a crazy pyramid, unyielding and slippery, but also, Frank realized, inherently unstable and dangerously close to the dockside. The child, intent on becoming King of the Castle was blissfully unaware of his own danger. Both the boy and the crates began to teeter at the same moment. The girl started to run towards her brother, screeching his name, but Frank was quicker and taller, and using every advantage of his stride reached the boy first. He felt the lower crates start to move as he leaned forward, arms at maximum extension and muscles taut. He battled the moving mass of loaded crates as splinters of plywood tore into his lower arm and he caught his chest against a metal covered corner. Finally, after several moments when time seemed suspended in the slow motion movement of the stack and child towards the water, he felt his fingers close around a tiny ankle. He grasped, grasped with all the strength he had, to ensure that gravity and churning crates did not rob him of his prize. The boy was shrieking in fear and Frank's brain wanted to shriek too, but his hands and arms fought on, securing his hold. His own body, acting as a counter weight, gradually slowed the falling pile and the struggling child. The child's ankle was so slender Frank's entire hand encircled it and he could feel his own finger nails embedded in the base of his thumb.

Securing the first ankle in one hand he reached for the other, and edged him backwards until he finally felt secure enough to trust the fabric of the child's trousers and yank him in by the belt. He reeled the terrified boy in like some struggling fish on a long line and finally pulled him to his chest and away from what remained of the stack of crates. God, dear God, he thought, thank you, I never want to see a dead child. Peering at the water he saw the boy's white sailor hat floating amongst the crates and filthy detritus of the dockland water.

Frank checked him for major injury, but once he was assured there was none, he lifted the now sobbing boy into a more conventional hold and with a gentle 'shush, shush now, you are fine, only a few splinters and bruises.' He carried the boy towards his mother and sisters, and set him down at their feet.

The whole party were stunned by how close they had come to disaster, and the mother, as mothers often do when a catastrophe has just been averted, began to scold her child for running away. His sisters were just crying with relief. For all his outward bravado and calm, Frank's heart was racing at the thought of the little soul sinking into that filthy dock trapped under a landslide of crates, knocked out cold, and drowning. It was worth a few splinters to have prevented that. As calm was restored and shouting dockers appeared to retrieve the fallen crates from the water, the mother began to mumble her thanks.

'Sir, what can I say, how can I thank you, that silly boy, so grateful, you put yourself in danger to save him'. Her voice gave way and she lost all coherence.

'Please don't mention it, Madam, it was nothing, I'm glad I was at hand. I know how lively boys can be, no sense of danger. Please can I help? Is anyone coming to meet you or may I help find you all a cab?'

'Thank you that would be most kind.'

Shock caught up with her and she collapsed on a suit case sobbing with the relief and as her older daughter moved in to comfort her, Frank strode off purposefully towards the dock gate. The elder girl rallied the small party forward.

'Come on Mother, Alan, Jean, up you all get, we can't sit here all afternoon, the young man has found us a cab.'

She bustled around, collecting up bags and boxes, urging the younger children on. As she came towards him and he listened more closely to the tenor of her voice, Frank realized that she wasn't the twelve or fourteen year old girl he had originally taken her for, but a petite and extraordinarily pretty young woman. He admired the way she took charge of the party, lifting that burden from her mother, who was still visibly shaken. She was brave too, spirited and athletic, he thought, he'd had only just beaten her to the pile of crates. Frank helped them load the bags and boxes and the young woman found time to enquire the name of her brother's saviour.

'Lawless, Mr Frank Lawless, Miss…?'

'Miss Gordon, Miss Hilda Gordon, newly arrived, complete with troublesome brother, from Hong Kong. How do you do?'

Beneath her hat Frank saw that tiny wisps of hair, of a gleaming brown, so dark it was almost black, had become loosened by her exertion, and had slipped down one side of her face, enticing further interest. She brushed them aside.

'It was a pleasure to be able to assist you all, Miss Gordon, would you like me to give an address to the driver?'

'Oh, the Larkspur Hotel, please, if you would be so kind, we will stay there for a few days until we get organised.'

Frank gave the direction and as the cab was about to pull away, Mrs Gordon recovered enough to say,

'Please young man, do call by the Hotel tomorrow, if you have time, perhaps join us for tea, I do not feel able to offer you adequate thanks for the service you have done for us today'.

Frank accepted with pleasure, Miss Hilda Gordon had caught his fancy and he was taken with her deep dark eyes, olive skin and pretty little face, full of interest and intelligence, which he felt he would be more than happy to see again. Just as the cab began to pull away and Frank was returning his raised hat to his head, he heard a man shout from the gangway of the *SS Miyzaki Maru.*◊

◊ **The** *SS Miyazaki Maru* continued to make regular passages between England and the Far East over the next four years. She was sunk by German submarine U-88 as she approached the English Channel on 31ˢᵗ May 1917 with loss of passengers and crew. Her Wreck lies 150 miles west of the Scilly Isles

'Miss Gordon, Miss Gordon, I wished to help you find a cab, you've forgotten to tell me where you're staying. The young man raced after the departing cab.

You're a bit late on the scene, thought Frank. He heard Miss Gordon call out 'Oh Captain Gates...' but the rest was lost as the cab pulled away. With his own package finally collected Frank returned to Oceanic House, his head full of ideas, scenes from the play he was planning, blending saving a child's life and an accidental encounter with a striking young woman. How do I make a scene out of all that? Perhaps just concentrate on her, put her in a story of her own. Maybe she could become the role-model for a governess, a secret mistress, or a heroine from an opera. She had a slightly exotic look, Italian or Spanish perhaps, with the olive skin and dark, dark eyes. He speculated about the length and thickness of the nearly-black hair, once it was released from its restraining hat, with an interest that was more than simply that of an author in search of a heroine.

The following day was Saturday and after a few hours in the office at Oceanic House, Frank was free to accept the invitation to tea at the Larkspur. He didn't require any further thanks for saving the boy, any man would have done as he had, but he was definitely pleased with idea of seeing Miss Hilda Gordon again. Frank liked to walk about London, especially after several hours in the office. His long stride took him briskly across Green Park, Piccadilly and Berkeley Square. He gave his name to a girl at reception and wondered for a moment if he was being presumptuous and perhaps had been forgotten. But within a very few minutes a small boy and a girl ran down the imposing stair, seemingly none the worse for yesterday's near miss, and closely followed by their elder sister. The boy ran up to him.

'Mummy says I must say thank you, sir, for saving my life.'

Frank stooped down and gave him a playful cuff on the shoulder.

'I'm glad all is well, but no more climbing on boxes, rotten tree branches or any other risky places; you gave your mother a terrible fright.'

Frank smiled when he saw the elder sister, she is really not much taller than the boy, he thought, she barely reaches my shoulders! He offered his hand and she tentatively outstretched her own and their fingers brushed in the briefest touch of greeting. The tips were warm and soft as a rustle of silk across his skin and he needed to exert all his self-control to wrench his mind away from that impression.

'Good afternoon, Miss Gordon, the young man looks fully recovered now, I am pleased to see.'

Her eyes were every bit as dark as he has remembered, so dark that their pupils were almost lost in their mahogany patina that seemed to reflect back the light towards him.

'Mr Lawless, what a pleasure to see you again, my brother is always troublesome, but I am glad he has thanked you himself.'

'It is the nature of small boys to cause trouble I think, especially when they have been confined to a ship for six weeks. I'm sure I might well have tried to do something similar at his age.'

'Well hopefully he'll be settled into school soon and then I'll no longer feel the need to provide him with air and exercise, it was like having a naughty puppy on the voyage, always into something unless kept fully entertained. Deck quoits never seemed to be quite energetic enough.'

Frank wanted to ask her more about her voyage, her family, her brother, anything to keep the conversation going, but her mother appeared and took over the role of spokesperson.

'My dear young man, Mr Lawless, we really cannot express our thanks and gratitude enough for your brave action yesterday. You undoubtedly saved my son's life. It was a truly gallant act.'

Frank reddened, and feeling the heat rise to his face and not wanting to appear silly in front of the young lady, brushed aside her thanks.

'It was nothing, nothing, ma'am. I am so glad to have been able to help, please, say nothing more about it.'

Over tea he heard a little more about the purpose of their visit.

'We live in Hong Kong, Mr Lawless, my husband has a business there, but these two youngsters must come over now to start their schooling.'

Frank looked enquiringly in the direction of Miss Gordon, hoping to be told she was too old for school.

'Oh, I left school years ago, my convent days are over.' Miss Gordon laughed. 'I've come to assist my mother on the passage and visit old friends in London.'

'Have you always lived in London, Mr Lawless? Do you work in Shipping?'

When Frank told them he worked for the White Star Line, Mrs Gordon remarked that these were awkward times for the company.

'The *Titanic* disaster must have affected everyone in your company deeply?'

'Yes,' Frank agreed 'now we're kept very busy with legal enquiries and court cases.'

She was glad, she said, that there were no icebergs in the Indian or China seas and that even though she had undertaken the journey so many times, she was still nervous at the start of every voyage. Miss Gordon concurred and said she was pleased to be settling in England for several months. The family hoped to be moving into a flat in Battersea within a few days.

Frank did his best to make polite conversation, but this tiny girl was a terrible distraction to a fellow's mind. There was a delicate little channel above her top lip which gave it a delightful bow shape and attracted his eye.

Frank rose to leave, offering them any further assistance with their move that he could, which was politely declined, they were indebted to him more than enough already. He smiled at them all, but held Miss Gordon in his gaze for several moments longer, then, with the slightest of bows, turned and left. Out of my league, way out of my league, he thought regretfully.

'What a delightful young man' mused Mrs Gordon.

Hilda had been able to take greater stock of Frank's appearance. At the dock-side she had really only ascertained that he was young, tall and very quick thinking. Now she had been able to look him in the face as she thanked him, and she had warmed to what she had seen. She thought of his voice too, which had rather captivated her, deep and mellow, with the smallest hint of an Irish lilt and the sound of laughter within it that you could have recognised even in the pitch dark. She sighed as she saw him slip out in to the crowded London streets. It seemed unlikely that their paths would cross again.

LONDON AUGUST/SEPTEMBER 1913

Frank returned to the routine of work during the following weeks. The London office, as Hilda's mother had noted, was exceptionally busy, dealing with the aftermath of *Titanic*. There was an on-going case, currently in the courts, where the company was being sued for damages. There was the need to rebuild public confidence following the disaster. Passenger numbers were only just starting to get back to their previous levels and senior managers were nervous. Extra life boats for all ships had been ordered and their installation had to be monitored. The atmosphere in the office was frantic and little episodes and outings, such as his trip to the Docks were rare. So it was almost a month later when he had time to give thought to Miss Hilda Gordon again and wonder how the family had settled down.

Frank decided to take a walk through Battersea Park late one Saturday afternoon, on the off chance of bumping into them. He walked the length of the park, circled the ponds and lingered to watch a couple of overs of a cricket match, all without success. He saw nannies with small children, families sauntering and elderly ladies walking small dogs, but there was no young lady trying to exercise an over exuberant younger brother. Perhaps the school term had started and the children were gone away, he wondered, vaguely disappointed that his idea had failed. Then he remembered, she had talked about a convent school. Perhaps they were Catholics. They would need to go to Mass tomorrow and so would he; he would locate the nearest Churches and find the times of Sunday Masses. Checking his London map later that evening, Frank found two churches in Battersea, the first dedicated to Our Lady of Mount Carmel and the second to The Sacred Heart, effectively one at either end of the park.

The number of variables was increasing and the chances of his seeing the object of his interest were lengthening. Two churches, three masses each, it could take him a month or more to hit the right one, but it was the only lead he had, so following his instinct and choosing the nearest end of the park, he opted for the 10.00am Mass at Sacred Heart.

It was a pretty, modern church, tall, red brick on the outside, with a copper clad steeple and painted within. Frank genuflected and slipped into a half full row in the gradually filling church. He knelt, crossed himself and tried to focus his thoughts on asking God's blessing on his enterprise. He laid his hat down on the seat alongside him and tried again to pray. Small beams of sunlight struggled to force themselves though the stained glass windows of the apse, splitting the prisms of light and sending the colours of the glass across the aerial expanse of the nave, capturing the dancing motes of dust. A pair of lazy flies rose and sank trying to reach the windows.

Frank's gaze wandered at will and took in the tabernacle, glistening in its copper gilt, studded with precious stones and with an unusual plaque at its centre, showing Christ as the sacrificial Lamb of God. Behind the altar there was a painted triptych and on each side, four niches, showing scenes from the life of Christ. At the end of the apse two unusual painted panels caught Frank's attention. He had seen nothing like them in any church, London or Liverpool, which he had visited. There, staring down towards him were a cherub and a seraph, wings spread to offer prayer and protection to all. It was a most unusual church and Frank was glad he had come, even if Miss Gordon did not appear.

The nave filled and the sanctuary bell announced the procession of priest and servers. The smell of incense grew stronger and smoke rising from the swinging censors mingled with the motes of dust in the shafts of light, carrying the prayers of the faithful heavenward. Frank imagined the flies coughing as the clouds of scented gas enveloped them. Was incense poisonous to flies, he wondered, waiting for them to drop. The congregation knelt as the liturgy opened and he heard the organ swell for the opening hymn. Frank looked for his hymnbook and searched for the number, but knowing the opening verse joined in automatically.

Faith of our fathers, holy faith
We will be true to thee 'til death
We will be true to thee 'til death.

The hairs on the back of his neck rose at the sound of a contralto voice that picked up the second line of the hymn, coming from directly behind him.

Clear and strong, it rose and rose giving a lead to the rest of the congregation. After four verses Frank knew he could have listened to that voice every day for the rest of his life and never grown tired of it.

Hillie sat down at the end of the first hymn and mechanically joined in with the responses of the Mass. Incense always made her feel slightly sick and to take her mind off the nausea she started to focus on the young man who stood directly in front of her.

She admired his height and the set of his shoulders, which seemed to tower above her. Looking upward she saw short, newly cut hair, pleasingly dark with a soft texture, which made her want to reach out and run her fingers through it and trace out the line of paler skin below the newly razored hair. She found herself counting the darker freckles which contrasted with the creamy whiteness of the skin on his neck; strong, muscular and attractive to her eye. She was shocked by the train of her own thoughts; in Mass of all places and times, what would the nuns have said? It would have meant an immediate confession for impurity! There was a certain familiarity about him too, which she couldn't quite place.

The bells marking the consecration at the heart of the Mass brought back her attention and she knelt and bowed as the host was elevated. As she raised her head she watched as the young man's hand fell to his side, a strong hand but gentle looking, with long masculine fingers, not calloused or labour stained. Not a farmer or a mechanic then, maybe someone who held a pen, a teacher or a clerk perhaps.

At communion time the congregation filed down the aisle and knelt in groups at the altar rail to receive the sacrament. Hillie found herself kneeling alongside the young man and struggled to accept communion reverently, attempting to glimpse sideways from under her mantilla to catch the profile of his face. Instantly she recognised the hero of the docks.

As Mass ended Hillie saw him kneel in prayer for a few moments and unconsciously delayed her own departure, fiddling with her gloves and missal until her mother finally whispered to her to get up. She reached the end of her bench at the same time as Frank and he stood back to let her leave. She smiled a demure thank you and looked up at him. They moved towards the door, joining the slow shuffle of worshippers making their way to the back of the church. As they reached the door she removed her glove to dip her finger in the holy water stoop at the door and dropped it. He retrieved it and as they emerged into the sunlight returned it to her with a smile that captivated her.

'Your glove, Miss Gordon. What a pleasure to see you again. I hope there have been no more unfortunate episodes for your brother?' She returned the smile and was uncertain how to extend the moment.

'Thank you, how kind. No, no more adventures or mishaps, thank goodness.'

They stood, surrounded by people leaving Mass, wanting to speak but not knowing, as virtual strangers what was allowed. Her mother arrived at her elbow.

'Come on Hillie, let's go, we will be late for lunch.' Suddenly recognising Frank, she greeted him as a long lost friend, but added,

'Sadly we have to go, we are lunching with friends.'

Frank raised his hand towards his hat in a slight gesture of farewell and with a final reluctant nod began to turn away.

Hillie decided boldness was her only option. She smiled once more at Frank and turned to her Mother, saying very audibly,

'What a lovely church, lets come back this evening for Benediction.' Her mother was slightly incredulous.

'Benediction? But you hate it, all that incense and we are having lunch and a walk with Captain Gates…'

'I should like to come tonight,' she said firmly, as they walked off together down the street.

Frank stared after them as the possessor of that lovely contralto sound walked away. She was definitely as beautiful as her voice, and that was not always

necessarily the case. The girl was barely five foot tall, how did someone so petite produce such volume?

He walked slowly with the sound of her singing replaying over and over in his head. He could slip back in the evening for Benediction, why not? In days like these it paid to be decisive, not coy, when you met someone who captured your imagination.

One Benediction and two Masses later, Frank and Hillie had exchanged shy smiles on three further occasions. In order to hear her sing he had resorted to stratagems. He had arrived early for services and then lurked in the shadows of the church porch waiting unseen until she arrived. He was then able to occupy a seat on a pew in front of her.

During Benediction he had learnt that she could sing hymns in Latin as well as in she could in English, that she had noticed his presence and whispered to her mother in a way that made him feel she was pleased to see him, but conversation was still limited to greetings and farewells and it was difficult to see how he could get to know her better. He would need all the help the cherubs and seraphs could offer if his boundlessly optimistic nature was going to succeed here.

LONDON AUTUMN/WINTER 1913-14

Frank took several 'accidental ' walks in Battersea Park after that and on the third Saturday afternoon, as he sauntered, carelessly admiring the trees and ducks, he heard himself called. Turning towards a small group of six or eight young people, men and women, playing an informal game of cricket, he saw a girl in the outfield waving enthusiastically. He recognised Miss Gordon.

'Mr Lawless, Mr Lawless'

Frank let out a breath that was somewhere between a gasp and laugh. He could not believe his luck. Not only had she recognised him from a distance, but she had called him over and wanted to see him.

'Mr Lawless, it's good to see you, are you busy? My team is a man short; would you like to play for a while?'

'I'm in no hurry at all; my time is all yours Miss Gordon. I was just enjoying an afternoon stroll.' I can hardly tell her I was scanning the park looking for her can I, he thought.

'Where is that young rascal Alan? Is he on your team?'

'Off to school, thank goodness, I really do need an extra pair of hands, and please, call me Hilda or my close friends call me Hillie. '

'Will your friends be happy for a stranger to join in?'

'Of course. If I introduce you, then you won't be a stranger, will you?" He caught the laughter in her eyes and returned it.

'We are not strangers to each other, after all, are we?' She stated.

At the next change of over, Hillie called the teams together and introduced Frank.

'This is Mr Frank Lawless, a friend of mine, he has agreed to be twelfth man and make up my team, if you are all happy?'

The men inclined their heads in a slight nod of acknowledgement and the girls, after giving him a more detailed appraisal, smiled and welcomed him.

'We are trailing badly 'said Hillie, 'I don't think we can save the match, but we can make the score a little more respectable'

'Where would you like me to play?' asked Frank.

'Oh, anywhere in the outfield, to save a few runs, maybe take a catch or two.'

'Let's not be too ambitious,' Frank said and walked towards an imaginary boundary line not too far from the spot Hillie had chosen for herself. He was treasuring the idea of being acknowledged as her friend.

The game ended tamely, with Hillie's side well beaten. The group of friends were gathering together, getting ready to depart and Frank was feeling rather spare on the side-lines when Hillie called him over again.

'We are all going back to my mother for tea. Do join us, she would be delighted to see you.'

'I would be very happy to come.'

Hillie began to introduce him in more detail to the group.

'Mr Lawless, this is my dear friend Jane, this is Mary Highford –Smith, we were all at school together, and her brother Monty. Jane, Mary can I introduce Mr Frank Lawless, he saved my brother's life.' Several more double barrelled names went past Frank until the final introduction; 'Marcus Gates, a friend from Hong Kong, he sailed over with us.'

Frank acknowledged them all and the group fell into easy chatter. He recognised Gates as the man from the dock side, who arrived too late to save the boy.

'Did you really save Alan's life?' asked Gates.

'Well, I managed to catch him before he fell into the dock when they were disembarking. I don't think that counts as a full life save, but he could have drowned I suppose.'

Gates persisted, 'you're not from London? What brings you here?'

'I'm in shipping, I work for the White Star Line, we are heavily involved in inquiries and litigation after *Titanic* - and you?'

'Royal Navy, China Station most recently, met Miss Gordon and all her family in the Club out there.'

'They seem a most pleasant family.'

'They are indeed,' replied Gates. There was something possessive about the way he spoke and looked at Miss Gordon that alerted Frank's instincts. He had never supposed that so lovely a girl could be without admirers, but this man Gates obviously considered himself in the front rank.

The group made its way through the park, the pairings fluid, with conversations starting then moving on. Frank eventually found himself beside Hillie.

'Thanks so much for joining in, it was jolly sporting of you with a group of strangers - I do hate to be whitewashed.'

Frank admired her competitive spirit, there was so much about this girl that was drawing him in.

'Do you play often?' he asked.

'Not so often, it was just such a fine afternoon and somehow this group of us just happened to be together. Gates called with his friend and the girls were already here and we just felt like going out. Is this a favourite walk of yours?'

'As you say, it's a fine afternoon, I was looking for inspiration for some writing, a walk often clears my head of work, helps me think plots or dialogues through.'

'How exciting! What do you write, novels, stories, mysteries?'

'Plays, when I can.'

'Do you think I might ever be able to see one performed in a theatre?'

'Well I try; I sold one in Liverpool before I came to London. I hope that being here I might get to meet more impresarios and theatre owners, other writers, that type of people. Meanwhile I sell my very best secretarial and administrative services to Mr Sanderson at White Star. Do you like the theatre Miss Gordon?'

'I love it, but in Hong Kong our opportunities are limited, mostly to our own amateur productions. In London we can enjoy professional concerts, opera, and plays, anything we choose. We try to go to something most weeks while we are here.'

As the group made their way through the hall of the house Mrs Gordon had taken in Battersea, Hillie rushed ahead calling out.

'Mummy, look who I bumped into, I've brought him home to see you again.' She turned to her friends,

'My mother has a very soft spot for Mr Lawless since he saved my incredibly irritating little brother from swimming with the rats in the murky waters of the Thames.'

Hillie's mother was warm in her greeting and Frank felt genuinely welcome but he sensed Gate's glare drilling into him as the story of the rescue was mentioned again. The young ladies present were keen to hear further details of this act of heroism. Frank, with self-effacing modesty said.

'Any decent man, present at the time, would have done the same thing.' He glanced at Gates and smiled.

Over Earl Grey tea, sandwiches and cake Frank relaxed and chattered around the group. All the girls were open and cheerful, more confident than the few girls in Liverpool that he had known. The men were polite, if a little stiff with the new acquaintance, in an English public school sort of way.

As teatime became early evening, the tea was replaced by a tray of gin and tonic circulating around the room. Frank had been quietly observing Hillie's interaction with her other guests. With her girlfriends she was close and giggling, with the men familiar but not openly flirtatious. He could see that the men were each trying to engage her in conversation when the chance arose, to hold her attention a little longer, but she did not seem to favour any particular one of them, even Gates, over the others. It was polite, well-mannered and fun, nothing more. Eventually Frank managed to manoeuvre himself close enough to start a conversation with her. Hillie was standing near her mother and he opened by saying how very hospitable her mother was.

'Oh there is nothing Mummy likes more than a house full of young people. She says it makes her feel alive, especially when she's away from home'

'Well thank you both so much for including me, it has been a most pleasant afternoon.' The ice in his gin brushed against his top lip as he sipped it, waiting for her reply

'It has been fun hasn't it; I hope you will join us again?'

'I would like that very much - how long you expect to be in London, Miss Gordon?'

'Oh at least nine or ten months - mother will stay another few weeks, then go back out East, then return again next year to see the children. My stay just depends on how I feel and when Daddy wants me back again.' She shrugged her shoulders and smiled ruefully.

'Have you always voyaged back and forth like that? I've never travelled further than London or Ireland; you sound a very well-travelled family.'

'My family are Scottish–Italian, Daddy comes from Clydeside, he's in engineering and steel works. Mummy's family came originally from Italy about sixty years ago and settled in Aberdeen. My grandfather came south to England then out to Hong Kong to make his fortune. There are lots of Scots in Hong Kong; my father founded the Caledonian Club out there. But as for the travelling, yes, we've been back and forth all my life, to Scotland, to London and Hong Kong.' Frank was in envious awe of the blasé, matter of fact way she talked of crossing half the world.

'When we were sent back here to school we had to stay for the holidays. I didn't go home to the colony for nearly five years, or see my father. But Mummy comes over every eighteen months or two years and stays for a few months. As well as seeing Alan and Jean she has other family. One of her sisters is a nun, here in London. My older sister and I often spent holidays at her convent in Hammersmith'

'Do you miss the East?'

'I miss Daddy, I miss my sisters sometimes, we are five, plus Alan. I do miss the warmth and colour and the food and the tropical gardens. And I miss the smallness of the colony where everyone knows each other. We have a very pleasant life.'

'But you have a pleasant life here at the moment?' he asked One of the girls walked by and Hillie waved a hand towards her before answering.

'Yes, I'm lucky to have so many friends from school, I'll stay with some of them when Mummy leaves. There is always something on, something to do. I hope we will see more of you at some of our outings, now we are friends. We are going to the theatre next week, five or six of us, perhaps you would like to join us? It's H.M.S Pinafore.

Frank felt his guardian angel must definitely have landed on his shoulder that afternoon. That this delightful girl, with her deep brown eyes and almost black hair (her Italian blood showing through,) should invite him to join her group of friends was beyond any expectations. She was lively, funny, engaging and beautiful. He was ready to throw himself at her feet if that was what she wanted. He suspected though, that, for the time being, it was much better to continue with friendship rather than startle her with too much admiration and, anyway, what had he to offer her compared to some of the young men in her circle? Time, we have plenty of time, let's take our time and see what emerges, he thought.

Frank waited, smart in his borrowed evening suit, outside the portico of the Grand Theatre. He had arrived early anyway, so as to not to appear rushed or out of breath when he greeted Hillie. Waiting and people-watching were never irksome to him. He was always curious about the audiences who visited theatres, anxious to absorb their interests and conversations, trying to pick up hints of what would appeal to them. A group of young people spilled out from a cab and into the road. The two young men were dressed in immaculate evening dress and the girls they were escorting, demure under the capes that covered their evening dresses, accepted the offer of an umbrella as they hastened into the foyer. Frank watched as the capes were shed and taken by the men towards the cloak room and then went forward to offer his hand, first to Hilda and then her friend. Hilda looked captivating in a close fitting silver evening gown, her hair lifted and swept into a French pleat revealing a neck that complimented the string of pearls she wore around it.

When the men returned and all greeting was over they headed into the auditorium. Frank found himself seated by Hilda's friend and he made pleasant and polite conversation as the orchestra warmed up. When the lights dimmed and the audience fell silent, Frank found himself absorbed into the music and the story of Josephine, the Captains daughter and her love for the unsuitable seaman Ralph.

Once or twice he stole an unobtrusive glance towards Hillie and then it was difficult to keep his mind on the music. Her neck, that elegant throat, revealed when her chin tilted upward with laughter, the pearls like tiny finger tips caressing her skin, were all imprinted in his mind.

From that point on Frank became a regular member of Hillie's circle of friends and family. There were tea parties, walks, cricket and picnics in one or other of London's parks and more visits to the theatre. Sometimes it was just a Variety performance, sometimes a play but most often a concert or an opera.

Frank was pleased to discover that Hillie shared his taste in music and it gave them endless opportunities for conversation. There were evening parties that often concluded in impromptu concerts. Mrs Gordon, Hillie's mother, was rather famous for her voice and often started the evening with Italian love songs. Hillie had inherited her talent and the whole group would stand around the piano as she played and sang for them. Sometimes the men joined in with duets and one evening towards Christmas Frank finally felt he knew the group well enough to join in with some carol singing. His voice took the small audience by surprise, a fine tenor, trained and modulated.

'Where did you learn to sing like that?' Hillie asked him.

'Years and years in church and school choirs, hymns, Masses, weddings, funerals, prize giving and assemblies, we sang them all.'

'Well, I 'm very glad you have finally revealed your talent, I look forward to hearing you again. What will you be doing for Christmas, can you join us all, we sometimes go to midnight Mass at Nazareth House, my aunt is one of the sisters there.'

'I would've liked that very much, but I must return to Liverpool. My parents will be expecting me, my mother particularly would be much hurt by my absence.'

'Have you a big family there, will it be a sizable gathering?'

'No, it will be my parents and an elderly aunt. I've two brothers, much older than me but they've both left Liverpool and emigrated to Canada. I haven't seen them for several years now.'

'So you're the only child in England?'

It was a commonplace remark and Hillie was surprised by the length of time it took him to answer, as if the effort was painful.

'I had a sister, Lily, just a year or two younger than myself. She died when she was twelve. I remember when she died, she was placed in the front parlour, in her open coffin, as if asleep, and the family and neighbours came filing past her, crossing themselves. I stood at the end of her coffin, watching her sleeping, praying for her to wake up, for my mother to stop wailing, for the candles to be put out. Next morning they closed up the coffin and carried her to church. We all loved her very much. I don't think my mother has ever fully recovered. She was very reluctant to let me leave Liverpool when the company asked me to come down here.' Frank shook his shoulders, as if to bring himself back to the moment.

'I say, I'm so very sorry, I didn't mean to come out with all that family history to you, please forgive me.'

'There is nothing to forgive 'said Hillie, looking at him intently. He sensed her compassion and she paused a few seconds before continuing. 'It is all so different for our family, we are close but once we were at school our parents might not see us again for many months or years. I am sure it hurt them, and us, but they always thought the sacrifice important for our education. But I think of little Jean now, just eleven, stuck away with the nuns at Isleworth, only seeing Mummy occasionally for the holidays and in the New Year Mummy will go East again. They'll miss each other and Alan too. Poor Mummy, leaving her babies behind, but at least we all know our separations are not permanent, we can write to one another, hear all the news.'

Frank returned to his family for Christmas, but work commitments ensured he returned to London for the New Year, and throughout the following spring their friendship grew. In late June Hillie found that her holiday in Britain was to end. Her father, finding that, unlike her sister Dorothy, she was not engaged to any British Naval officer and therefore had no reason to remain, decided she should return to the Colony. Reluctantly she took a passage back to Hong Kong.

Finding Frank

I HAVE THE SCRIPTS NOW, of two of your plays and I wonder if the first act of 'Ferdie' is autobiographical, reflecting how you felt about Hilda and her social world in those early days of your acquaintance.

You tell the story of Ferdie, a bright young engineer working in London, who has fallen in love with Dora Page, a well-connected young woman on the London social scene of the day. Ferdie has only his salary (or in Edwardian parlance his 'screw') to live on. He has no inherited wealth, no country mansion to offer her. He has a 'big idea' which he believes will make his fortune but he is terrified that the social gulf between them is still too wide.

You believed in your writing and were optimistic you could make a good living in those pre-war days, but all the family traditions say there was a social gulf between you and Hillie to be overcome at first.

AN EXTRACT FROM 'FERDIE'; A PLAY IN THREE ACTS BY FRANCIS H LAWLESS

Two Friends, Monty and Ferdie are discussing Ferdie's romantic predicament.

Ferdie. Oh Monty! Isn't it too cruel? Isn't it just the Devil's own work… this…this …barrier between us…this obstacle…this I don't know what?

Monty. It's quite plain what it is! Perfectly. It's your own wild, unhealthy outrageously precious scruples.

Ferdie. Oh, no, no, no, it isn't! It's something quite real. Something concrete, I can feel. You don't realize… Whenever I touch her, even when I am speaking to her, I feel it there between us, pushing us apart. Something that only grins when I scowl at it... I try to think that, after all, the whole affair is so simple. That I am a man and she a little woman, and we share this earth and love each other...!

Monty. Quite right. Nicely put.

Ferdie. It's no good. In bed at night, when I think of her, it sits on my pillow, and spoils those sort of dreams. Sometimes it looks like a Colonel, sometimes a stern Governess, sometimes it's a Parent, sometimes that accursed friend of hers, the Baronet's daughter.

Monty. One would think, to hear you talk, you suffered from the D.T's

Ferdie. Always pushing us apart- this great ugly devilish thing. The Incarnation of the Socially Unobtainable.

For Freedom and Honour

On the evening of Bank Holiday Monday, 4th August 1914 Great Britain declared war on Germany. At that point Great Britain had a regular and reservist army less than one quarter the size of Germany's.

The following day, 5th August, Lord Kitchener became Secretary of State for War and on 7th August Kitchener appealed for 100,000 volunteers to serve in the army for the duration of the war.

On the 19th August Lord Derby wrote to the local papers in Liverpool asking for a first tranche of volunteers.

These initial volunteers, mostly from agricultural, unskilled or semi-skilled occupations, and the unemployed, formed the bulk of the earliest recruits. They were to be paid one shilling a day, to serve for the duration of the war.

The better educated, white collar urban dwellers that ran the commercial life of the Empire from Liverpool and other cities had not yet been targeted. They were just as patriotic, but it was more difficult to give up a salaried position or walk away from a lifelong profession into the unknown. Office clerks, lawyers and accountants did not necessarily see themselves as natural soldiers.

The military situation became grave. Between 22nd August and 26th August the regular army of the British Expeditionary Force fought the Battles of Mons and Le Cateau. The casualties were enormous with nearly ten thousand men of the British Expeditionary Force (B.E.F) killed or wounded.

On 24th August Lord Kitchener and Lord Derby discussed the concept of a 'Comrades Battalion,' where men who volunteered together, alongside their friends and colleagues, would be allowed to serve together.

Lord Derby immediately decided to raise such a Battalion in Liverpool targeting the professional and office workers.

He said *'The desire to serve their country was predominant amongst Liverpool men and I voiced the wish expressed to me by many would-be recruits, that they be allowed to serve alongside their friends'*

Finding Frank

So HERE I AM, 98 years later, with a copy of your Military record on one side of me and a pile of regimental histories, including Maddox's meticulous *Liverpool Pals*, on the other. With these I'm able to trace your footsteps through those early days of the war in Liverpool. And as I learn more about the Pals, I remember the small silver badge that used to lie, broken in two halves, at the bottom of my grandmother's brown attaché case, where she preserved it alongside all your letters. It was a small badge, about the size of a fifty pence piece, with the crest of an eagle and child. The eagle had broken away from the child in the nest. The ribbon banner carried the words *SANS CHANGER*, on the bottom and your name and number 15438, were engraved on the back.

I did not know when I looked at it then, that each of those earliest volunteers had been personally presented with their badges by Lord Derby, who had ordered them at his own expense. The silver badges were not intended to be worn, but were proudly given to wives or mothers for safekeeping.

LIVERPOOL AUGUST 1914

On the 27th August word was sent to all White Star offices, in Liverpool and London. The country's need was great. All employees between the age of 18 and 30, who were keen and eager to serve their country, were encouraged to enlist, with the full support of the company. They should meet in Liverpool the following evening to answer Lord Derby's call for volunteers. These volunteers would serve together in a Battalion of Comrades.

Frank headed to Euston station that same afternoon and caught the train to Liverpool. The train was packed full of other young men, heading home to sign up. Like a biblical census, each man heading to place of his birth to be counted. Frank found it difficult to rationalise his own feelings. Like most of his friends he had read the papers, followed the news and observed the outbreak of war without feeling particularly personally involved. Britain and her Empire were all powerful, a war would soon be over, be nothing more than a headline in yesterday's paper. But as August had worn on and the early battles fought, the calls for volunteers had gone out. Frank and every one of his friends had been keen to do their bit and give the Germans a very bloody nose. There was a sense of euphoria, of pride, of being part of something great.

At 7.30 pm on the 28th August Frank joined hundreds of other eager young men, answering Lord Derby's call, at the Headquarters of the 5th Battalion, The Kings (Liverpool Regiment) at St Anne's Street in Liverpool. Frank was one of the earliest to arrive but the hall was soon overflowing, men standing in the aisles stairs and doorways. The crowd was so large a second room was commissioned. The atmosphere of excitement, tinged with danger heightened as the minutes passed. Like young men everywhere, they were invincible, oblivious to possible death or injury.

Lord Derby arrived and received a wildly enthusiastic welcome. Frank, standing towards the front, watched as he stepped on to the platform. The men, filled with a deep and genuine patriotic fervour, stamped and cheered and threw hats into the air. The cheers redoubled when Lord Derby announced that his brother, Ferdinand, would command the new Battalion as Lieutenant Colonel F C Stanley.

Derby was humbled by the tremendous response his appeal for volunteers had generated. Even on that first evening it was apparent there were more than enough men to form the new Battalion. He spoke in moving tones to the men, praising their response, telling them in a speech later widely reported:

> *'This will be a Battalion of Pals, a battalion in which friends from the same office will fight shoulder to shoulder for the honour of Britain and the credit of Liverpool. I don't attempt to minimise the hardships you will suffer; the risks you will run. I do not ask you to uphold Liverpool's honour; it would be an insult to think you could do anything but that. But I do thank you from the bottom of my heart... You have given a noble example in thus coming forward. You are certain to give a noble example on the field of battle. '*

The volunteers were invited to return the following Monday morning, to St George's Hall, Lime Street, to complete their enlistment.

Frank joined his colleagues from the White Star Line early that Monday morning and together they marched from the company's office to the recruiting hall in Lime Street. The troop of clerks and office staff wore their suits and boaters, and as they made their way through the streets they were joined by groups of workers from other businesses, trades and professions, all heading in the same direction. There were men from other shipping offices, the Stock Exchange, Cotton Exchange, Provisions trade, Charted Accountants, the Law Society and many others, all civilians with no experience of military service or the reality of war. When they arrived at St George's Hall, Frank's group waited patiently outside and by 10.00am the first 1,000 men had been allowed through the doors. All needed to be attested and medically examined and this took time. Those outside were reluctantly told to return in two days' time.

On 2nd September, following a second march through the city, Frank finally entered St Georges Hall. Within the huge neo classical basilica areas had been set aside for each trade or business. Frank went to the shipping area where the White Star Line had set up a table for their own staff to enlist.

At the table each recruit was asked the same questions and the same Attestation Document was completed. At the top was written:

Three years general service

Name	Francis Lawless
Place of birth	Liverpool
British subject	Yes
Age	22 years 290 days
Trade or profession	Clerk
Rate payer	No
Previous military service	No
Willingness to be vaccinated	Yes
Married	No

Height, weight, complexion and religion were all duly recorded and after an examination Frank was passed as fit for Military service with no distinguishing marks or scars. Frank was asked if he understood all the questions, he replied in the affirmative and signed the form in the presence of witnesses.

Over written at the bottom was; ***For the Duration of the War***

None of the men and boys who enlisted that day could have imagined they were signing away four years of their youth, their limbs and, for more than a third of them, their life. As the day progressed men began to be sorted into groups or companies, they were asked about any previous useful skills or experience in organisations such as the boy scouts. Frank acknowledged that he knew how to handle and fire a gun. His older brother William, a veteran of the Boar War, had a keen interest in guns and had taught Frank to shoot and to clean and handle a weapon. That, together with a good school and employment record was enough. By the time he left the Hall that evening, Frank had *'taken a stripe'* and been promoted from

Private to Sergeant. The new recruits were dismissed and told to return home and await further orders.

Recruiting continued for several more days and by then Lord Derby had over 3.000 men prepared to serve, more than enough for three Battalions. Now he just needed to turn the inexperienced but enthusiastic civilians into serving soldiers.

By mid-October a fourth Battalion had been raised. These Battalions were known as 17th, 18th, 19th and 20th Service Battalions of the King's (Liverpool Regiment) also known as 1st, 2nd, 3rd, 4th City battalions of the KLR. They were affectionately known as 1st, 2nd, 3rd, and 4th Pals Battalions. Further reserve and training Battalions were added later.

The one thousand earliest volunteers were allocated to the 17th Battalion and Frank was amongst them. Some initial sorting and training took place in Sefton Park in Liverpool and then, on 5th September the recruits were called to a riding school in Aigburth and were organized into regular companies within Battalions. The men were taught some basic drill, 'Quick march' and 'Halt!' then formed into columns to march back into Liverpool, led by Lieutenant Colonel F C Stanley, of the 17th Battalion.

The people of the city turned out in force to cheer on the new recruits, still in their office wear of suits and summer boaters and a review was held in front of St George's Hall.

Frank felt nervous but elated by the crowd and the cheering. The straw from his boater prickled his newly cropped head, the short brutal hair cut was still unfamiliar. The white exposed skin on the back of his neck caught the late summer sun. Again the men were sent home, until barracks, equipment and training staff could be organised.

Frank waited quietly at home, spending time with his parents, catching up with old school friends and colleagues from his days in the Liverpool office, who had joined up alongside him. He wished he had had the chance to discuss enlisting with Hillie, but her boat had sailed east two months ago and all he had of her were occasional postcards sent from ports along the way, Malta, Suez and the last one that reached him just before he left London, from Calcutta. His Mother had seen it on his bedside table but had refrained from commenting and now he carried it in his pocket to each of the marches.

In the meantime officers were found and sergeants from the Grenadier Guards reserves were employed to train the new recruits. The 17th Battalion, as the first to be raised, was the first to be found permanent accommodation in a derelict former watch factory at Prescot, just outside Liverpool and within marching distance of Lord Derby's estate at Knowsley. Men were sent in to make the building safe and the Shipping companies, Cunard and White Star, offered to provide the white-wash to help make the premises, where many of their employees would be housed, habitable. The 18th Battalion moved to tented accommodation on the racecourse on the Wirral and finally the 19th were to build a temporary camp within the grounds of Knowsley Hall. Until all these arrangements could be finalised the men were billeted in their own homes or those of local people.

Whilst the men waited for their uniforms and equipment to be issued much discussion was taking place about the badge the new Battalions would wear on their caps. Eventually it was agreed that as Lord Derby had raised the units, his family crest, The Eagle and Child, would be the insignia of the Pals battalions.

Frank stood, towards the end of the year, outside Knowsley Hall, with all his companions and each of them was presented with a silver badge by Lord Derby himself, showing the crest of an eagle standing over a nest containing a small child and inscribed with the words 'Sans Changer'. The men admired their badges and many talked of leaving them for safety with mothers, wives or girlfriends. Frank turned his over and over in his hands. He would be reluctant to give it to his mother and had no way of asking Hillie to keep it for him unless she returned.

Colonel Stanley managed to equip his troops with decent uniforms within a few weeks but arms took a little longer. Over the winter of 1914 and into the spring of 1915 the Pals battalions remained in Liverpool, learning military discipline, drill, company formations and as much musketry as possible with the few aged weapons that they had. They maintained the barracks, took sentry duty and went on route marches in the area. Stanley was delighted when the four battalions were finally able to train together and were formed into a single Brigade with himself as Brigadier.

The weekends were free and Frank often went back into Liverpool to spend time with his parents, have a bath and take in a trip to one of the the-atres which were offering reduced prices to the volunteers. He thought of all the plays and concerts he and Hillie and their group of friends had enjoyed in London, all the walks and picnics and cricket matches. None of it had had the same appeal once Hillie had left, but those carefree parties seemed very distant now with the imminence of combat.

By early spring army commanders realized that trench warfare was becoming a permanent feature of the campaign and the new Battalions needed to sharpen up their digging skills. Lord Derby lent an area of his estate and Frank and his comrades often found themselves helping to landscape the grounds. There was camaraderie and sometimes laughter amongst the men as they trained, and tales were told of horses 'borrowed' from the peer's stables for evening rides, of forays into the kitchen gardens and pleasure grounds and of the classical statuary that adorned the grounds of Knowsley Hall being embellished with appendages of priapic proportions, made from the clay which the men were continually shifting. Frank, as a sergeant, often turned a blind eye to many of his men's escapades.

**Sgt Frank Lawless second from left, Knowsley Hall Liverpool 1914
The recruits here are shown wearing the White Horse
of Hanover cap badge of the Regular KLR**

By the spring of 1915 Frank and his companions were reaching good standards of both fitness and military bonding. They still lacked decent rifles but were becoming restless and wanted to move on. They had, after all, joined up to be soldiers, not landscape gardeners. Christmas had passed and the war showed no sign of ending. Casualties amongst the reservists who had been called up to the Western Front were rising and still the Pals Battalions were unused, held in comfortable barracks close to their own homes. The local mood in Liverpool became restless also. The men were ready to fight for King and Country, to don their chafing uniforms and test their newly polished boots.

On 20th March, as a way of lifting morale, a huge rally was held in the city. Twelve thousand locally recruited men, in full battle order paraded down Lime Street past St Georges Hall to be reviewed by Lord Kitchener himself, local dignitaries and a crowd of local people reportedly 100,000 strong. Lord Kitchener was impressed, remarking to Lord Derby; *'They are splendid, we must have more of them.'*

In April orders were finally received for a move of the entire Brigade to Belton Park in Lincolnshire and on the 30th April, Battalion by Battalion, the Pals Brigade marched to Prescot Station and entrained, in twelve special trains, for Grantham.

Frank's parents were among the thousands who gathered at Prescot to cheer on the volunteers and wish them farewell and good luck. Frank hugged his mother goodbye and shook his father's hand, he was sad to see his mother cry. Everywhere he looked there were mothers holding back tears and girlfriends waving handkerchiefs and blowing kisses. He wished Hillie had been there but then laughed inwardly to himself, Hillie was so tiny he would never have been able to pick her out in such a crowd.

Belton Park, the estate of Belton House, had been lent to the War office by the Brownlow family. A purpose built camp already existed, although conditions there were deeply unsanitary by the time the Liverpool Battalions arrived. The first job awarded to Frank and his companions in the 17th, was to shovel away the top two feet of heavily polluted mud from around the barracks, a legacy left by the previous occupants who had insufficient latrines for the numbers of men. The mud stank, a repulsive sewer which made them heave and gag with every barrowful they moved. Clouds of flies followed the barrows as the filth was moved and pink tails of rats disappeared at speed beneath the barrack huts. It was excellent preparation for the trenches.

The young lads from Liverpool soon became popular in nearby Grantham, with local people even offering the use of their baths to the troops. They often offered accommodation, to parents and families visiting from Liverpool. The officer cadets were also allowed occasional weekend leave.

It was at Belton that that the four Liverpool Pals battalions were formed into the 89th Infantry Brigade, and serious training as an entire Brigade regularly took take place. The troops were re–equipped with good clothing and boots and were issued with modern rifles. From early summer 1915 senior officers made trips to the Front, so they were fully informed about conditions there.

On the 27th August 1915, almost exactly a year after they had joined up, the Pals battalions of volunteers were taken over by the War Office and accepted as fully functioning units of the British army. Orders were received for the units to proceed to Larkhill Camp and its surrounding areas on Salisbury Plain, where large numbers of other troops were also training, prior to their deployment on the Western Front. Most left Grantham by train on 6th and 7th September. Frank left for Larkhill with the 17th Battalion, expecting to leave for the front within the following few days.

KENT MAY 1915

The extent of her pleasure in seeing Frank Lawless again took Hillie by surprise. He'd always had a way of popping up when least expected and to find him in her drawing room one Sunday within a week of her return to London was startling.

'Mr Lawless, Frank, I had no idea you were in London, what a pleasure to see you. I thought you must have been posted to the front by now.'

Frank's smile at seeing her again after so many months was irresistible, sending warmth through her and making her realize just how much she had missed his laughter and cheery presence.

'Miss Gordon, Hilda, I do so hope you don't mind my calling, I just wanted to exchange greetings, to know that your passage home had been safe and leave my compliments to your mother.'

'Oh Mummy is around somewhere, she will be delighted to see you and know that you are well. You must stay and have tea with us. Have you been posted yet? How is it that you are in London, How did you know we were back?'

He looked well, fit and tanned but his uniform was that of a 'Tommy', a common soldier, albeit a sergeant. He would look even more handsome in an officer's uniform, she thought.

Frank saw the glance at the uniform but misread it.

'My apologies for appearing in this' he said 'but if men of my age appear on the streets of London in a suit they tend to be offered the white feather, not a pleasant experience. So it is preferable to travel as a soldier. I have weekend leave and I heard there was a chance you may have arrived in London so I took the opportunity to call on a few friends and hoped to see you too.'

'How is it that your Battalion is still in England?'

'It's taken the better part of a year to find us barracks, equipment and uniforms, never mind training a bunch of clerks and office lads to become soldiers. We've moved from a watch factory in Prestcot to barracks on Lord Derby's estate at Knowsley and we spent days 'entrenching', digging lines, landscaping his grounds, filling them in, then digging them out again. Last month we moved to Lincolnshire, to Belton Park to create more chaos on another peer's estate. The lads are desperate for action, to see the whites of the German's eyes, but our next move is Salisbury Plain, to practise warfare. Then hopefully we will head to the Front.'

To Hillie it seemed incomprehensible that anyone would *want* to go to the Front, she knew the papers were prone to report only good news but her Father had taught her to be sceptical and read between the lines of the reports. People were dying in large numbers and the war did not seem to be going as well as the government hoped. London was bleak with news on every newspaper hoarding and all the young men of her circle had gone to volunteer. The war had already lasted longer than anyone had believed at first and Hillie had heard of some friends killed or wounded since she had returned from her months in Hong Kong. Now she realized she would dread hearing from Frank that orders had been received to leave for the Front.

'Keep in touch as long as you can, don't go without letting us know' she told him and he was grateful for her interest.

A week later Hillie was in Kent. Her mother had begged her to come when she took Alan to the coast for his half term break. He needed young company and with all the family scattered, Hillie was the closest to hand. And besides, her mother would be returning to Hong Kong in the autumn so Hillie was happy to spend as much time as possible with her before then.

The heat of the midsummer's day, that had caused Hillie's face to glisten with perspiration, was beginning to fade a little and she willingly agreed to her brother's suggestion that they go for a long walk on the beach now the tide was going out. Alan, like most ten year old boys had surplus energy at all the wrong times, was beset by hunger when he had just been fed and was both the great pet and a complete puzzle to his mother and five older sisters who had known nothing but female children and siblings, prior to his rather unexpected arrival several years after the girls.

Mother had taken a set of rooms in one of the grandiose Victorian guest houses that lined the sea front. They had the first floor and a drawing room of a tall terraced house, with an ornate cast iron balcony that looked out over the sea.

Hillie loved the Kent coast. When she was at school, she and her sisters had spent all the holidays, when Mummy was in Hong Kong, in the convent guest house run by the nuns from school. It was always fun, she recalled, despite the rules. There were no lessons, the nuns were more relaxed and kind and there were many friends, whose parents, like hers, were overseas. The girls had free range of the beaches for picnics and exploring. They took long walks, from Margate to Botany Bay, from Westcliffe to Reculver, painted, drew, held amateur theatricals and wrote long letters home. They had been happy days. Alan dug her in the ribs.

'Get on Hillie, stop daydreaming, it will get dark soon, let's get out on the beach.'

They left mummy, book in hand, sitting by the open balcony window and waving them off.

Heading towards the harbour, Alan kicked off his shoes and tied them by the laces and hung them over his shoulder. Hillie watched as he raced over the corrugated sand, kicking up small splashes as he went. She looked at all the pent up energy and recalled the day on the docks two years earlier when that energy had nearly been the death of her brother. If Frank had not been there to save him from drowning... Hillie shuddered. Such small moments change lives, not just saved them, she thought.

Her thoughts turned towards Belton Park and the King's Regiment but she shrugged them off and chased after Alan towards the receding sea. The first small fishing boats were already lying high and dry upon the sand, as the tide left them beached. The sunset behind the town was beginning to tint the sky with palest pinks and oranges. Hillie knew why she loved to come here, you had to climb high hills in London to escape the built up streets and see a sky like this, wide, streaked with evening colour and trails of cloud.

Alan picked up stones, flat flints and pieces of rounded chalk pebbles,

'Come on sis, I bet I can skim these further than you,' and he dumped a pile of weaponry at her feet.

'I win, I win!' He shrieked after his sixth throw bounced, hitting the water five times before it finally sank.

They walked on, jumping the mooring ropes of small craft fixed to the harbour wall, then scrambled up the steps onto the wall itself.

'We must pay our respects to the Sea Gods, for luck,' Hillie said, walking towards the end of the harbour wall and staring out to sea. She thought of all the other women who must have stood there by the light house, fishermen or sailor's wives looking anxiously for the return of their husband's ship. Hillie threw a handful of the shells she had gathered on the beach into the sea as an offering to the gods. The indigo and opalescent of the mussels, mother of pearl from the oysters, faint pinks and whites of the tiny clams and winkles glinted as they fell and acted like tiny mirrors magnifying the evening light.

Standing on the end of the harbour wall they looked south. The next beach, framed by great chalk cliffs, white and strident, brazen and muscular, proclaimed 'England' to the point at sea where the English Channel and the North Sea met and led to France and the continent beyond.

She shivered slightly as she thought of all those young men gone across the water, maybe only thirty or forty miles from here if you were an albatross or a gull, but a world away if you were a young woman, anxious for news of your friends. That last conversation with Frank came back to her, it must be soon, his deployment, it must.

The gaslights in the streets behind them were flaring up and houses and hotels and inns were beginning to show their evening illumination. The wet beach reflected the lights from the sunset that suffused the sky with vivid pinks that faded into oranges and yellows at the edges of the horizon. The smallest wisp of a new moon was rising and that too was reflected in the darkening blue of the sea. On the beach below two children were playing a last game with their small brown dog, which barked and yapped around their ankles as he chased a ball with teeth and nose. Suddenly the dog stopped barking, and the children's voices fell. The dog stood, transfixed at the water's edge, gazing out towards the point where the sky and the sea met on the darkening horizon. Hillie and Alan followed the dogs gaze and stood as motionless as statues, bewildered by what they saw and heard.

The low hum of an engine drew closer and in the sky, out over the sea but drawing nearer and nearer at tremendous speed, a giant silver shape floated towards them. It was cylindrical, pointed at the front, sleek and windowless with silver flanks that were glowing in the setting sun. At the end of the cylinder tailfins gave the impression of a giant whale or shark that had suddenly escaped the sea and broken bounds with earth to take flight across the skies. To Hillie it appeared alien and fantastical, straight out of *War of the Worlds*, something unknown and utterly sinister.

'What is it, Alan, what is it?'

The engines had cut out and the great silver ship drifted noiselessly towards them. There was a moment of inexplicable silence broken only by the sound of Alan's ingressive breathing. The silence broke when others on the beach and esplanade saw the shape looming towards them and screamed in panic at the alien aggressor. Alan, like many boys too young to fight, had taken a keen interest in the weapons of the war.

He let go of his breath, 'It's a Zeppelin- an airship, they're armed, maybe ready to attack. Get down Hillie, along the wall, creep down and along.'

Hillie had never felt true fear until that moment. The hair rose on the nape of her neck and she felt her pulse race as her shaking hands reached to her little brother for reassurance. The airship seemed to have eyes that were fixed on her, searching for her, waiting for her to slip, or cry out or somehow present herself as target. The warmth of the evening evaporated in the sweat of her terror.

The pair made their way slowly back, scuttling alongside the inner wall, pressed up flat against it when they needed to catch breath, never taking their eyes from the Zeppelin which had come slowly in towards the town. Suddenly though, it seemed to change direction and headed round, laboriously westward, as if it had decided Margate was not its intended target this night.

Hillie and Alan took a circuitous route back to the guest house, avoiding the exposed esplanade. They turned into the small jumble of little streets that led towards the market place, ducking beneath the old and overhanging shops and up into New Street. There they veered right into the High Street, weaving and turning until they had finally to cross the open road towards the seafront hotels again. All the while people were coming out of pubs and houses and looking skywards as word spread of the horror in the sky. Church bells started ringing a warning and far in the distance they saw search lights, vainly raking the sky for the elusive craft. Mother met them at the door, anxious and drawn, and they joined the other guests who had all taken refuge in the wine cellar. Some two hours later, around midnight, they felt safe enough to come up and gaze upon the now empty sky.

Hillie lay for several hours unable to sleep, fixated by what she had seen. She had no idea that war would come to the very shores of England, that people could be threatened and in danger in their own homes, fields and beaches. Then her thoughts became angry. Wasn't it enough for the Germans that British men were going to war in Belgium and France, going to fight and to die? Why was this not enough, why were they now attacking civilians from the skies? Feeling her own fear at the unknown danger, at the threat of sudden, unexpected death or hideous injury, made her think too about what all those young men who had joined up must feel when they first landed in France. Her friends, like Frank, worked in everyday occupations; they were lawyers, shipping clerks, teachers, actors and musicians, not professional soldiers. They had never expected to have to take up arms and fight and kill for their country, but when told to go they had, in their hundreds of thousands. Did these great airships fly over their barracks or trenches and drop bombs? Did the soldiers' fire back at them? Hillie began to long for the reassurance of Frank's company. She longed to hear his laughing voice telling her not to be afraid, they would all be safe, he would be their lucky mascot, protecting them from this new terror in the sky. She thought of Frank, tall in his uniform, armed and alert. It was a consoling image to cling to as she finally fell asleep.

In the morning mother cancelled the rest of their holiday, much to Alan's disgust, as he was desperate to see more of this new phenomenon. They took the twelve o clock train back up to Victoria. Hillie herself was not sure they would be any safer in London but she reassured her mother that it was probably the wisest thing to do. The war was close to home now and they would all have to get used to it.

◊ On the Evening of 31st May 1915 Airship LZ38 left Evere in Belgium, crossed the channel and was seen off Margate. It turned west towards Southend then followed the Thames towards London. Over one hundred incendiary devices, grenades and bombs were dropped, seven people were killed, thirty five were injured and a large number of properties were destroyed by fire. No searchlights found LZ38 and no British guns were fired in response to the raid. Throughout the war the towns of the Thanet peninsular, Margate, Ramsgate and Broadstairs which were in in the British Front Line of home defence, suffered deadly, destructive air raids. Attacked both by Zeppelins on their way to and from London and later aeroplanes, it was estimated that 396 bombs and 343 shells were dropped on the district with 45 people being killed and 93 injured. Extensive direct damage to property was caused and the coastal towns lost all the tourist trade upon which they depended. On quiet nights, when the wind was blowing from the south east these towns could hear the rumble of distant shelling.

For Freedom and Honour

THE INNS OF COURT OFFICER TRAINING CORPS 1915-16

THE INNS OF COURT OTC was founded in London in 1914 specifically to provide Officers for the New Army. Numbers were already insufficient and the rate of attrition amongst the very young men enlisting from the public schools made the rising need for new officers acute. Boys of 17 and 18, trained in old fashioned types of warfare in the cadet forces of schools such as Eton, Fettes or Shrewsbury, found themselves serving in the trenches at the Front, leading platoons and with a life expectancy of around six weeks.

The OTC later removed from London to Berkhampsted in Hertfordshire because of the need for much greater outdoor space for training purposes.

The call had gone out to Battalions in training to look for suitable officer material amongst their NCO's and other ranks. Indeed General Errington, Commander of the Inns of Court OTC, records in his history his regret that so many excellent men of officer calibre had been allowed to enlist in the ranks and how difficult it was to get them out again. Many men of educated, professional backgrounds, like Frank, had joined the Pals regiments and had eschewed seeking a commission preferring to enlist and serve together with their friends in the ranks.

General Errington was very aware that these were a new type of officer that he was training. They were older men, many of whom had spent a year in the ranks and all of whom had had experience of life, of the world and working alongside others. Errington selected his recruits carefully, and what he was looking for, he records, was moral strength and leadership potential.

Errington devised a curriculum that differed widely from the one more typical of Sandhurst and pre-war days. The new Officer's education acknowledged their previous experience, was more compressed and more urgent. The men spent a lot of time on field exercises by night and day but also had classroom lectures, particularly when poor weather precluded outdoor manoeuvres. Errington records many of the subjects covered including; Discipline, Sanitation, Musketry, March Discipline, Entrenchment, Tactics, Advanced Guards, Attack, Defence, Trench Warfare, Map Reading, Scouting and Reconnaissance, Night Operations, Village and Woodland Fighting, Messaging, Wire Entanglement, Military Law, Principles of Strategy and Tactics, and History of the War (from Mons to the Marne).

Errington was rightly very proud of the Officers the Inns Of Court OTC produced. The foreword to his *History of the OTC* shows some of the statistics. It was thought that some 130,000 men were interviewed for selection and about 1 in 10 was accepted. In the course of the war between 11,000 and 12,000 men were trained and received commissions. Of these 2100 were killed and 5000 wounded. Honours gained in the theatres of war were about 2,800 including 3 Victoria Crosses.

Finding Frank

FRANK LEFT FOR LARKHILL ON Salisbury Plain with the 17th Battalion but did not remain there long. He had been selected for Officer Training and was discharged from the Service on 9th September. Four days later he re-enlisted at the Inns of Court Officer Training Corps.

Frank spent his first few weeks as an officer cadet in familiar territory in London, billeted near Wimbledon. Many field exercises took place on the Common. The recruits marched round ponds, practiced woodland fighting around the forest cover of the Windmill and 'took' the trenches around Caesar's camp. Drill was practiced for a few hours each day at the Temple. After the move to Berkhampsted the training became more intense and filled both days and nights for several months. Frank bought a motor bike and still found time to make regular visits back to London to see Hillie.

On November 5th 1915 Frank wrote to his brother Charley;

My dear Charley
....The battalion went abroad yesterday and I am cursing my luck as I have to finish my course here and prepare to spend the winter at home. The adjutant has written and said he will send for me when they get out there, but I am much disappointed at the way things have worked out.... Anyway I suppose I've saved my life for the time being.

...I have invested in a motor bike so slip to London quite easily, to meet a pal at the cathedral, or for tea. (Hillie). There is a minor opera

season running under Beecham's auspices at the Shaftesbury....Madam Butterfly is one of their best productions.

London is indescribable now after dark and awfully danger-ous... Theatres now give their performances in the afternoons, except on Saturdays. There have been two bad air raids just before I arrived. Women, of course, are fearfully scared and many have cleared off to the country.

I was at the opera with a lady, when a stage gun went off.....it's identity, like all stage guns was perfectly clear, but she wouldn't be re-assured until I had made myself generally unpopular in the row we were in, by going into the street and gazing at the inky sky to see that the Zeppelins hadn't come to drop souvenirs again. Joking apart...the German mind responsible for blowing busloads of women into little bits, must be a particularly foul one, There is no apparent military end to be gained....

Am just off on an all-night operation, must get some sleep
Frank

Frank was initially commissioned into the 21st Battalion, Kings Liverpool Regiment which was a training unit, and spent further time back at Knowsley and Formby, training new volunteers and going on specialist courses himself. He wrote to Charley again, in July 1916, from The Western Command Grenade School at Prees Heath, in Shropshire.

Dear Charley
...I am here on a bombing course......During the day we sling live bombs about, demolish trenches with guncotton and amuse ourselves quite successfully. What a school boy affair war is. I would have been in seventh heaven if I could have possessed a revolver and set off slabs of Gun cotton - at 15!! Now it's rather a bore after a bit.

However I expect to go to the front any time now. The 'Pals' are heav-ily engaged in this furious fighting on the Somme and I am to go on my final leave as soon as I get back to Liverpool.

They may make me a specialist when I get back, a 'bomber'. I hope not as it would keep me back from the Front and I am anxious to get out. I am long overdue, tho' goodness knows I've done my best to go.

I have just sold my motor bike, it was a wrench as it was a topping 'bus, but I have no more use for it now. I bought it to take 'French leave' to visit London at the weekends.......
With love
Your affectionate brother
Frank

In mid-July 1916 he received a commission as a 2nd Lieutenant in the 18th Battalion KLR.

HINDHEAD SURREY JULY 1916

Frank had six precious days of leave before taking up his commission, long enough to head to Liverpool to say goodbye to his parents and then, he hoped, back to London to say farewell to Hillie. He worried the remaining time would not be long enough for his real, immediate battle, to convince her that she was in love with him before he went to the Front.

'Why must you leave Liverpool so soon, when you still have four days of leave left?' his father asked, as his mother sniffled and wept at the prospect of his departure.

'Your mother is distraught at the thought of you finally going to the front, what is it that is so important in London that you must spend these last days there and not with us?'

'Don't talk as if I'm never returning Dad, you must help Mother not to worry. I'll be home in three months. Officers get leave.'

Frank knew his parents, his mother particularly, were jealous of whatever they believed it was that drew him back to London. He tried to explain.

'I've met a girl, Dad, I believe I'm in love but I am not sure how she feels about me or if she returns my feelings. I need to convince her that I'm worth her interest. Being an officer has increased my chances, but she has other men following her. If I don't go maybe someone will steal her from under my nose. I would have nothing to fight for then.' He tried to sound light-hearted.

His father shook his head, tutted and was sternly unconvinced.

'Your mother needs to see you Frank, she worries, all mothers worry at these times. It's selfish of you to go away when you could stay longer, just to pursue this unknown young person in London. She sounds like a flighty young woman to me, who cannot make up her mind. How do you know she isn't just stringing you along for fun, to amuse herself?'

'It's not like that, Dad, honestly, she just doesn't know me well enough yet, and if I'm not there, she never will know me. I promise you, she is truly beautiful and good. You would both like her; I have to try for her while I can.'

So despite being under something of a parental cloud, he left Liverpool and arrived back in London. Within two hours he had called on Hillie and was invited to join them all for a picnic in Surrey, the following day. He liked the prospect of a day out in the English country side before leaving for the Front. Hillie and her sister Dorothy together with Dorothy's fiancée the naval officer Bill were all to get the train. Several of their friends were to join them, including, Frank thought, his main rival for Hillie's affection Marcus Gates. If she was that keen on Gates, would she have invited me Frank asked himself.

Frank made his way to Waterloo Station. They had arranged to rendezvous there, on the platform, to catch the eleven o'clock train to Haslemere and then get a couple of cabs to take them up to Hindhead Common. They planned to walk, explore the hills and woods, have a picnic and enjoy a day out of London.

Bill, Dorothy and Hillie arrived together, the girls carrying a picnic hamper between them and Bill with an awkward sports bag and umbrellas. As always Frank's heart lifted when he saw Hillie and his hand was offered to her first, with a smile of greeting. The train was standing alongside the platform and he took the hamper from her. They all boarded the carriage, chatting about the weather.

'Will it hold fine for the day Bill, do you think?' Frank asked

'I come prepared for all eventualities, we have raincoats and brollies and a cricket set, what more does one need to make the most of the English summer.'

The train pulled out, whooshing steam and smuts of soot as it laboured out of the station, gradually picking up speed as it headed south. Frank felt he had spent too many of his last few days and hours travelling. The speed of the wheels, their rhythmic metallic clunk along the rails, all seemed to be carrying him closer and closer to the Front at an unnerving pace.

At Haslemere, the rest of the party met them and they headed for the hills. Frank had seen the uplands of the Lake District and the Welsh mountains too, but Surrey was relatively unknown to him. He was faintly surprised to find these substantial hills so close to London, in part gently undulating and covered with close cropped grass, in others, deeply wooded, with sudden drops and steep inclines. The cabs laboured to reach the top and set them all down at the picnic spot. Bill arranged with the drivers to return for them at five in the afternoon.

'Shall we come sooner sir, if it rains?'

'No, no, we shall be fine, we will take shelter.'

Their group of four had been joined by three more naval officers, amongst them the dreaded Marcus Gates, all friends of Bill's, a sister of one of the officers and two other old school friends of Dorothy and Hillie.

Frank, feeling his task was to try to keep himself between his rival and Hillie as much as possible, went briskly to greet him and kept a shoulder between them. The party broke up into smaller groups to go exploring and Frank instinctively followed Hillie. He succeeded in being next to her when they reached a particularly muddy patch and was able to offer his arm as she negotiated puddles, hitching up her skirts to keep them out of the mud. Somehow he just forgot to let the arm go and managed to steer her to one side of the main group. She didn't seem to mind, which was promising, he thought.

'The sky looks threatening, those deep dark clouds. Will they blow over do you think, or will we get rain?' Frank asked her.

'They must blow over, this is too attractive a place to be ruined by weather. It's beautiful, this common and woods, with the gorse in the banks and the heather just coming through to flower.' Hillie brought her face close to pick up the faint, honeyed scent that the heather gave off.

'Let's pick some, it will make mother think of Scotland.' She said.

'Not yet,' urged Frank, 'It will dry out by the end of the day, wait until this afternoon, just before we leave. It all reminds me of the Lake District. We used to go walking there among the fells when we were youngsters, with Dad and my brothers. Have you ever seen the Lakeland fells?'

Hillie hadn't.

'The highest hill I know is the Hong Kong Peak, very different to here. We live half way up, you can walk, but it is a stiff climb and now you can take the Peak Tram, which carries you to the top. You pass through tropical gardens, forest trees, tall with huge vivid flowers. Maybe the heather is just a tiny reminder of that contrast. England often seems to me to be just varying shades of green.'

'I envy you those sights' Frank told her.

He wanted to make her laugh so he could see that smile which seemed to irradiate her face, and succeeded with silly anecdotes of his fellow soldiers and his view of the pomposity of senior officers. They managed to get themselves a little lost amongst the birch and oaks of the woods and they were the last to get back to the picnic spot for lunch. The rain held off and they covered the damp ground with their raincoats. Hillie went to sit beside her sister to supervise the picnic.

Hillie and Dorothy were laughing, saying it was like a scene out of a Jane Austen novel, a picnic on the Downs. Frank, who had lost his place beside her to Gates, just hoped it would end more happily than the scene in *Emma*. We must avoid conundrums at all costs, he mused.

Gates is a good looking enough fellow, mused Frank, and maybe she prefers the Navy, The Senior Service, how can I know. He seems to be holding her attention, what is he telling her about, his brave deeds on the arctic convoy? We can all be brave.

Frank thought for a moment about his former comrades in the 17th, in their trenches. In two or three days, he would be amongst them. Officers from the OTC had visited the Front regularly. They brought back clear descriptions of the conditions that were to be faced, the mud, the duck boards, the guns, and the tension and fear men endured as they waited for a battle to begin, or to be sent over the top. He thought he knew what he would be up against, but he wasn't sure if he really knew what bravery meant any more. He thought of friends and colleagues who had 'caught it' and would not take their leave again, and his mother worrying all the time about him. But he <u>had</u> to be here, he had to try for her. Time to break up the little tete a tete.

'Anyone for cricket? Bill, girls, will any of you play?'

Hillie jumped up immediately. 'I will.'

Bill chose Dorothy, Hillie, Gates, another officer and his sister for his own team. Frank rallied his troops, won the toss and elected to bat first.

Bill bowled a very gentlemanly over towards one of the ladies and she was allowed to take several sedate runs between some branches knocked into the ground as stumps. She was bowled out at the beginning of the second over and Frank took her place at the wicket.

'Come on Frank, we want a captain's innings from you,' one of his lady team mates called out in encouragement. Frank bent over his bat and watched as Gates took over the bowling at the other end.

Heavens, he looks as though he's firing a shell at the Hun! The ball came flying down the make shift crease, hit the uneven ground and bounced up in front of Frank's face. He leant back on his heel and took an almighty swing at it, more in defence than sport and the ball sailed away over the Downs.

'A six,' shouted one of his delighted young ladies, 'definitely a six!'

Frank was actually considering that cricket might be more dangerous than war. By the time they were all out Frank's team had amassed a healthy score of 35 runs. The clouds had been gathering for some time and spots of rain were beginning to make the ground slippery.

'We should call it a day,' Gates said.

'It's nothing, call this rain? We must finish the match,' cried Hillie.

Frank was delighted by her spirited approach, it was one of the things he admired about her, she seemed so game, so up for anything that people suggested, with a sense of fun that sometimes defied decorum.

Frank put one of the other naval types in to bowl first and Dorothy made a delicate attempt at hitting the ball; she seemed quite relieved to run out on her second attempt. Gates came in next and was still muttering that the ground was too wet, it was stupid to keep playing, they should give up and shelter, the girls would get damp...

Hillie got impatient

'Come on Marcus, just play your innings then you can hide under a tree if you want to.'

Gates scored a couple of singles then Frank took over the bowling at the other end. I'll show him how a gentleman plays cricket, with skill and a decent temperament. The ball was heavier in the damp and he took a couple of throws to judge its weight and distance. Gates ran two off the first ball and hit what was judged to be a four off the second. But by the third Frank had his measure and clean bowled him with a shout of triumph, 'Owzzat!'

'That was a bouncer, Lawless,' complained Gates,

'Can't be helped on this uneven ground old chap.' The uneven ground proved to be Frank's downfall however.

Hillie came in next, and stood, rather like a sporting angel before the wicket. Her ankle length, cream raincoat was flapping open gently in the breeze like an angel's wings. The rain was heavier now, but nothing compared to the tropical storms she was used to. He watched her as she shrugged it off, wiping the water from her eyes and brow and taking a firm grip on the bat, she waited for him to bowl the first ball.

He sent it accurately but at moderate pace, not wanting to patronise her, and she hit it full on and yelled at her partner to run. They took two whilst one of the opposing girls fumbled to retrieve the wet ball from the long grass. As Frank approached his run up he became distracted by her laughter, her wet face glistening, almost like tears but with eyes glowing with fun. He was wary of making her his target and released the ball carefully. She hit it again and was awarded a four.

She taunted him. 'Come on Frank, you can do better than that.'

He smiled back, took his run up and let the ball go much faster than he intended. It fell short and then reared up with that uneven bounce. She bravely defended her wicket but instead of hitting the bat, it penetrated the folds of her flapping rain coat and struck her at full tilt on the shin. Hillie squealed with pain and started to hop around on one leg.

'Really Lawless, I told you it was stupid to go on playing in the rain, I knew one of the girls would end up hurt,' Gates sniped.

Frank was utterly mortified, the very last person on this entire earth he would have wanted to injure was Hillie, he must have really blown all his chances now. He rushed over to her.

'I'm so sorry old thing, are you alright? Are you badly hurt?'

'It's nothing, a tiny bruise that's all, nothing to make such a fuss about. I told you to try harder.'

'Yes, but I did not mean to hurt you in the attempt.'

'I shall finish my innings,' she replied.

'You are out, leg before wicket,' came Gates's sour tones. 'Now let's finish this confounded game.'

Frank gave up the bowling and went to take up a position in the outfield, whist Bill and one of the officers battled out the final wicket. Frank watched as Hillie lent back against a tree and occasionally rubbed the injured shin.

That must have really hurt her, it must, I heard the crack. Yet she's not making any fuss, just playing the game.

His admiration for her courage grew and when she smiled an encouraging smile in his direction, he knew he didn't have to give up all hope yet. Yet it's a strange way to try to win some one, by cracking them on the shin.

He backed off and let Gates fuss over her and help her into the cab as they made their way back to Haslemere. He sensed she hated the fuss and his rival was doing himself no favours. At least, I have a fine excuse to call round tomorrow and see how she is. I can take flowers, apologise again, see where it takes me.

Frank was at Hillie's door early the next morning and felt obliged to apologise for the earliness of his visit.

'I must leave this afternoon; I have to report to Pembroke Dock tomorrow morning, I couldn't go without knowing that your leg wasn't too badly hurt.'

'It's nothing, nothing at all, please don't give it another thought. Is this really your last day in London?'

'It is. I expect to be at the Front within two or three days.'

He saw her shiver and the expression on her face turned his heart over. She was gazing at him, deep into his face, looking for love, or fear or what... He just couldn't be sure. Frank stood, paralysed by indecision, not wanting to make the wrong move but too unsure to make the natural one.

'I have a favour to ask of you' he said at last, 'I will need your prayers. And please, can I ask you to keep this for me?' He held out his hand towards her and lying in the palm was a silver cap badge, the Eagle and Child, with its motto, *Sans Changer*. Like my feelings he thought.

Hillie took the cap badge from his hand and held it briefly to her lips, such a slight gesture that he almost missed it.

'I will look forward to returning it safely to its owner in a few months' time. I will take care of it. I will pray for you, we will all pray, for you, for every one of you. I have something for you too.'

From her pocket Hillie drew out three small medallions, one each of St Martin, St George and the Archangel Michael.

'They've been blessed, they're the soldier's saints, and I hoped they might help to keep you safe.'

Frank held out his hand and she placed them there, the warmth of her pocket still within them. He could not find the words to thank her, and they both looked at one another with the beginnings of tears, just held back.

'I must go now.'

'I know, but when you get leave, if I am not here, my aunt, Sister Margaret will always know where I am. Perhaps you could write to me sometimes, to let me know how you are. Take care Frank and God Bless.'

For Freedom and Honour

1ST JULY MARKED THE BEGINNING of the Battle of the Somme. Unlike many of the other Pals battalions, the Liverpool Pals were not 'wiped out' in the early days of the Battle of the Somme and in general achieved their objectives.

On 4th July the 18th Battalion was relieved at the Front by a South African Battalion and moved back to tents and huts at Bois de Tailles. On 8th July, as the 18th again moved forward they suffered heavy casualties, including the loss of their much loved and respected Colonel Trotter, at Train Alley Trench. On 13th July the whole Brigade was relieved but was warned their period of rest would be short. Frank joined up with the battalion around this point.

The average life expectancy of a junior officer at that time was said to be six weeks. Frank lasted four before he was wounded.

On the 29th July an attack was made by the brigade on Guillemont, but the 18th was held in reserve. The attack failed and the losses for the other three battalions were over five hundred of the Liverpool men. All battalions experienced a gassing attack. The Pals battalions entrained for Abbeville on 2nd August to rest and regroup and then move to Givenchy.

A week later the 18th re-joined the Front Line and on the 12th August Frank was wounded for the first time.

Letter 1 From Frank to Hilda

33ʳᵈ   (field ambulance station)   BEF (British Expeditionary Force)
France
August 12th (at least I think it's the 12ᵗʰ!)
My dear Hilda
　　I suppose it's just possible they may stick my name in the paper as lost so this is to say it's nothing and I feel top hole.
　　In fact I've got my doubts whether or not it'll be a 'blighty' case. I hope so but won't know until I get to the clearing station, probably tomorrow,
　　The hun sent over some rifle grenades last night and one of them knocked out six of us—but we are only scratched thank goodness and mine is the worst.
　　Isn't it rotten luck?
　　I was just finding my feet and getting along fine in the battalion.
　　However I always said war was dangerous you know!
　　So with luck and by dint of blathering the RAMC, I may see you soon. In any case will let you know the prospects
　　Just chance.
　　Excuse this little note old thing, but the idiot here made me lie down and this is 'on the sly'
Love and heaps of remembrances
from Frankie
Ps your mascots did what I always knew they would, for it was a near thing I suppose.

For Freedom and Honour

It was not uncommon throughout the war for groups of soldiers to be found within dugouts or shell holes, dead, but with no visible external injury. They had died from concussion caused by the blast waves of shells or other ordinance exploding close by. Those who did not die often suffered long term neurological effects and sometimes shell shock.

Frank was lucky on this occasion, his concussion was short lived and he did not get a 'blighty'. After a period of recovery in a field hospital he returned to the 18th in the autumn of 1916 as they took part in the ill-fated Battle of the Transloy Ridges. In December he was able to take leave back to England.

LONDON DECEMBER 1916

Frank was not even sure Hillie was in London when he stepped off the boat train at Victoria, on a rank December evening. Leave had come through unexpectedly, and he had grasped at the week he had been offered and taken a place on the next troop train home, hardly bothering to pack even a change of clothes in the small kit bag he took with him, just a gas mask, his compass and revolver, his papers and a pay book. His mind for weeks, months, past, when he had time to think at all, had been fixated on that tiny girl, her dark eyes, so enticing with laughter, the voice that ran through his head in the darkest moments in the trench. When the fear came he often found the best way to deflect it was to focus on Hillie, to hear her singing, something from Gilbert and Sullivan maybe or an aria from 'Butterfly'.

> *'I am like the little Moon Goddess*
> *The little Moon Goddess who comes down by night*
> *From her bridge in the star lighted sky.'*

Those lines he played over and over in his head and could recall them at will. If he was lucky he could drown out the shelling and achieve sleep, or, if action was needed, he could imagine her proud of him, as his company did well under his leadership.

The journey had been vile and the troop train overfull of injured men, all getting 'a blighty', groaning and laughing by turns, smoking hard to dull the pain and believe they might just make it home. The channel threatened in the dark, the luminous crests of waves breaking over the troopship, coming out of utter darkness, sea monsters emerging from the fogs that hemmed the ship in, as she heaved and lurched her way to England.

Frank loathed these channel crossings. If anything would put him off a future career in shipping, it would be these. Mean ships, he thought they were, dark and airless, smelling always of coal and steam and vomit, stale clothes and unwashed soldiers. He gritted his teeth and collected a cup of tea and an unpleasant ham sandwich, and then was unsure if the nausea he was experiencing was caused by the boat, the sandwich or his nerves at possibly being able to see Hillie again.

Frank had realized months ago that he was deeply in love but hardly knew if he would ever summon up the courage to ask her to marry him. There were so many more worthy fellows around, richer, braver perhaps and he could never be absolutely sure that she preferred him. Often he believed she did, when he saw her laugh at one of his silly jokes or when she chose to sit beside him at a dinner or when they shared a duet at one of their impromptu concerts; then it had seemed that he really did have a chance with her. But then he thought how penniless he was, about how his life without the war was full of promises, dreams and ambitions but with little in the way of concrete livelihood. Or how his life within the war had a high chance of death, why would any girl want to marry a soldier in these days, when she had more chance of becoming a widow than a wife and mother, or worst of all, a widowed mother?

Frank's spirits had sunk into a trough, deep and gloomy as the trenches he had left behind and the freezing fog that greeted him at Victoria station did nothing to lift them. He stepped off the train and intended to shake off the stench of steam and smuts as he reached the street but the sulphurous film, heavy and clinging, that encased him outside was worse than the station. A million stinking coal fires were belching more smoke than the express engines, trying to heat the draughty homes of London on the coldest night of the year. The pall of smoke had settled and sunk to street level with no wind to disperse it in the frosty night. So it hung in droplets off Frank's nose and chin, coating every surface he touched with its acidic gleam, isolating each man from his fellows, leaving them to feel their way around the streets. For Frank there was no fear in this, just frustration at the delays it caused. The cabs had deserted London and the underground was closed, there was no alternative, he would try to find a hotel room nearby and then visit Sister Margaret in the morning.

With early morning a chilly breeze got up, but the fog, reluctant to clear, rolled and crept closer to the ground. With the daylight Frank felt more positive, and the warm water of the bath he took, seeped in and eased his spirits. He took a loofah to his back and feet to cleanse away the ingrained dirt and stimulate his skin. Each action of raising his arm to reach and stretch and scrape seemed to invigorate his mind as well as his body. As his skin began to glow from the rubbing so his resolve strengthened. Each stroke of his razor, each tightening of a button on his shirt confirmed his plan.

Stay in London. Seek her out. Tell her he loved her and see where that led to.

Put aside the other great fear, what if he proposes and she says no, she does not love him in that way? Will that kill their friendship and leave him hopeless, with nothing? No future plan to take back with him to Flanders?

But if she says yes, she loves him too, what then? All the futures he ever wanted, if he can survive this war.

Breakfasted, Frank set out for Hammersmith and the convent. Nazareth was a place of angels and annunciation, of peace and refuge for the Holy Family he thought, perhaps Nazareth House will be the same for me. He was too late for morning Mass, so there was no hope of using that as an excuse for calling. There was nothing for it but to knock at the main entrance and ask the Sister Porteress if he might please see Sister Margaret Mary. The sister seemed unfazed at the sight of a young soldier asking for one of the nuns, if it was unusual she showed no sign of surprise. Instead she showed him to the Visitor's Parlour. A small December fire burnt there, a speck of brightness amongst an atmosphere as stiff as a dentist's waiting room. Frank felt the anxiety, when you sit, with a stomach full of butterflies, waiting for the inevitable unpleasantness that would follow. There were uncomfortable chairs, net curtains and a forlorn looking parlour palm on the mantelpiece. To remind you of the sacred nature of your surroundings there were religious scenes on the walls, here a picture of the Madonna and Child with St Anne, there The Head of St John the Baptist upon a plate. Frank felt stifled, watching the tiny hand of the small clock above the fire tick out each passing second. Sister Porteress remerged, bringing him a cup of tea and a very plain biscuit.

'Sister Margaret Mary will come as soon as possible; she is engaged with the children.'

Frank drank the tea, took in all the convent smells, of floor polish, boiled cabbage, old hymn books and stale habits. He read the religious tracts upon the wall and finally heard the sound he was waiting for, swish, swish, rattle, swish, swish, rattle. It was the unmistakable sound of a nun's full length habit sweeping along the ground accompanied by the click and rattle of the rosary beads around her waist. The brisk footsteps ceased momentarily outside the door and as it opened Frank stepped forward eagerly,

'Sister Margaret Mary' He held out his hand, uncertain of his welcome, but there was no need for his anxiety.

Sister Margaret Mary welcomed him with a broad smile and returned his handshake heartily.

'It's good to see you safe and well Lieutenant Lawless, have you a leave?'

'I got in last night on the late boat, we had no notice, leave came up unexpectedly and I took it, please,' he said, after a slight nervous pause, 'call me Frank.'

The nun looked kindly. She knows why I have come, he thought.

'Well Frank, how does it go with you, is your Battalion at the Front, how have they fared?'

He gave her the latest news from Flanders, but all the time he felt his heart racing, surely beating so loudly that she must hear it too, his palms were beading with sweat and he thought he would rather face the Hun than a nun in full regalia. It was not an experience he was used to.

'I was hoping to see Hilda, erm, Miss Gordon, whilst I was in London, she told me that you would always know where she was. I wondered...'

He stumbled and mumbled and the speech petered out. His eyes drifted downward, picking out the specks of dust upon his boots. He shuffled his feet, shifted his gaze to the dancing flames of the fire and wondered if this was it, was all hope finished now?

'Well, Frank, I do know where she is staying and she told me she is happy for me to pass that information on, if ever you should ask.'

His heart soared, Sister Margaret Mary was a good nun, a kindly nun, not fierce or judgemental or stern, but one who understood the power and the need of love. He looked at the scrap of paper she handed him, Cleve Hall, Denmark Hill, Camberwell. Puzzled, he glanced at Sister Margaret Mary;

'She has a room there, she will be pleased to see you and tell you herself all about it. She will be so pleased to know that you are safe.'

'Thank you Sister, thank you, can I ask for your prayers for my Battalion, we will need all the assistance we can muster.'

'My prayers and those of all the sisters and residents here go with you and all you young men, who risk so much for our sake.'

Frank felt his spirits lighten as he left Nazareth House. The fog had lifted completely, Hillie was in London and the Thames, at full tide, sparkled and winked conspiratorially in the bright winter sun. London seemed alive this morning and optimism drove each step Frank took as he made his way across the city.

Denmark Hill was new to him, almost the countryside, widely spaced and lined with mansion houses set well back from the road in their own grounds, all built about fifty or sixty years ago by wealthy Londoners, merchants and banker types, all keen to remove themselves from the city to the fresh air of the new suburbs. Cleve Hall, when he found it, turned out to be mock Tudor, red brick with black and white timber facings and diamond paned windows. It stood three stories high and was surrounded by leafless trees, the only greenery now a couple of holly bushes and occasional conifers which lined the drive. A peeling wooden sign stood by the gate and Frank read, *Cleve Hall Residential Hotel*. As he approached he sensed an air of dilapidation around the building, weeds in the gravel of the driveway, grounds unkempt and windows dirty, a house, even one now turned into a hotel, too big, too expensive for its owners perhaps, in these days of uncertainty. But what on earth was Hillie doing, living here. Frank took the stone steps up to the massive timber doorway two at a time, determined not to lose his optimism, despite the gloom of the surroundings, and rang the bell rope. He felt like some kind of knight approaching the drawbridge of a medieval castle, demanding to fight a dragon to gain the fair princess.

The bell echoed within the hall and he could feel it reverberate with each thudding beat of his heart. Here were his nerves again. Why was he so nervous? She was only a girl, a harmless girl, with no power to injure or kill him, why then such anxiety, such knots in his stomach such panic in his pulse rate. There was a sense of having made a definitive movement, of going 'over the top', a point of no turning back.

He gave his name to the parlour maid who answered the door and enquired for Miss Gordon.

'One moment sir, I will find her.' That was it, dice thrown, she was in, he had committed himself. How would she greet him? Frank kept his eyes fixed on the stairs, inwardly counting the seconds that passed in an effort to control his breathing, steady himself, keep his equilibrium. A small squeal of laughter could be heard from upstairs and then, from two stories up, the sound of small footsteps, eager, excited footsteps, like a child running down on Christmas morning. He wanted to run up the first flight himself and throw himself towards her, catch her, catch her as she came down. All heaven is up there, with one small angel descending. But he didn't dare move and fixed his eyes on the staircase as the speed of the footsteps increased. He saw her little feet first, then the dark hem of her silk skirt brushing her ankles, her tiny waist, her figure, her beautiful neck and throat and finally her face, with its halo of dark hair, was revealed.

'Frank!' a pause, small, breathless, latent with excitement, 'Frank, how utterly delightful to see you.' Hillie held out both hands towards him, it was just the welcome he had hoped for, warm, excited, concerned. Immediately her smile was replaced by an anxious frown.

'Are you well, safe, no injuries?'

'I'm well. Leave opened suddenly, so I took it and came, I arrived last night and your good Aunt gave me your address this morning'

Hillie looked genuinely pleased and relieved to see him. Her gaze travelled up and down the length of his person, as if she did not quite believe his assurance of wellbeing until she had personally checked every inch for bullet holes or shell marks.

'Honestly, it is genuine leave, not 'a blighty.' I have one week.'

Hillie led the way into the drawing room and they sat down, awkwardly, in distant chairs, longing to be close but each slightly wary, taking time to weigh up the full implication of this unexpected meeting. She asked him again,

'Are you fine, no hurts at all? And your company, your men, do they do good work?'

Frank fidgeted in his faded, mouse-nibbled armchair, the anti-macassar chafed the back of his neck and he stood up and did a ceremonious twirl.

'Look at me, I'm top hole, nothing to worry about at all and my men, the whole Battalion, do fine work. We have not lost many fellows these last few weeks.' Hillie giggled and the tension broke with the suddenness, the crack, of ice breaking on a dry winter puddle, when a boot goes through.

'When did you arrive, have you been to Liverpool, how are your parents, how much leave do you have?'

The questions tumbled out in rapid succession at machine gun speed, as if she felt there might not be time to answer them all, before he disappeared again, as suddenly as he come. He really had survived the Somme. So many questions! Frank began to answer some, and then, when there was a slight pause, asked one of his own.

'This is an unusual choice of a place to stay, Hillie, so far out from town, why have you chosen this?'

'Mummy has gone back East, I'm by myself, there are lots of girls here, we rent rooms and volunteer in the hospital.'

'Which hospital? Why?'

'Champion Hill Infirmary, we are VADs, volunteer nurses. We help out with those who have been wounded and are brought back here to Dulwich. They are Belgians mostly, who cannot get home. They come here for treatment and to recover. They do very well, we do not lose many. I came originally to Denmark Hill Hospital for some training, but when they found I could speak French I was asked to help with the Belgians.'

Frank was surprised. The idea of her working unpaid as a volunteer nurse, in a military hospital had never occurred to him.

'We just try to do our part' was all she added

'Well Nurse Gordon, may I take you out to lunch so we can catch up at leisure?' Would she agree to lunch with him alone, or insist on a friend joining them? It would be quite understandable if she did that, but not at all what he wanted. His desire to have her to himself was overwhelming.

'How lovely, I 'll get my hat and coat'

With Hillie well wrapped up against the bitter day, they left the house. Frank offered her his arm and she took it without hesitation. He loved to feel her there, weightless, no burden, but under his protection. The difference in their height meant it was just her tiny hand and forearm that rested against the crook in his elbow. A nanny with a large pram came by, occupying most of the pavement. He drew the arm closer to him, nonchalantly, with inward daring and it was not withdrawn.

If you were to ask either of them later what they had ordered and eaten that afternoon, they would not have recalled it, or even remembered what cafe they had gone into. There was no time for thought or analysis. There were so many questions, so much to exchange; family news, friends, other's losses and liaisons. It seemed trite to Hillie, to ask, 'How is the war going?' She read the papers every day, scanned the lists of names for killed, wounded or missing, looking for those she knew, always dreading she would one day see Frank's there, always relieved when it was not. She followed the reports of actions and battles, successes and difficulties and still she could not quite believe he was here, had sought her out on his first day in London and was safe, at least for the time being.

So they did not talk of fighting or the war. He had survived so far, it was enough to know that and he would not have dreamt of telling her any of the horrors he had seen. If she asked him a direct question he would dwell upon the bravery of the men, the outstanding moments. But all the time they skirted around the big issue, their delight in being with each other again. Her voice, laughing, sparkling, lilting up and down as she regaled him with anecdotes of naughty brothers, silly friends or awkward matrons, steeped into his brain, soothing yet exciting him. He was able to look her full in the face, watch every movement of her eyes, every tiny crease change as she smiled. He took in her lashes, the dark, dark eyes themselves, her tilting little nose and her cheeks, dabbed hurriedly with face powder before she left, pearlescent in the winter light, like icing lightly dusted on a cake. They sat, close and intimate across the small table, so close he could feel her breath on his face and smell the gentle scent of lavender from her clothes.

Sometimes, when the conversation paused, he relished the tiny silences and lengthened them by delaying his responses, because it gave him precious seconds to gaze longer at her face. When lunch was over and they emerged into the fading light of a midwinter afternoon, she replaced her hand in his arm and he appropriated it. It was a natural, easy movement and no words were needed. Frank was vastly reassured. She does want to be with me, she feels safe with me, she cares about me, I will tell her, I just need the perfect moment.

When they reached the front door of Cleve Hall they hesitated.

'One day of my week is gone, may I see you tomorrow?'

'Come in, come in. I am on duty tomorrow, it is too late to change my shift now, but tomorrow evening we are having a concert, an entertainment for the veterans, would you come? Your voice would be very welcome in the concert party, and then I can try to swap my shifts for later in the week.'

Frank had to be satisfied with this, she wanted to see him again, that was the main thing, and he would get to hear her sing, but one whole day lost…

'What will you sing?'

'Something cheerful for the men, Gilbert and Sullivan perhaps, how about you?'

'I haven't sung anything for many months now, but the men have taught me some songs, or something from an Opera maybe, '

'Something popular' she suggested, 'so the pianist knows it and the men can join in. Some Christmas carols would be good.'

They chattered on, planning the songs as the maid brought tea, but at seven a bell rang.

'A curfew,' said Hillie, 'all visitors must be out of the house by seven.'

Reluctantly he took his leave, their eyes holding each other as long their tentative handshake lasted and their fingers slid gently and slowly apart.

Frank turned and headed down the drive, seeing, in his mind's eye, his smallest angel, dressed head to toe in white, a red cross emblazoned on the bosom of her apron, hair tucked demurely under a nurse's cap. It was brave of her, there was no need for her to give her time this way, she could have stayed in fresher, more fragrant air, than in a hospital of wounded soldiers, gangrenous and crippled. He knew how soldiers' minds worked when they saw a young woman, especially one as pretty as Hillie, he wasn't sure he liked the idea of those men eyeing her as she ministered to them. He sighed. Perhaps tomorrow at the concert he would get the chance to be more protective, show the men that she was 'spoken for', not available to a group of soldiers lascivious thoughts. He knew her better than to try to talk her out of her chosen role, she would stamp her small foot and say 'It is what I choose to do'.

Besides he had no 'rights'over her at all, it was not his place, to offer advice or suggestions. That could only be her father or her husband's role. He chuckled to himself too, if I was lying in some French or Belgian hospital I am sure I would recover more quickly if my brow was mopped by some pretty mademoiselle, rather than an old battle-axe.

Frank spent the next morning writing letters home, explaining that his leave was so short he didn't have time to travel north. He was well, no injuries at all. The 18th Battalion had done fine work, Liverpool should be proud of them. They had not suffered losses on the same scale that he had heard reported for some of the other northern Pals battalions. He knew the Accrington lads had been very badly hit. The brigade had moved and his company, No 3, were the best of the best. They had lost one or two officers and a few other ranks and horses but reinforcements were on their way. They were now 'out of the line', training and resting, and his parents were not to worry, he would see them again very soon.

He found a barber near his hotel for a really decent haircut and hot shave and he went shopping for shirts and fresh under wear. Finally he went to Buzzards, the famous cake maker in Bond Street and bought a splendid cake to take to the injured veterans in the evening.

And all the while Frank's head was full of Hillie, how she'd wanted to see him again, how pleased, how excited she'd been at his sudden, unexpected appearance. How relived she'd seemed that he'd not been wounded again. It was topping, absolutely top hole, just what he wanted. Now all that was needed was the right moment.

LONDON DECEMBER 1916

Frank was prompt to his appointment at the hospital and joined a small stream of visitors invited to join the choir or do a 'turn' to entertain the wounded. They filed into the canteen to find it filled with men, in pyjamas and dressing gowns, some on seats, some in wheelchairs and some still even in their beds which had been wheeled down from the ward. They were directed towards tea and biscuits and Frank delivered his cake to a small collection of similar offerings for the troops. There were some nurses and VADs flitting around and fussing over the patients, straightening sheets, plumping pillows, offering tea and cake, but Frank could not see Hillie amongst this uniformed flock. Then he picked out her tiny form emerging with a sheet of paper from behind a doctor in a frock coat. She waved him over enthusiastically.

'I have put you towards the end Frank, yours is the only voice I am certain of, have you chosen your final songs? Frank suggested 'Mademoiselle from Armentieres' and a chorus from *The Pirates of Penzance.*

'I thought maybe we could coach these young Belgians in some verses of 'It's a long way to Tipperary' and then finish with a couple of carols, not 'Silent night', too Germanic, 'Oh little Town of Bethlehem' maybe and then 'We wish you a merry Christmas'.' Hillie was more than satisfied with his choice and went off to let the pianist know.

Frank watched her trot off with her little list, efficient, caring, and adorable. All organised, she rang a small bell for silence and the frock–coated doctor welcomed them to the evening's entertainment. It opened with popular music hall songs led by some of the orderlies who were followed by three girls he assumed were nurses, giving *'three little maids from school'*. Clad in kimonos, faces whitened, they received a rousing cheer.

When Hillie came forward and sang a solo from *The Gondoliers* a profound silence fell on the audience and Frank watched them as they watched her. His writer's eye seeing the woman he loved transfix her listeners with every inward breath, every rising, falling cadence of her love song. To hear her sing again had been beyond his wildest hopes for this short week, to hear that voice, the sound filled his brain, in all its glory… He heard the tiny momentary wobble as she started the song, under-rehearsed with an unfamiliar accompanist, but they got into their stride together and as she ended, bowed and smiled to her soldier audience who, to a man, burst into enthusiastic, prolonged applause and demanded an encore. And he heard too, her sing the words from the aria in *Rodelinda*, a song from a girl who thinks her husband is lost and then finds him again,

> *'While I embrace you, Oh embrace the child.*
> *Thy sighs, thy sobs, my love give o 'er,*
> *my heart is now no longer sore,*
> *and grief and pain shall feel no more.*
> *Seeing thee pleased,*
> *has hush'd my care,*
> *come to my breast, its pleasures share*
> *Now love has fix'd his dwelling there.'*

Hillie declined the encore and ushered forward the hospital choir to sing and then one of the doctors told some music hall jokes. Neither Frank nor Hillie were sure how much the Belgian soldiers would have understood of the English humour, but everyone laughed politely. When Frank's turn came he stepped forward, sang his opening songs and gradually worked his audience into joining in, practicing each line of 'Tipperary' and going over it until he had full participation for two good verses. The room was full and warm and suffused with a sense of security, if not happiness. When he came to the carols Frank looked around and behind, seeking out Hillie. When he caught her eye he held out a hand and she came forward to join him and they sang with a single voice, joined for the second carol by all the medical staff and helpers.

> *Angels from the realms of Glory,*
> *Wing your flight o're all the earth...*

As they ended she looked up at him and smiled her thanks for helping making the concert such a success. Frank stayed to help stack chairs and move tables back into their proper positions and when Hillie reappeared immediately offered to escort her home. He had seen one of the younger doctors working his way towards her and moved fast to get his offer in and they moved towards the door together. It unnerved him that despite her obvious pleasure in being with him, other men still hovered, wanting to take their chance with her. Did they get encouragement too, was he being presumptuous, he just couldn't tell. They wandered out into the gas lit streets of south London, frosty with their breaths hanging in the air, intermingling as they spoke. He offered his arm again and she took it.

She began to thank him for coming, for the pleasure it had given to the men, but he stopped her, 'You will never have to thank me for helping you out, especially if I get the opportunity to hear you sing, I would come every night of the week if you wanted.'

She laughed. 'I don't want you to come to the hospital again, but I've managed to get the rest of the week free by promising to cover for the others over Christmas, so I have time if you want to spend it with me.'

He tried to control his excitement at the news, 'How wonderful, what shall we do, where shall we go? No picnics in the park in this weather but we can do lunches and walks and dinners and a concert.'

'Are you absolutely sure you don't want to go to Liverpool?'

'I am absolutely sure that I want to spend this leave with you if you will have me.'

They reached steps leading up to the front door of Cleve Hall and she was feeling in her pocket for a key, when she let go of his arm and climbed one step ahead of him. As she turned back to say goodnight he found himself at her exact eye level. They gazed intently into each other's eyes and Frank reached for and took back the tiny hand that had slipped from his arm. The depth of her gaze disarmed him, he had meant to rehearse this not just come out with it like a babbling idiot.

'Oh Hillie, Hilda, you know that I love you don't you?'

She nodded and leant forward and kissed him gently, oh so gently, on the forehead.

'Till tomorrow,' she said and slipped inside the door.

After the kiss, the lightest touch of lips to brow, Frank went off, feet trailing reluctantly through the crunching gravel. He stopped at the end of the drive, and looked back at the house, watching for an upstairs light to go on, hoping to identify her room. Nothing happened for at least five minutes and he began to think she must have gone to discuss her evening with one of the other girls, to laugh at his love making perhaps? What had that nod meant? That she knew he loved her and was sorry, but she could not return his affectation? Or she knew he loved her and wanted time to think before she answered. Or was that little kiss a sign of love, real passionate love like his, or just kind, sisterly, a blessing bestowed on a man going to war? A light came on, he was reassured and went back to his hotel. He was tantalisingly close to his objective.

Hillie's feelings were in tumult. She sat down on the end of the stairs, arms wrapped around her knees and her chin on her hands, sighing, trying to think, but excitement made her restless. She stood up, sat down, stood up again and finally climbed up to her room, locking herself in, not wanting any of the other girls to pop their head around the door or ask nosy questions about her visitor.

How to decide her own feelings, that was the question. Men had told her they loved her before, on more than one occasion. But she had laughed it off politely, not because she did not think they were serious, but because she did not like them in that romantic sort of way. There were men whose company she enjoyed, who made her laugh, who were good company. Almost all of them were richer or better connected than Frank Lawless. And yet for him she knew she had felt something different, even if she had not fully examined what it was. Why else had she left her new address with her aunt so that he could find her if he wanted to? Why else did she scan the papers, searching in trepidation for his name? Nevertheless, she had not seen him for five months; did men change in war time? What future would he offer? She knew he didn't really like his pre-war job and wanted to make a living as a writer, but it was precarious.

Anyway he hadn't proposed yet and maybe he wouldn't, perhaps he felt he had nothing to offer her. Love and ambition alone were hardly enough to satisfy her father of Frank's suitability as a husband. But Hillie knew too that her mother and sister liked Frank, everyone liked Frank. Everyone who knew him enjoyed his company, his charm and his intellect; she had no doubts that his ambitions would be fulfilled. She felt like the young Anne Elliot, heroine of Jane Austin's *Persuasion,* whose faith in her Captain Wentworth proved justified by subsequent events and ambitions realized. Anne Elliot regretted her early caution and was lucky to get a second chance. Hillie went to bed, turning over her feelings as often as she turned her head on the pillow. What if Frank did propose, what would she say? Or worse, what if he didn't, should she encourage him to come to the point? And the war, what of the war? She already knew one friend who had lost a fiancé and another who had been widowed, the future was surely a lottery for them all, no certainties anymore, just the unknowns of battles and no current signs of peace.

Finding Frank

I'VE FOLLOWED IN YOUR FOOTSTEPS out of Cleve Hall, down Champion Hill, across the road and into Denmark Hill Station. What were you thinking that evening as you walked up the steps to buy your ticket, how did your mind run? Love and war, war and love. You'd spent six months on the Somme in the trenches, engrossed in the mud of war, but now, in everyday London, the girl you love has nearly said she loves you.

Denmark Hill. One of the prettiest stations on the South East line. It's a listed building now. How many times did you both walk up those steps, under the cast iron fringe and into its glazed pavilion? The pretty Victorian ticket hall, with its air of an orangery attached to a stately mansion, is a pub and coffee shop these days. Did you look up and see the cornices and tile -covered walls with their Italianate décor and then saunter down glassed -in walkways to the platforms below.

I've followed you down the stairs and sat waiting on a platform bench, hoping that, perhaps, you might step off a ghostly train that stops here on its way from Clapham Junction. Can I spot you, tall and upright amongst the alighting passengers? Maybe you sat on this bench that evening. Could you have occupied this very space and gazed up, absently, at the painted capitals that support the roof, or stared, in a dream, at the colourful brick work arches. Do we all leave traces, impressions of our hopes and fears in the places where we linger? Your heightened awareness of the closeness of death and the intensity of love must have left some kind of aura.

I think I can see you now, getting up from the seat, pacing the platform, stepping into the train, hoping, praying, for life and love tomorrow.

LONDON DECEMBER 1916

Frank turned up at Cleve Hall promptly the next morning with a plan for how they would spend the day. A train up to Town, some Christmas shopping, lunch in a pleasant hotel, a walk in Green Park in the afternoon then the theatre in the evening. Hillie agreed to it all, and to spending an entire day in his company, without any friend or chaperone. She reached for his arm before it was offered and nestled up towards him in the queue at the ticket office or whenever they needed to cross a busy road. It felt right, comfortable and where she belonged. In Oxford Street they wandered amongst the crowds, and bought presents for their mothers. Together they chose a book and a set of soldiers to paint for Hillie's brother, and a box of assorted toys for Sister Margaret Mary's orphans at Nazareth House.

Over lunch Hillie said, 'There is one person I wish we could see this week, before you return. Alan would love to see you, he hero worships you, he's always asking if I have any news of you. Could we take him out for tea do you think, term is nearly finished, I'm sure they would release him.'

Frank was happy to agree but argued with the word hero, 'I am just one among many, he mustn't think of me that way. '

'You are the one he knows well and is fond of, who we all speak well of, he needs some heroes to look up to, you are an honorary brother to him,' she laughed, 'with so many older sisters he needs one.'

Frank was flattered and moved and Hillie realized her words probably carried a more significant meaning to both of them.

The next afternoon saw them at the doors of the college, with Hillie asking Alan's housemaster for permission to take him out to tea. Alan appeared, ecstatic at the unexpected visitors. He gave Hillie a fleeting hug and hurled himself at Frank. They headed first for the park. It was too cold for cricket or boating but they found a ball amongst the leaves and amused themselves throwing and kicking it around, intercepting, chasing and in Frank and Alan's case, tackling each other. Once Frank and Hillie collided and came face to face, hands touching as they scrambled for the ball, pausing for a moment to take in the intimacy. Alan sensed the pace had slowed down and urged them forward, shouting and demanding, 'C'mon Hillie, throw it!' They pulled apart and she grabbed the ball and hurled it with all her might and sent Alan into a heap of leaves, searching.

Frank caught her hand, 'Hillie, what I said last night, I meant it.'

'I know you did, I'm thinking of it all the time.'

The conversation got no further, they returned to schoolboy games, then took the lad to a café and fed him as much toasted tea cake and buns as he could eat.

Alan asked Frank, 'When do you go back, will I see you again before you go?'

'I don't think so, old man, I only had a few days, they're almost gone.'

'When will you come again?'

'I have no idea, when the Generals let me I suppose, if your sister is kind enough to want to see me.'

'You will Hillie, won't you. You always want to see Frank, don't you?'

'I do, and I'm sure when he next gets leave, Frank will come and see you too.'

The following day was Sunday and after meeting for a late morning Mass and then lunch they started to walk along the Embankment. Frank told her about his latest idea for a play, about his fellow officers, anything to keep her amused. She listened, always alert and interested. They watched small boats scurrying up the Thames, schoolboy crews sculling, ducks, swans and cormorants bobbing and diving, and on the riverside path, squirrels searching for the last few gleanings of the year. They brought a bag of stale bread from an old lady to feed the ducks and watched as they fought and jostled each other for pride of place close to the bank, nearest the source of largesse. It was a gentle, peaceful afternoon, a million miles away from the noise and munitions of the trenches.

As darkness fell they reached Westminster Bridge. Big Ben stood tall and shadowy as it chimed out the quarter and the Houses of Parliament cast their own dour reflection. The lamplighters were making their way across the bridge and as each street lamp was lit its reflection hit the inky water beneath the bridge, rippling and disseminating into a series of orange shades upon the water. The bridge was busy, Sunday strollers, hospital workers, parliamentarians, the men directing the war. Who knew who the scurrying people were, anonymous in the enfolding December light? Omnibuses, occasional motor cars, all lit at road level, and the breath of all this life rising in the winter chill to shimmer in a surreal cloud over the Thames.

Frank and Hillie began to cross the bridge, slowly weaving amongst the crowded walkway. Somewhere near the middle, her heel caught in a crack in the pavement and she stumbled. Frank caught her tight by the elbow and no damage was done but as he turned to ask if she was unharmed he caught her eyes again, glittering under the glow of a street lamp. He bent down closer, closer, drawn irresistibly to her face and realized he did see love there. When he kissed her she didn't draw away but held him closer.

'I do love you Frank, I do, I know you meant it, I know that we have probably loved each other for a long time.'

'Will you marry me Hillie, will you? I'll do anything to make you happy.'

'Frank, I love you, I am not sure about marriage just yet, in the middle of a war, I need time to think about that, but I do love you.'

And with that answer and the promise that she would write to him, Frank had to be satisfied when he returned to his battalion in Flanders.

For Freedom and Honour

64 OFFICERS AND 1274 OTHER ranks of the Liverpool Pals Battalions gave their lives in the service of their country in the course of 1916. The 18th Battalion was in the front line near Bienviflers and Berles as 1917 opened and although a quiet time for the Battalion in general, Frank was wounded for the second time. He received a gunshot wound to the chest and seems to have been lucky, in that the bullet was slowed or diverted by the pay book in his pocket. This wound was serious, requiring hospital treatment and it earned Frank a 'Blighty'.

LONDON AND LIVERPOOL JANUARY 1917

Hillie was surprised when the handwritten note reached her at work one afternoon. It came from a sister at Denmark Hill Hospital, 'A new patient here is asking for you, please come across when you can.' She was flustered and distracted from her work, rolling bandages badly, dropping a dressing bowl and attracting the unwanted attention of her own ward sister. Denmark Hill took in newly arrived casualties from the Front. Who was asking for her by name? Who knew where she worked? It could only be Frank. Then she did almost give way to all her worst fears. This was the man she loved, the one she had written to, only four weeks ago, agreeing to marry. The one she had pledged her future to, for better or worse. The man to whom she had written, *'yes, yes, with all my heart, I do love you enough to want to marry you and to marry as soon as we can, not wait until the end of the war, not wait until you can offer me a suitable home, but now, as soon as my Father has given his permission. My fears for your future, for all our futures, are buried in my love. I have confidence in the strength of our affection, which it will get us through all difficulties, fears and danger. I love you and only you.'* That confidence was nearly wavering now.

Hillie changed out of her uniform as rapidly as she could when her shift ended and started the walk across to Denmark Hill. Sometimes on these dark evenings she was nervous as she walked home, but tonight a different type of fear caused her to stumble the more she tried to rush. Every horror, every injury that she had seen and nursed on other soldiers raced through her mind. She couldn't bear to think that Frank, her beautiful, handsome Frank might be badly wounded. 'Wounded' could mean anything from loss of several limbs, a head injury, facial damage, to gunshots through any part of the body. But he had been able to speak to the nurse, and that was promising.

She was directed to the Officer's wards and found him, sleeping quietly. After watching him motionless for a few minutes she took in that there was no visible head wound, no facial disfigurement, he had two arms and hands, so far, so good. She looked around for the Sister in charge, to get more information.

'He has a serious chest wound, a bullet has been removed, it missed his vital organs and we are hopeful he will do well. It seems there was something in his pocket, some sort of book which slowed it down and helped protect him.'

Hillie stood there, keeping her silent vigil, sending up prayer after prayer of Thanksgiving for his survival. Their engagement was only a month old and had already come close to a catastrophic end. Frank might have died before her father had even received his letter requesting his consent.

Hillie reached out then and took Frank's hand, stroking it, kissing it, holding it, willing her health and energy to transfer to him, offering it in exchange for her own, and finally he woke to find her there. The moment he recognised who held his hand, Frank returned the grasp tightly, 'Now I really do believe in angels,' he said.

Hillie visited Frank every day for a fortnight after that, as his fiancée she had a right of interest in him. He told his parents his wounds were minor and not to travel down. He wanted no one but Hillie and so she came, whenever she was allowed access to the ward, sitting by him, watching as his wound was dressed, fearful always of infection and delighted as each dressing came away cleaner and dryer. She knew he was in pain but he made little fuss and maintained he had no memory of the incident that caused his injury. Hillie helped wash, feed and finally dress him when he was well enough to leave his bed.

One evening visit, Frank was immensely cheerful when she arrived. 'The doctor says, if I have some help, I am well enough to go home to recuperate. Could you come with me on the train to Liverpool, come and stay with my parents for a while. It would be a splendid opportunity for them to get to know you. Can you get time off?'

'I'll make time.'

So they travelled together to Liverpool, he reluctant to accept any help, she terrified of him over exerting himself and risking his wound.

Hillie wasn't sure what to expect of Frank's home and family. He told her they were comfortable but not rich, his father well-read and kindly, his mother religious but always saddened and grieving for her lost daughter, her emigrated sons and unknown grandchildren. Hillie hoped to be liked and to like them and Frank tried to reassure her that this would be the case. Nonetheless she was uneasy.

When the cab drew up outside 33 Harthill Avenue and the chill, dank north -western air hit her, Hillie felt a pang for Hong Kong, for London, even for her old convent school. She was used to warmth, warmth and most of all space. Big rooms, high ceilings, corridors and gardens were her natural habitat. Her childhood had been spent in spacious colonial bungalows, school days in vast echoing convent halls and dormitories. Even the mansion flats her mother rented had twelve foot ceilings and roomy corridors. The semi-detached house in front of her was smaller than any of these.

Frank's parents greeted their wounded soldier son with loving concern but were stiff in their reception of Hillie. Did they think it was somehow improper of her to have nursed him or accompanied him on the train, she wondered. Frank had written to them weeks ago, asking for their congratulations on his engagement. Perhaps it was just her imagination, but she felt in the way, as if they wanted him to themselves. Hillie tried to reassure herself it was just anxiety about his injury. Frank had been so insistent on her presence. In hospital he could hardly bear to have her leave his sight. For his sake she decided to ignore the frosty atmosphere and focus herself entirely on him.

Over the following weeks, whilst Frank's health continued to improve, Hillie's relationship with his mother did not. 'Can I help with dinner in any way?' she had offered one early evening.

'We will be having tea at six o clock. You can help peel the potatoes and carrots,' came the sharp retort. And Hillie stood over a sink in the back scullery staring at a pile of muddy potatoes without an idea of what to do with them. Frank came up behind her, laughed, put his arms around her waist and showed her, knife in one hand, potato in the other, how to pare away the skin.

Frank's mother was disgusted, and upbraided him later,

'Who does that young woman think she is, not able to peel a vegetable?'

Frank tried to explain, 'In Hong Kong they had servants and at boarding school no girl would be allowed near a kitchen.'

'How will you live if she cannot cook, if she is too smart to clean up, how will she take care of you?'

'Mother, she is warm, loving and intelligent company. I will take care of her. I will earn enough to pay people to do the work for us.'

On another occasion Frank's mother had sneered at Hillie.

'Did your Mother never teach you to cook, does she never cook herself?'

'She cooks well,' was Hillie's response, 'She cooks the Italian dishes of her childhood when she can get the ingredients. Frank enjoyed the macaroni, didn't you Frank? In the Colony it would have been seen as bad form to do the local servants work for them, it would have deprived someone of a job. But I'm sure if Frank needs me to cook for him, I can learn.'

Hillie was well aware of the snort of derision produced by her future mother-in-law. Nor did his mother want Hillie's help or advice in nursing Frank or changing his dressings.

'I have nursed him all his life. You see that kitchen table? I stood there, where you are now, when he was just two years old, gasping for breath, suffocating with the diphtheria. I laid him on that table and the doctor came and cut into his throat to allow him to breathe again, to bring him back to life, turn his face from blue to pink, when I thought he had gone. And I cleaned that wound and kept it clear and open and nursed him then and I will nurse him now. I need no help from you, young lady.'

Hillie could see how hurt Frank was by his mother's reaction to her. It seemed so petty and pointless in the midst of war, that people couldn't just try to get on, to spare him the atmosphere of resentment, when he and his friends risked life and limb to protect them all, on a daily basis.

Breakfast time was a blessed relief each morning. Frank's mother went to Mass but she often came back more saddened and depressed than before. Each day it seemed, as well as praying for her lost daughter she listened as prayers were said for her neighbours' sons listed dead or missing and those 'whose anniversaries occur about this time.' Hillie found it gruelling enough every Sunday listening to the forlorn and ever lengthening list of lost sons, fathers and husbands but to listen, as Frank's mother did, on a daily basis, was more than she could contemplate.

Frank and Hillie made it their business to leave the house as often as they could. They walked to build up Frank's stamina as well as clear their heads of the poisonous atmosphere at home. When the weather allowed Frank showed her the streets of his childhood, the White Star office in James Street, the

Docks and the Liver building. They walked down Lime Street past St Georges Hall. Frank never dwelt on what he had seen at the Front but he tried to describe the excitement he had felt, all his friends had felt, in those earliest days of enlistment, when fighting for your King and Country had seemed a grand thing to do.

Being out of the house allowed them time to explore an early physical intimacy that being engaged now permitted. When they were unobserved they reached for each other's hands as they walked. One evening they went to a concert at the Empire and within the safety and darkness of the auditorium, their hands had sought each other and began a slow fingertip journey. His roughened forefinger tracing lines across her palm, each individual finger and finally the soft skin on the inside of her wrist. She returned the movement, her tiny fingers travelling the lines of veins, feeling the hairs rise on the back of his hand. Enthralled by each other and enveloped in the music of Tchaikovsky they left the realities of their wartime situation and entered a semi dream world of their own creation, warm, safe, intimate and totally private. Coming out into the chill of a February night Frank wrapped his great coat around her and they moved as one. In a quiet and shadowed spot Frank had stopped and kissed her, gently at first and slowly, then passionately. Within the strength of her attraction to him Hillie felt her own desires rising too. A new feeling, exciting, frightening, bewildering but pure and loving. Hillie knew she had made the right decision and Frank was utterly certain of it. They would marry as soon as humanly possible.

They headed to a café and ordered grilled chops for a late supper. As they ate, the plans for their future life together tumbled out. They would go abroad, somewhere warm, Frank would write, his plays would be masterpieces, agents would be falling over themselves to sign him up. They would be comfortable and love one another for all time. Nothing would ever come between them.

Letter 2

'33' (Harthill Avenue Mossley Hill Liverpool)   ***Feb 15ᵗʰ***   1917
My own darling little Hillie,

How can I say how sorry I am, my darling old Hillie, about that letter not reaching you yesterday. I do hope you got it by the last post.

Beastly nuisance about the letter from the 'East' isn't it? I too am rather on tenter hooks until I hear from your father. I hope to goodness he won't be furious. If he is then I really will ask you to elope! — I know you believe that I am a dreamer, don't you Hillie? You shall see my dear.

No word again today from the War Office... Bless their hearts! I think it most generous of them to give me another day to work at 'Yvette'. Hillie! I am simply crazy about this play. I think it will be splendid. I can praise it up safely as it is Maupassant's and not mine. When it is finished and if you think it's fine, I'm going to send a copy to Mair (and Bocher... ask him to talk to Scott about it, and let me know if it is likely to interest Puccini as a libretto. My first idea for it was as a libretto... Then Mayer must be consulted about copyright. If permission can be obtained from the great Guy's executors to 'do' a play from one of his novels...As an Opera book, it would be top-hole. Dances, Love in the Moonlight, Serenades,, Roses, Love all the way, Passion, Deathbeds!... Everything, you see!◊

I started yesterday morning as the sprit moved me strongly to get up and make a start. I'd planned it all out the day before, so I started translating big chunks of the book, to provide the expository matter. Got on fine, when after lunch, Lo! Another d... woman floated in for a gossip and tea... A nice girl, this time, a friend of my brothers, but Oh didn't I scowl and curse... Lost three precious hours, so after dinner, to prevent further disasters I went up to 'your' bedroom and attacked it there before a huge fire. I worked for hours and did all the first scene... Today I'll

---

◊ Yvette is a short story by Guy de Maupassant. It is a moral tale of a mother who is a Courtesan, who tries to keep her daughter in innocence of her profession. When the daughter finds out her mother's true way of life there is much heartbreak and sadness. Frank is right; it is the type of story that would have suited Puccini well as the basis for an Opera.

go on and should finish the first act, that means it's a quarter finished doesn't it? Topping!

I think I'd better not send you any of it until it's finished. You'd do better, I think, to read it all at once and besides I want the thing by me, whilst I'm working on it' to refer to.

If only it isn't too questionable a theme, I think we are onto a good thing this time, Hillie dear, with a bit of luck.

My darling old thing! I am hoping you won't dash off down to Weymouth right away, tho' if I am sent to Pembroke, it would be a lot nearer than London wouldn't it? It is too decent altogether of your Mother to promise to wait until my Medical Board before deciding. I'm very sorry to hold up your plans so, but I must hear from them soon I suppose.

Hillie! You darling little thing! — I am so very jealous of every-body…. The people at '21', the crowds in the street and shops and buses. They can all see you and admire you and enjoy your voice and your smiles and … And I can't!

Isn't it a stupid old world?

Do you think they all love you as much as I do, Hillie? They may say they do and think they do, but I feel quite, quite sure they don't you know.(I know it sounds frightful cheek to say that). I was reading Victor Hugo over my breakfast today… (Bad manners but you taught me to read over meals didn't you?). In a letter in 1822 to a woman, he said he felt quite certain no one before had ever felt such tremendous love for a woman as he felt for her…He had a great mind and a great soul, yet I believe he married this woman and his affection cooled — I think of Emily Dentruss and the crowd at '21', Lottie Madigan and Halacida… all so different, yet all so intensely ugly in their little amours and alike in that. Hilda! Hilda! Do you think I could ever be cool towards you? I shall either love you truly, or I shall hate you. There can be nothing in between…and I don't think I shall hate you, you know, if big souls cool off in their affections, thank God for little ones, say I…

Perhaps ambition spoils these people…Hugo, his poetry, Dentruss, her voice, Halacinda his ability to turn hits….. My ambition is to be always near you, anyway, anyhow… in the best place possible, but if you are given to me, then nothing else matters to me. I'll try hard to sell 'Yvette' and get a good job, but if I fail…alright! What matter, so long as you don't mind –

Goodbye darling Hillie, for today. The letter ends but my thoughts go on… From the first impressions of you at '29' through to the months of Peace and War, to that kiss as the train went out of Lime Street last week… and further still, right up to this moment, when I wonder what you are doing and envy those who are near you.
A kiss and all my love
Frankie

Letter 3
'33'   **Feb 18**th

My own darling little Hillie

Thank you so much my own darling, for your letters of yesterday and today…they bring me near to you, dear, and while I read them I am happy and content.

I have got my orders at last… Write to Chester and report to the G.O.C. of the Western Command, who, in his turn will instruct me about a Board 'to be assembled for the purpose of ascertaining the state of my health, at an early date.' After that, when I have received their decision, be it leave, Home Service, light duties or active service, I 'will proceed <u>at once</u> and report personally to the O.C 3rd King's at Pembroke Dock, for further orders'. So that's alright…

Now a bit more military news… in a letter this morning from one of the 18th Officers, he says the 'soft job' he previously mentioned as waiting for me was not the Musketry one at all, but that the Brigadier wanted me to train for staff Duties, was going to send me somewhere to learn all about it, and then going to put me on his staff!

This would have been a big compliment, as it isn't Stanley of course, of the 89th Brigade, (who made me the offer when I was wounded in August), but Morgan, our own fellow, of the 21st—the Brigade of the famous Wilts and Yorks…

Isn't it extraordinary luck that I should have missed a staff job twice through being in Hospital?… So just to make sure Hillie, that I have missed it, I've written a note to Claude Hyson, who's a pal of mine on the staff, to ask… I enclose it, so that if you don't want me to do anything to accelerate going out, you can tear it up… I wouldn't, for one single instant, darling Hillie, do anything to go out there again, unless you want me to, but this staff job would be a fairly safe one… and a real godsend after the line…. No 'going over the bags' anyway… and it is pretty plain now I shall get out again sooner or later, isn't it, dear old thing?

I recommend you post it, but you know I shall be quite happy what-ever you do Hillie, 'cos I am only happy when I please you and if it makes you happier for me to do nothing, then burn it...I promise I shall have no regrets, so don't think I will now, will you?

'Yvette' is finished, bar a visit on Monday to the big library in town to get hold of some words I can't find in my little dictionary, and if pos-sible find a copy of Conrad's translation of 'Yvette' to see what he makes of some weird idiomatic passages, which rather stumped me... Then I'll send it to you... I'd like to think it isn't too 'blue' for a licence... I'll drop a note to Mayer to ask him if he will read it... I've already written to Mrs Allen to ask if she's ever heard of it being dramatized in Paris. I don't think there's any likelihood of it being done in England before.

It would be a perfect joy to produce it. It lends itself so well to decora-tion, the artists would like the parts and the producer could really find some use for his intelligence and feelings.

I've never met the lady you mention — who criticises the great genius who wrote the thing so heavily... she must be an authority to speak so dog-matically I suppose, so I can't contradict. I must confess that I don't know his work well. The little I do know I admire tremendously and certainly do not think it immoral. Besides, what is 'immoral' work? I'm d... if I know, Hillie old thing. You will hear of people who find the nude, in painting, shocks their sense of decency... Then I am indecent, for I am not shocked if the painter is an artist ... I don't believe you are either. When the Lord Chamberlaine wouldn't licence 'Ghosts', as he found it 'indecent'... and 'Ghosts' is a powerful appeal for purity.

'Tristan and Isolde,' to some minds, is obscene! It is all lunacy and igno-rance! To appreciate virtue one must know vice, I agree with Oscar Wilde's 'there is no such thing as an immoral book. There is only good or bad art.'

If a book is horrible and the only effect the author can foresee upon its readers is to stir their basest instincts, it may be 'immoral'. I'm sorry to dash the authors hopes ('Victoria Cross' and her school of writing) but I'm afraid they are only disgusting and rather 'moral' really as they merely succeed in inspiring a feeling of loathing, on the whole, for the vices they try to glorify.

This sounds like a sermon…I'm awfully sorry, but I feel like defending 'Yvette'. It is well written, extremely interesting and, as one of the characters says

'After all, life is what it is and we can't change it, my dear…'

Very true… for small souls.. (And most of us have small souls I'm afraid)… but why be cowards and refuse even to look at life, particularly when an artist like Guy de Maupassant offers to shew us round the show?

But your friend would appear to wish to deny you the pleasure and I think that would be a shame, don't you.

I reckon she'd box my long ears if she heard my horrid comments on her advice to you, so for goodness sake, don't tell her any of my views on the matter, will you Hillie?

I'll send you the MSS as soon as I've done with it. Early next week I hope.

All the snow has gone now, thank goodness… I became very tired of it.

It is interesting to see the working of this allotment scheme in these parts… all the people are renting, for a few shillings a year, so many yards of otherwise waste land, and planting potatoes and other vegetables, in order to supply their own requirements at a moderate expense of money and some little energy in their spare time. It seems a good scheme, don't you think? All the waste land at the back of this house is being dug up by the perspiring neighbours, fearful of the threatened prohibitive prices… If it draws that man next door to plant potatoes, in his spare time, instead of striving to emulate Robert Radford or Sammarco, I'll be one of the very first to yell 'Hurrah! It's a topping scheme!.. for he's a d….nuisance and played the devil with poor little 'Yvette' when he started yodelling.

I feel for you in your antipathy to young babies! One always expects you to kiss them and I hate that… You feel so ridiculous…If you could only get them ready made at say six or seven years of age, when their features had taken on some sort of order and they've given over yelling and saying 'dad, dah ' all the time. That's all I know about babies I'm afraid.

Hilda! My darling... I think you are a little bit mean about those letters you know... I burnt all yours on condition that you burnt mine. Those Ghent letters are most uninteresting ... I wish you would say that every letter I write is uninteresting compared to what I tell you with a kiss, because I try to tell you then so much more than I dare attempt to write... So please burn everything Hillie dear, for everything is inadequate and unsatisfactory...save to see you and hold you tightly and kiss you.

Hillie! How careful I shall have to be in taking care of you.... I love to think of you as a flower, for you are so sweet and fragrant... But if you are given over to my care, I often wonder if I am skilled and clever enough to keep you so fresh and beautiful as you are now, for flowers are so fragile you know... But I shall love and adore my little flower and try so hard to keep all unkind winds away and if it will nestle up very closely to my shelter and sometimes allow me to enjoy its own rare fragrance, I feel quite, quite sure we will weather everything and laugh at any bad times that come along.

Darling Hillie! One of the people in 'Yvette' says...'.but a woman's soul is always as far from your own as the stars...' and I don't believe that either ... Until that wonderful night when I sat in a dirty billet at Ribancourt-sur-L'Ancre, and read those words of yours which made all life joyous for me, I believed you were as distant as the stars, Hilda. I used to look at your eyes – and wonder if any man would ever dare to think he saw an invitation in them... At your lips and wonder if any man could ever be found who would dare to kiss them... I used to wonder if God could possibly have given you a heart which would love anybody, for I thought you were rarer than anything to be found on earth and the idea of you condescending so far was almost annoying to me...

But the stars came down to me, as my ambition could not soar so high, and Oh my Hillie... my own, darling, beloved little girl, whom one day – very soon - I pray I will call little wife - I have looked in your eyes and I've held you and kissed you - and I feel you love me a little - sufficient to make me say 'Oh darling Hillie!'

My own, my love, my life, I want you to be by me always, and have perfect joy and peace, but now, even now I am very, very, happy my dear! Goodbye and a kiss.
All my love
Frankie

Finding Frank

I OFTEN THINK OF YOU as I transcribe your letters - committing them to the memory of machines, your writing scanned, stored, numbered and transcribed.

And you, as you wrote them - I see you sometimes in a trench -leaning back against the earthen side, field notebook propped up against your knees -writing in pencil, pages numbered and commas precise even then. The paper has a translucent quality after a hundred years -but the pencil is firm, purplish in colour, easy to read.

Sometimes these pencil notes are hurried, brief, but others continue page after page, your thoughts as they arise, conversations with an absent partner, questions answered two weeks later. The length depends on what time you have, how late in the day, how close to posting time, whether things are quiet or shells are falling close by.

Sometimes you must be writing at a desk, perhaps in your billet in the cure's house, or maybe you have carved out an office for yourself in a covered trench. I see you, writing in pen, inkwell close by, steady handed, no blots or smudges. The pages, paragraphs and lines are firm and clear, gradually fading as your ink runs dry. I see you sigh, refill your pen and start again, each letter reinvigorated by fresh ink.

Did you write your letters of love longhand to have that connection with her, in those long empty days and hours when you were not required to fire your guns or rally troops. I think you had a little typewriter too, to write your orders and send replies and chits and reports home and then clattered away into the night, to help drown out the rumbling of the distant shells

I wonder too if I will get to know, without your saying, but merely by the pressure of your pen, when you are tired or sad or sick of mud. When, despite all your efforts at cheerfulness and positivity your melancholy on the pointlessness of war, the filth and death of the trenches creeps through.

And if I can know, she who knew and loved you most must have recognised it too and redoubled her prayers for you.

How she treasured those letters, stained some with tears, horded them, stored them through the rest of her life and handed them on, her only legacy of you, for us to find.

For Freedom and Honour

WHEN FRANK RE-JOINED THE BATTALION they were based around Agny, alternating between trench duty and training. Frank was selected for promotion to adjutant, the senior Captain's role, and spent several weeks at Third Army School. He was also issued with a horse named Blackie, who went with him through several battles over the next eighteen months. He became very attached to her and mentions his 'fat old mare' in several letters. The Battalion went to fight the opening assaults of the Battle of Arras throughout April.

Letter 4

Third Army School   B. E. F. France
March 26th 1917
My own darling Hillie,

I couldn't write yesterday, Hillie darling, as most of the day was spent in a motor bus, coming down from the line to this place, and we arrived too late for the post.

I always seem to be writing these wretched excuses for not writing, and feel so very ashamed, but you know, Hillie, don't you, how I love the privilege of writing to you?...It is the next best thing to talking to you, my darling, and I curse pretty strongly when I am prevented.

The team and I had a most exciting journey. The road was so bad that I thought, sometimes, the old bus would topple over.… Two or three times it sank into the ruts and we had to get out and push!

Of course I couldn't help feeling a bit sorry at leaving the Battalion again. So soon after my arrival, but I know my own darling little Hillie won't worry the least little bit for five whole weeks now, will she?... and so I am going to say I am very pleased too 'cos I never want her to worry about anything.

They go 'in' on Tuesday. I do hope they have good luck. The conditions in the line now have changed so much that the fighting is different to the old days in every way, and one can't quite imagine what it's like. I was speaking to a fellow yesterday and he said, on his bit of route they had pushed on a whole day and not seen a single German.

Graham, when I spoke to him yesterday, said they were getting it 'very hot', but other people who were up in the line then say it is quite cushy. Perhaps Graham isn't a very good judge of frightfulness yet!

Anyway I hope the old 18th doesn't get knocked about.

What horrible weather, Hillie! It's bitterly cold down here, but I've a comfy billet, with a bed, sheets and an eiderdown, at the house of the Curé's sister, so I can afford to laugh at the hail and rain. I am pitying poor little Hillie, tho' 'cos I know how she hates the cold!

What about that sweater Hillie dear? Has anyone else admired you in it yet? I don't care what Jean says, I think you look most perfectly sweet in it, Hillie… you do in everything, of course, but a woman always looks a fright in a sweater. You are the only one who can wear one.

How mean of you to rub it in again about the macaroni! I do think you ought to apologise for my rudeness to your mother, give her a kiss and say I didn't mean it…'cos I didn't! Then she would forgive me or put it down to my narrow mind!

I've been imagining the dish of spaghetti you describe, Hillie. How I should have just loved to have been there. Of course, of course, you silly little Hillie, you should enjoy every single thing that reminds you of those happy times we have had, 'cos they will bring to your mind a vision of the days ahead… Which are going to be happier and even more wonderful than those we are inclined to mourn sometimes.

I've just been talking to a French officer, wounded at Verdun and invalided out. He says he feels quite sure the war can only last a few months longer…He has seen everything, from August 1914, so knew what he was talking about. Of course, I nearly fell on his neck and hugged him.

I shall get a letter from you quite soon, won't I Hillie? For I feel quite sure you will have posted one to this address? I am going to look out for it very anxiously, for today, somehow, I would give anything to hear you say again that you love me…

I am reading over and over again those letters I had from you on Saturday, Hillie, sending me a kiss and the sweetest message in the world, but I want to hear you tell me all over again that you love me…

Oh darling Hillie! I do want you, dearest.

I am praying every day that I may see you soon again, for I feel sometimes I simply cannot bear it any longer and that I will make an effort to get home to you… But that's all cowardice and nonsense I suppose. We must just wait and wait and trust that our dream of 'June' will come true. I feel sure it will, you know.

What a dirty dog I am to write in such a melancholy strain. As if it isn't ten thousand times more difficult for my sweet Hillie.

Hilda, my own darling, forgive me, I'm not melancholy at all, really… I'm tremendously happy…but savage…more savage than I can say because I want to be near you, and this stupid war is interfering! My darling little Hillie! I wouldn't want the gateau if only I could have you … I want nothing else from fate but Hillie. I love her so much that I have no love left for ambition, money, or anybody or anything else.

Hilda! I promise I shall not forget that you want me to come back safely, and I will dear, whatever my job.

This prospect of going as Adjutant does away, I'm afraid, with my chance of going on the Brigade, but it is as safe or perhaps safer, than 'learner', so, you'll have to pray, dear, that it comes off, won't you?

When I was leaving yesterday the adjutant said, 'Goodbye… and I hope you're not recalled before the five weeks are up…'

That looks as though his brother, the second-in-command, was going soon to England.

I hope he does, 'cos if I'm going as adjutant, the sooner the better, eh?

I hope the stunt at your old school passed off alright Hillie dear. Of course I should have just loved to have asked those old nuns if they weren't very proud of a certain dark eyed little ruffian, who wouldn't be a holy angel. If they'd said 'no!' I'd have tweaked their pious noses and said 'damn!

Anyway, you've promised to take me, haven't you, Hillie.

My dear old thing! You are simply forbidden to burst all your screw at Buzzards! … so there, and defy me if you dare(Iron will!)◊

Truly Hillie, you are a darling to have sent off another topping cake, but no more while I am at the Army School, at any rate, 'cos the Mess here is quite good. It hasn't arrived yet, but I expect the fellows on the C'oy will eat it anyway. That's the usual arrangement. If it's like the first one, it's awfully good.

Hillie! I can't help thinking of that poor wretch that Dorothy Cartwright told us about… the man out here who babbles immoderately of 'Hilda Gordon'. You can't help being the most adorable little person in

---

◊ burst all your screw i.e spend all your money

the world, any more than I can help being the luckiest... And we can't help the fellows miseries can we? But do give him a kindly thought, Hillie dear, 'cos I've thought about that same little 'Hilda' until my heart nearly burst and I'm full of sympathy for him.

All the same, he shouldn't babble about you, should he, Hillie?

Father will have your letter by now won't he, Hillie, poor wretch. I'm less sorry for him tho', I think, for calling you 'my dear young lady' patronising idiot!

This is the weirdest letter, I know. I feel quite unable to catch hold of my thoughts today, Hillie. When I am thinking of you a great deal...and I lay awake last night, dreaming and dreaming of the days that are past and are to come...and when I am loving you so much that I feel I shall die if I don't see you soon, Hillie...It is no use my trying to write properly, 'cos I can tell you nothing, no matter how I try.

If only you could walk into this dingy little room of the Curés sister this afternoon! How I should jump up at the rustle of your skirt and the sound of your brisk little steps. My own darling Hillie! I would run to you, as you ran to me that afternoon in December when I came home, and I would tell you absolutely everything dear, for I would offer you the tenderest kiss a man could ever give.

Never mind Hillie! I shall kiss this little letter, 'cos your sweet little hands will really get it then, and you know I have a particular devotion to your hands, don't you Hillie?

I am thinking of you every moment, darling.
Every bit of my love
Frankie

Letter 5

Third Army School   B E F   France
April 10th

My own darling little Hillie,

.... even in serious things, the most serious things that you can possibly imagine, you know you have only to call me don't you. And I shall come and put my arms around you. And give you a little kiss, (if you will let me,) so that we can weather the storms together?

If only you will let me take on every single one of your little troubles, Hillie! Will you? My own sweet Hilda! You know I will do my little best to cope with 'em don't you?... and as for 'sticking up for you'...! Oh Hillie! If the whole world was against you, I should only be the prouder to have the honour of hearing your dear little voice cry out for me.

Of course, of course, I do honestly believe the war will be over soon, perhaps before June or July. I am going to tear out a few bits from today's 'Journal', just to buck you up dear and show you we really are nearing the end.

Besides, how splendidly we have done, so far ... and the French news hasn't come yet. I am hoping it will be wonderful!

I don't think our division will have been in this first 'push', but I don't know. They are sure to 'go in' very soon, tho', so there will be a good many changes in the Battalion, I'm afraid, by the time I get back. Do spare a prayer for the 18th, won't you, in the coming weeks, that they may have good luck, do their job alright and not suffer too much? 'Cos you know, you really can help in that way, I am sure of it.

Of course I shall give to you, Hillie, my Easter Communion. I shall go next Sunday and offer it for your own intention. I promise it shall be the most decent Communion I am capable of, for I really want you to get your intention very badly---- I have an idea it is the same as mine!

They were saying in the mess tonight that Officers are going to get a very decent gratuity at the end of the war. At present it stands at 2/3rds pay for every year of service since August 14. That'll be very useful to us, won't it Hillie, and put us well in funds for our world or Arran trips!

Yes! I often think, too, how splendid our Christmases and Easters will be, Hillie, and your birthday, and our wedding anniversary! They will all mean so much to us, won't they?

Hillie darling! I know so well that our life together will be just one splendid dream of happiness. Write and say, dear, that you feel so too. And we are praying for it so hard that I know it is going to come soon.

Darling! I shall never forget, tho', in those happy days, how hard it has been for you in these terrible and dreary long days of waiting and how patient and keeping brave, my Hillie has been... For every tiny tear, darling, I shall offer you a million kisses and for your sighs, my whole life's love and service. Will you have them, Hillie?
The sweetest kiss tonight, darling, and every bit of Love
Frankie

Letter 6

Envelope post mark 1917 field post office

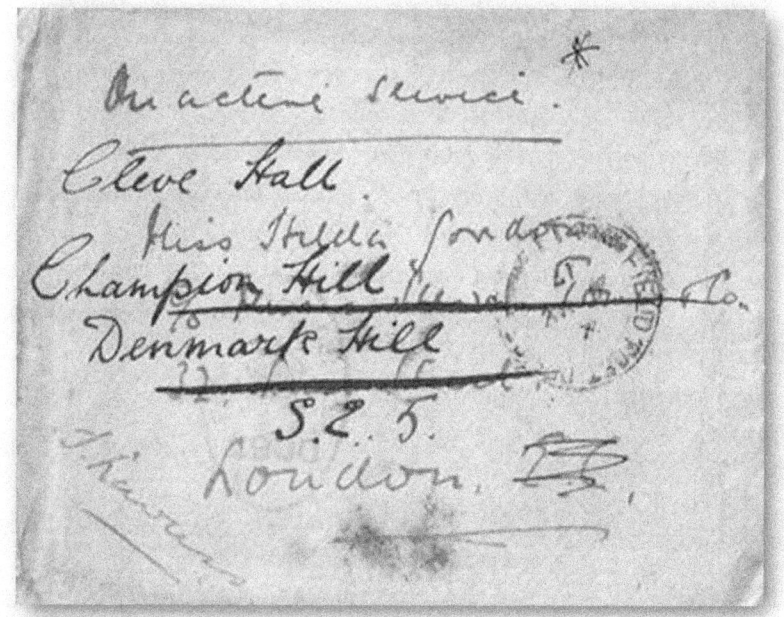

18th   B.E.F

30th April

Darling Hillie

Just one tiny line, my darling to send you a kiss and say I've re-joined and we have come out of the line.

Am O/C No 3 again and there is a terrible lot of work to do today pulling things together.

It has been a lot worse show than I had thought and the poor old company has lost a lot of fine men. Only one officer left, a little fellow named Jacobs, isn't it too bad Hillie?

I don't think we'll be going back to the battle any more. They say we will be sent off now to a quiet spot to hold the line

Heavens Hillie! Isn't my luck just wonderful? Only for that army school..!

Forgive this tiny chit, Hillie, won't you, and I'll try and write a decent letter tomorrow darling.

Good bye and the very sweetest kiss for you. Frankie

Letter 7

May 2nd   18th B.E.F France
My own darling Hillie,
    I did get a letter yesterday after all. It arrived quite late and so, being unexpected, I loved it all the more. It contained the one you had received from Gates, which I'm not tearing up, dear Hillie, 'cos somehow, it's a nice letter isn't it, and I'll let your dear little fingers do the work of destruction.

    Poor old chap! He must have felt Oh so very, very, sore when he wrote it you know, 'cos I've felt that way myself. However I can't keep his misery, I'm afraid, can I Hillie? These things will happen even to the most cock-sure people!

    (just a tiny whisper: I'm so glad, you darling little Hillie, that you are going to love me and not Gates. I'm sure I would have shot him as dead as mutton if he'd won.)

    Your letter was an awfully sweet one Hillie darling, and cheered me up tremendously. Yes ! I do want you to be tremendously selfish when I come home and there is nothing more I can ask of life than that you should keep me by you all the while ... and I promise very faithfully not to run away and play billiards with anybody and no golf with my Father, eh! Well! I promise that too.

    But I can't imagine any one being terribly frightened even if you 'put your foot down' ever so hard, Hillie, cos you see dear it is such a tiny little foot, isn't it? All the same, I so love it very much, you know. Is it the same little foot you scalded and wouldn't write and tell me how it was getting on, tho' I asked ever so many times.

    We move again tomorrow Hillie darling, but only to another 'back' village. The Brigadier told us this morning we shall be 'out' for quite a little while 'training' and getting up reinforcements. We have a draft today of officers and men.

    I got one officer... a little, tiny man from St Helens. He looks a little wretch, but one can't be over particular these times I'm afraid.

Topping weather again, getting fearfully sunburnt. Wasn't it Peg who hated freckles? I always get heaps in the summer, so I'll confess now, Hillie, in case you would like to repent while there is still time. There's not very much time all the same, Hillie darling, 'cos it won't be long now before I am back will it?

This last fighting has been terrific. I did not realise until I got first-hand account of the various 'stunts' how terrible it has been. The newspapers give one no idea at all of the operations or how the fortunes of war went. I'm afraid we didn't have it all our own way but the Hun has lost a lot of men and I hope he will realise the cost is just too heavy to go on. The U boats seem to be bringing us to the same state of mind, I'm afraid, don't they Hillie? The English ministers seem to have 'the wind up' badly about our food supplies.

It all means that as soon as someone cries 'Peace' again, we will all listen, doesn't it Hillie? Let's keep on praying it is soon shall we?

My own dear, dear Hillie!! I will love you always, darling. How could it be otherwise, old thing? If only I could tell you how I am just living for the day when I can hold you very, very close to me again and threaten never to release you, Hillie. Would you be dreadfully frightened I wonder? You would have to ransom yourself then.

Can you guess what I should demand?

I have made a tremendous hit, Hilllie, in this billet. Her name is Marguerite and she is very dark and pretty and oh such a charming little voice. Do you think she can be the dreadful creature Mrs Cavanagh warned you about, dear?... She is not very dreadful, tho' Hillie dear, 'cos she is only about ten. I 'helped' her last night with her home lessons and provided incorrect answers to her sums, for which she was tremendously grateful, though I did 'em wrong purposely, poor little beggar. Then she wanted me to play her mandolin for her... a present from a former occupant of the billet... but I introduced her to the gramophone instead and she was vastly delighted with my comments on the music. She says my French is 'Tres Drole'... the little imp!

'Half past eight' she likes better than, Tchaikovsky's 'Pathetique'.....
and rightly so, cos didn't you and I hear it at the L'pool Empire, darling
and enjoy a chop at that funny little cafe afterwards? Do you remember?

Don't say you don't like Marguerite, Hillie darling, even if she is a bit
of a flirt (I saw the fickle miss making eyes at the quarter masters sergeant
this morning, but she denies it of course!)   She wears a funny little black
frock and I wonder if the one you wore at Gumley when you were ten was
anything like it. I think it was a bit. Why didn't I know you then Hillie,
I wonder. I promise I should have fallen tremendously in love with you,
just as I did when you were twenty -one.

'Tubby' is calling me to go to a concert he's got up for the men, so I
must bunk, darling, for this time...

Just one wonderful sweet little kiss, and I send you every tiny, tiny bit
of my love, dear, for you to keep always, if you will... and it is to tell you,
please that I want you to give me a real kiss, Hillie, very soon now.
Do you promise?
Good bye sweet Hillie
Frankie

P.S.
I agree 'My Dear Young Lady' looks awful in writing.
I emphatically deny you are any thing of the kind. Hillie sedate! Never!
I should hate it even if she punches me ever so hard.

Finding Frank

I HAVE READ ALL I can to follow your trail through the summer of 1917 when you went with your battalion to the Ypres Salient.

For three years the British Army had attempted to hold the Ypres Salient. Described as a bulge in the Front Line of trenches which encircled the ancient city, it was surrounded on three sides by the Germans who held the high ground all around and could overlook every movement of the British troops.

The names of the ridges that surrounded Ypres are synonymous with some of the worst horrors of the war; Messines Ridge, Pilkem Ridge and Passchendaele.

The ground was reclaimed land, much of it below sea level, with no topsoil, only claggy clay. The agricultural drainage systems had been destroyed by three years of shelling and every trench flooded within eighteen inches of being dug. Men were lost and sometimes drowned in the mud and flood waters.

For the British to be there at all was a political decision, not a military or tactical one. The army would have been better placed by withdrawing to the Flanders Hills. Withdrawal, however, was not a political option. The decision to hold the Salient *'was to consign the British Army to nearly four years of unceasing warfare, unspeakable conditions and almost indescribable horrors'* (Maddocks)

The Liverpool Pals Battalions arrived at Brandhoek in the Salient on foot at the end of May 1917, marching through the destroyed city to be billeted in vast camps around the area. The trenches in the area were immovable and both sides took to tunnelling in an attempt to dislodge the other by planting explosives beneath their positions. On June 7th enormous British mines 'evaporated' German positions on the top parts of the Messines Ridge. 50,000 German troops simply disappeared. The success of this manoeuvre was followed by intense German bombardment from other areas of high ground.

All the Pals Battalions alternated between serving in the front line trenches and being withdrawn for working parties and training.

On 24th July the 18th Battalion moved up to the front line once more and were based at Chateau Segard. The 31st of July was the first day of the Battle of Passchendaele, the third Battle of Ypres. The 18th remained in the Front Line around Passchendaele for a month. The following letters from Frank to Hillie cover those weeks.

Letter 8

June 18th   18th   B.E.F   France
My Darling Hillie,

   I have such a lot of your delightful letters in my paw. Let me count now! Five no less.

   I feel a wretch for not writing to answer them my darling, but yesterday, after another 'dose' of the line I was so dog–tired, that I just flopped down, dirty and unshaven, and slept all day, and I wasn't feeling very bright either, and I hate to be dull when I write to my Hillie, who is all brightness.

   We got a bad time, my darling and poor old No3 left a good number behind- including little Platt. All wounded, thank heaven, except for one man who is still missing. We've searched for him but he has vanished utterly. I felt most extraordinarily confident coming through the shelling, Hillie, tho' it was a hot shop and the boys were dropping around me. I thought of you all the while and knew I should be alright.

   My Darling Hillie! I know now so well that no harm can come to me whilst you love me. So love me always, to keep me safe. Will you darling? And I shall love you with all my heart.

   We're ' out ' now, I've no idea for how long, Hillie, some days yet anyway, I believe, then a little time in the line: tremendously good news, I am praying, for you — and then 'out' again for a long while — Perhaps never to go in again, if all our hopes are realized.

   'No Winter Out Here'! I am sure, sure, <u>sure</u> of it my Hillie.

   No, we aren't at Loos. We are at the place of which I sent you a book of postcards.

   Oh Hillie! The deserted streets ruined houses are so pathetic, one thinks of all the happy, busy families who used to live there. The desolation is most affecting.

   But things go well. We've been talking over lunch today of Peace. Jacobs, my 2nd in Command said 'six weeks' and I offered him a big whisky on the spot!

I enclose an amusing letter from old Humphrey, an old 17ᵗʰ pal of mine. A splendid fellow and you must meet him, Hillie darling. Nothing like Wather and no moustache, I assure you.

Hillie! I think the morning of your communion was the morning we were so badly shelled. How wonderful your prayer was, darling Hillie, 'cos no one could understand how I escaped! I know tho'

I am putting in one of my Corporals for a medal for the brave way he looked after his men and cheered them on. It has been sent in and I hope he gets it, don't you, eh Hillie?

I am very alarmed to hear you were caught in the aeroplane raid last week. Oh Hillie! Nothing, nothing - even the very tiniest thing – must ever happen to you. I know I should die if any harm came to you because life wouldn't mean anything to me any longer. Hilda! Promise me, my darling, most faithfully, that if ever again you are near a raid you will go to cover at once, if possible to a cellar, because the danger from splinters of the bomb and falling bricks and debris is very great indeed, and even if you only go inside a shop or a house, the chances of your being hit are thousands less. Promise, Hillie, won't you, 'cos then I shall be happier. You must be my very own lively little Hillie always and no harm or un-happiness must ever touch you.

Do you remember our cricket matches at the Oval in '13, Hillie? I felt so proud to be with you there, all alone in the big crowd- but I felt a bit sad too, 'cos I wanted you to myself for ever, and thought that a fan-tastic dream which could never be realized. But it is coming true soon, Hillie, isn't it?

Hillie! You say you prayed for us while we were in the line. We were in a bit of trench-No 3, and all around us, on both sides, The Yorks, the Manchesters, took it badly. No shell ever came on No 3. The Yorks and Manchesters had men knocked out every hour. Why was our little trench so spared? Some say one thing, some another (I've talked it over with the Brigadier, he bursts with theories!) but I can't very well explain the real reason, can I eh? That little Hillie was out with us all the horrid six nights.

The greatest problem in my life, Hillie, is to decide how in the name of goodness, when I hold you to my heart again, I can ever let you go. I don't want to, Hillie. I want to hold you in my arms for ever and look into your eyes and feel your arms around me and taste the sweetness of your kisses, Hillie, 'cos all that is my Heaven and who wants to give up Heaven, eh?

Must close now as I have promised to play in a game they are mad on nowadays.

A sort of tennis, but instead of rackets and balls, you use a quoit and throw it at each other. When it is 'buttoned' it counts a point. Judging by the tears in my shirt I think I must be hot stuff. I've also got a darkish eye and a bruise on my cheek!

The very sweetest kiss for you Hillie, darling to tell you I love you, and am longing soon for our marriage.

Awful soon now, Hillie, I know.

Goodbye, my very own darling,

Frankie

Letter 9

June 19ᵗʰ   (1917)   18ᵗʰ   B E F   France
My darling Hillie

The mail hasn't arrived yet, but I think there is going to be a letter today, my darling.

There is not very much news up to now, since I wrote last night.

There has been a very bad storm of wind and rain and it has played old Harry with our tents. Mine blew down altogether. I did curse and that helped to dry things a bit!

Then the Hun commenced to shell a hospital on our right with a high velocity gun, which was rather exciting. Thank heaven he was short. He hit the Manchesters camp with one shot and gave a man a blighty. I don't think it was Fritz's fault entirely, because the stupid hospital people had put up their seventy odd big tents, before they hung out their Red Cross flags and signs and so Fritz no doubt thought it was an ordinary camp.

Got two new officers yesterday. One isn't so awfully bad, as they go nowadays–an actor fellow who has been on the music halls and also with Miss Horniman. An effeminate looking youth, with the vilest Manchester accent but I think he will turn out well in the line. He's been out before as a Tommy.

The other fellow, by a terrible whim of the Gods, hails from the same place as little Platt- He looks a rough, uneducated fellow and has been combed out of the R.A.M.C. Poor old No. 3! When I think of Tubby and Walters and Twemlow -Allen and all the rest of our splendid men of last year I nearly weep.

Never mind, Hillie, they may be alright, darling. We won't despair eh, especially as the war is so nearly over now?

Our Band is playing away, somewhere in the camp, despite the rain. They are improving and I am sure we shall all do our march past, at St George's Hall, in better style, with our own proper Brass Band to lead us.

You will have to stand on the steps of the Hall, Hillie darling, and wave your hand as No3 goes by. I shan't be able to wave back, but I shall see you alright.

And you must promise not to throw anything at little Pinnie, 'cos he really is a good little soldier- even when he gives No 3 all the dirty jobs!

Lunch just on Hillie, so I won't write any more until afterwards when the mail will be in perhaps. Just one tiny kiss, my darling little Hilda, for luck and because I love you and want you so much.

<u>*Afternoon*</u>
My sweet Hillie! I knew I should get a letter–and it is such a fine one too. I got it in the mess tent but I went away with it, hugging it ever so tightly, so that in my own little tent I could press it to my heart and kiss your lines again and again. I adore you my darling and want to be with you again.

I am so happy because you say it is alright for our wedding to be on my next leave, Hillie darling! That is the best, most wonderful, wonderful news you can send me, and I am overjoyed.

Oh, I shall try and get my leave soon now. After the next push, 'the' push – it will be easy.

Yes, let it be soon, Hillie eh, so that you and I can go away and spend every moment together. I don't care where we go, Arran, or where you like. It will be heaven, in any place, darling Hillie, where you are.

Yes! And you will have to let me know what I must do, 'cos I've never been married before, haven't read any books on the subject and in fact I know d.... all about it. I've read G.B.Shaw on 'Getting Married' but he did anything but tell you how to do it.

Of course the Pater would be only too glad I should think, to make whatever arrangements are necessary. Will you let me know Hillie, what you manage to find out, eh?

I haven't the faintest idea what Banns are for. I only mentioned them because I remembered going to Wavertree Church to hear Charlie's read out, about the consanguinity, affinity stunt when Kittie Madigan was going to Canada to marry him.

I'm glad Hillie darling, you are getting my letters again. I can't think why there was a break in them. But I told you before some got blown up, didn't I, eh?

How horrid–but Fritz is a nasty fellow sometimes.

I think we will do one more short tour in the line soon Hillie, and then go right back– well out of range. Topping!

You can't imagine the relief to get away from the individual crashes of our guns and go somewhere where they only reach you as a low, confused mutter– and to get away from the whines and screams of Fritz's stuff! Why! That is a splendid day. I don't worry about them hitting me. I know quite well they won't…but some people stop them and that makes one saddish.

But I'm wrong to say 'you can't imagine,' Hillie, 'cos you can, my darling, can't you?

In everything I do I feel you are with me, sharing the work and bits of sadness and bits of pleasure–

When we are shelled, I know Hillie's sweet little face looks troubled as mine is, and her little jaw is set quite tight and hard.

When No 3 gets the pat from Pinnie or any one, I go 6 feet and a bit and Hillie looks a tremendous little girl at 5 foot and a bit. When we are playing 'Push the Puddles' a weird game the new Doc has brought into fashion I know Hillie is just as keen and harum scarum as I am. We are going through it together aren't we, darling, darling Hilda, every (dash this pad for tearing!) inch of the road– just as we will do everything together, eh?

I love you Hilda, I love you, I love you and want to see my sweet wife very badly.

The most perfect kiss I can send – for luck– and to tell you it will be soon now.

Frankie

Hillie! Love me always, my darling, won't you? I never, never, never can leave you again, when this is all over.

Letter 10

June 20ᵗʰ   18ᵗʰ B.E.F   France
My adorable Hillie,

Such a sweet letter today, Hillie, and I love my darling for sending it to me.

But I shall hate your Mr Scott intensely if he does take you up in his plane 'cos I should be so frightened, if I knew you were in danger. Hillie darling! Do be very good now for my sake, and do nothing dangerous, old thing – 'cos if you knew, even a tiny bit how broken hearted I should be if you were ill or unhappy, I feel sure you wouldn't. My darling, darling little Hilda! I am coming now ever so quickly, to give you the tiny kiss you want and to beg one from you in return. Don't come to ...... for it, because it is a horrid spot.

I've got a souvenir for you, Hillie darling. Ever since I came to France again, I have been trying, every time I draw money from the cashier, to get a new book – but until today, they'd only agree on condition I gave up my old one. The one today was a good fellow and gave me a new one, so here is the old one, Hillie dear, with the bullet hole in it.

You should have gone out on the river, Hillie, really. I just hate to hear of you declining all these invitations – but Hillie, it will be alright soon, eh, and we will have lots of days on the river – perhaps with a lunch basket, eh?- and in the very quiet parts, if we have lots of good looks around, do you think we might have one little kiss, Hillie?

How I have sat before you so often on those old Battersea Park benches, Hillie, and longed to take you to me – and daren't!

Hillie, I've got to go. I'm sitting on a Field General Court Martial tomorrow and I have to see the adjutant.

Goodbye, my own darling Hilda, I am thinking every moment of our marriage and how much I shall adore my sweet wife and guard her.

The sweetest kiss, Hillie, because my heart is always yours.
Frankie

Letter 11

June 22nd   18th   BEF   France
My Darling Hillie

We moved last night rather unexpectedly linewards, but it is support and not front line, and I think with luck and your prayers for us, dear Hillie, we will have quite a cushy time.

It is quite an interesting spot. An old chateau, just a bit of the building's still standing and the park and woods not too badly churned up by the shell fire. It has been a topping place I should think with pretty gardens and ornamental pools, but the gardens are honeycombed with trenches now and the pools are littered with bully beef tins and all sorts of rubbish. It is too wicked, isn't it Hillie?

We have quite a good shelter in which to sleep and mess, made of sandbags and corrugated iron. Of course it is quite safe to walk about 'on top', except when fritz is shelling or his planes are overhead... We were glad to come here as a matter of fact, for our 'rest' camp was becoming very unpleasant and we could get no rest on account of the shelling. We lost some men and some valuable horses, so after that we used to evacuate the place and spend the night in the fields – not too pleasant –and it is so undignified to trail around muddy fields and tracks at 2 am in pyjamas!

So far (touch wood!) this place is a great improvement.

Won't it be splendid to get right back again. Oh Hillie, I shall send you really good long letters then.

I've got all my pictures back up on the wall again, to cheer things up. Of course Hillie, you shall have them when I get home.

I got Hutchinson to send me out some paints, for making maps, and have been amusing myself today by painting two pictures with them... One was 'war' and was a great success and the other I called 'peace' – and it was a failure and I have torn it up.

Danalby, the artist man, of No 4 says 'war' is good so I'll keep it for you eh Hillie? I know 'Peace' failed because the subject baffles my imagination. I can't imagine what it will be like. Peace means Hillie and how could anyone describe such beauty or such happiness?

A topping letter came up with the rations, Hillie, and I loved the kiss it contained for me.

The little officer has got a blighty posting and also Jacob my second-in-command. The two new men who replace them look alright. One is an actor called Futuoye (?) and the other, from St Helens, is called Graham. The actor man will be a good fellow I think, he's quite amusing which is a blessing

No! I am never, never, never going to let you go from me, Hillie darling, after I come home to you soon and I am so happy when you tell me that you won't ever want to go. Dear old Hilda! The prospects still are quite bright, even though our June is slipping by. I <u>know</u> there is a splendid chance of the end coming soon. Just hope and trust my darling, darling, Hillie and

'it will all come to pass as I tell you'

Fancy 'Butterfly' coming into my mind!

What glorious hours we have spent together, Hillie, listening to old Puccini's music. I do 'feel' music tremendously Hillie, 'cos I have lived through, in my heart, everything these composers have written in their scores – because I love Hillie, so very, very, dearly.

Goodbye Hillie darling, with the tenderest, most precious kiss I can send you.

Frankie.

For Freedom and Honour

THE 18ᵀᴴ BATTALION FOUGHT THROUGHOUT July 1917 on the Front Line in the Battle of Pilkem Ridge. Records give a detailed account of the actions, bravery, fortitude and endurance, especially of No 1 and No 3 companies. The 18th was also at the front for the opening days of the Battle of Passchendaele, although unable to achieve their objectives. During this time the Pals Battalions lost 11 officers and 223 men of other ranks. In addition 21 officers and 625 other ranks were wounded. On 2nd August the 18th Battalion were relieved in the line and returned to Chateau Segard for rest.

Leave for Officers finally opened and Frank went home to marry Hilda.

SCOTLAND SUMMER 1917

Hillie sat on the train from Glasgow out to Ardrossan, watching the incessant raindrops chase each other down the smoke stained panes and blot out the dank and sodden landscape of south west Scotland. She remembered coming here as a child and even then, after the joy of seeing her grandparents, her one abiding memory of the area was the rain. Even at the height of summer Ardrossan was a bleak and uninspiring sight and she was glad to think Dorothy had suggested trips to Arran, with picnics and fishing and walks on the hills and beaches. Getting away from this place must be a main priority if the sun ever shone. But really, she thought, what does the weather matter, if only Frank can get here quickly. She clutched his letter in her lap and opened it once more, to check again that he really had said he was coming, that his leave was confirmed, and they could get married immediately he reached her side.

Getting married had seemed to Hillie to be a simple thing to do, but organising it when everyone involved was all over the place had been easier said than done. She and Frank had wanted to marry as soon as Hillie had accepted his nervous and hesitant proposal, but he had to return to his Battalion at the Front and had then been wounded. Also they needed to wait for her parents' permission. The post was agonisingly slow; she knew it would take at least twelve weeks for Frank's letter to reach her father in Hong Kong and then come back with the response. She had known her parents would agree, her mother had liked Frank, thought him clever and entertaining and kind, but Hillie knew they would be concerned about her marrying a man whose chances of being killed were high and rising with every day that passed. But she couldn't think like that and she was certain that Frank's desire to marry as quickly as possible was born of love, not fear about his future survival. They had their correspondence and both lived for each day's post. But finally the letter from her father had reached Frank in France, giving his blessing, and Hilda had received one too, with his love and congratulations. So from then on it had been a question of waiting for Frank to be able to get leave long enough to come home and for them to start to married life together somewhere. Weeks had passed with no news of a leave and his

Battalion was at the Front Line, involved in serious heavy fighting. But Frank was always optimistic that leave would open soon.

The original plan had been to have the wedding in London, but Cleve Hall wasn't the ideal place from which to marry. And bombs were raining down on the city. It was her newly married sister Dorothy who finally worked out the best solution.

Dorothy's husband had been posted to Scotland by the Navy and she had gone with him. But it was a lonely posting, with few other officers' wives around as they waited for his ship to complete its refit. Why didn't Hillie come and join her in Ardrossan and wait there for Frank's leave to be announced? The priest where she went to Mass was friendly and approachable, she was sure if Hillie came and talked to him he would help the young couple, so that the marriage could go ahead immediately when Frank arrived. Their Banns had been called in Liverpool. There was only Frank to wait for. Hillie wrote to him with the plan and then made arrangements to go to Ayrshire to stay with Dorothy. She was happy at the thought of spending a few days with her sister, thinking they could take trips to Glasgow for tea and shopping. She would need some shoes for the wedding and a small trousseau. Dorothy had the advantage of being a newly-wed and knew what was needed. Mother had promised to bring her a wedding outfit from Hong Kong, made up of the silks she could buy there. Hillie had been insistent, not white, not in wartime, something pretty and feminine but restrained, no veils, a hat maybe. Frank eventually wrote that leave was imminent, mother's ship was due in Southampton any day and they started to pray for fine weather on the 25th of August.

So here she was, on the train, shoebox in hand but thoughts very far from her feet. She was still not quite sure of the exact nature of marriage, what it fully entailed. She and Frank had pledged to live together for the rest of their lives, in one home, alone. That included sleeping together. She was not afraid of the physical intimacy she knew it involved, but she just didn't quite understand it. She had tried to ask her sister about wedding nights, but Dorothy had seemed so shocked by the question and utterly embarrassed by the concept and had only replied 'ask mother'. Unfortunately, mother wasn't here yet. Another concern was babies. Her mother seemed to have spent her life in one eternal pregnancy, with six live children and one or two lost, and Hilda, as the eldest had been aware of the inconvenience this had involved, even in the Colony, where her mother had aya's and wet nurses and nursery maids to help her. But what would happen now, in war time, if one had a child, with a husband at the Front? Hillie wasn't keen on the idea of babies, they seemed the one big drawback to marriage. So many things to ponder, she reflected, when really the only thing that mattered was that she and Frank loved one another and he survived this monstrous war.

SALTCOATS AYRSHIRE AUGUST 25TH 1917

Frank and his parents arrived at the church in excellent time, walking from their boarding house on the sea front after the kind of Scottish breakfast Frank was sure would come back to haunt him for the rest of his wedding day. His mother had urged him to eat, rumbling stomachs in church were a sign of nerves or faulty faith to her, as if one could help them! So he had forced down porridge and some good Ayrshire bacon and eggs, and coffee of dubious quality and his nerves had steadied as his excitement rose. He had never imagined having to get married in uniform but now he was anxious that his tunic didn't smell of bacon or cabbage water or anything unpleasant at all. His mother had taken the tunic the previous night and brushed and brushed it, rubbing at marks, polishing the buttons and pressing the seams. She had hung it out of the window in the sunshine and sea breeze to freshen, and given how opposed to his marriage to Hillie he knew his mother really was, he was grateful for her efforts. His father tried to sooth the ill feeling between the women and support his son.

'You look the part of an army officer in these, son, I never thought the army would suit you so well.' he said, as he and Frank sat on the back step of the guest house, polishing his boots.

'War doesn't suit me, Dad, but if I have to do it, I try to do it well. I only want it to be over and to be with Hillie and to live a life together.'

'It's what we all want. Your mother is just saddened that even after the war you will be so far from her. I think she always hoped that at least one of her children would live close to home.'

Frank shook his head and looked out towards the sea.

'I don't see any future for us in Liverpool, Dad, and it's not Hillie's fault the others have gone to Canada. Mother must stop blaming us for that. For now I just want to stay alive.'

Boots buffed and shining they had shaken hands.

Frank shook off all awkward thoughts as he and his parents walked towards the church. All he wanted was to marry Hillie and begin their great adventure together. He checked all his pockets one more time. Clean handkerchief, money in an envelope for the priest, wallet and train tickets to Glasgow for this afternoon, cap on, Regimental badge polished, gloves in hand. The ring! Safe in Father's breast pocket. None of Frank's friends could get leave at the same time and his brothers were both in Canada, so Dad was his best man.

Surrounded by small, rather mean little houses, and so close to the railway line each passing train interrupted prayers, the little church, dedicated to Our Lady, Star of The Sea, was nevertheless an attractive spot on a late summer day. The small garden which united the church to its presbytery was neatly lawned and ringed by trees which cut out the view of the road and railway. It stood on a slight rise and behind it was the sea and distant views of Arran and Ardrossan harbour. With its rosebeds still in full bloom and daisies in the lawn, you could just about imagine you were in some romantic country spot. Anyway what did it matter where one got married, the only thing was that he was here and Hillie, he fervently hoped, was on her way.

Father Bernard met their small group at the door. 'All set young man?'

'Thank you, Father, yes, all set.'

They followed the priest into the dim interior to the front of the church where candles were already burning on the altar. The scents of pervasive, lingering incense and candlewax were freshened by the smell of sweet peas placed in vases last night by Hillie's mother. He knew Hillie loved flowers and he was delighted to see that Mrs Gordon had managed to find some, somewhere, to brighten up the church. Frank sat with his parents in the front row, waiting while Father Bernard bustled about around the altar, arranging vessels, opening books and smoothing out the altar cloth. Two kneelers were arranged in front of the altar rail, with chairs behind, one for him, one for Hillie. Where was she? Nerves caught up with him again. Was she late? He picked up his gloves and a prayer book left on the bench in front turning them over and over, until eventually he dropped the book and it clattered to the floor

'Steady on Frank, she's not late yet. Try a prayer,' his father reassured him.

Frank knelt and bowed his head and heard Fr Bernard turn and walk up towards the church door. More sunlight entered as the door swung back and Frank heard voices in the church porch. He stood and turned as Mrs Gordon and Hillie's two sisters walked towards him smiling and took their seats on the opposite side of the aisle.

'She's here', whispered Mrs Gordon, 'don't worry.'

Frank turned towards the church door and watched where Hillie's diminutive figure, clutching the arm of her brother-in-law, stood. She *had* come, she had, and he really was going to be able to marry her.

Hillie looked so tiny but so determined to Frank as she walked firmly down that aisle, no hesitation, no doubts about what she wanted to do. He couldn't see her face just yet, hidden beneath a cream lace mantilla, but he heard the rustle of her frock and coat as she walked and the striking of her heels in beautiful satin shoes on the tiled floor. There was a glimpse of a stockinged ankle between the shoe and the hem of her coat and Frank thought she had never looked so beautiful. He just wanted to hold her, to take her and rush from the church and kiss her. His excitement was barely containable and he started to shake.

At the priests signal his father nudged him out in to aisle and he removed his cap and laid it down on the bench. Hillie came forward and stood, looking at Frank from under the little veil and Father Bernard indicated he should stand beside her. She handed the single red rose that she carried to her sister and then she and Frank genuflected in front of the altar steps.

'Brothers and sisters in Christ' began Fr Bernard and the marriage service opened.

Finding Frank

Poor Saltcoats. The shipyards and coaling stations at Ardrossan that brought you here are long since closed, except for the Ferry to Broddick that you took the following day. That still takes tourists across the water. Perhaps it was as good a place to marry as any other, all you needed was a church and a priest willing to marry you at short notice when your leave came through, maybe that was easier in Scotland too. Perhaps you hoped that the setting of such a crucial part of your wonderful romance would somehow be prettier or grander or more charming, and even in 1917 it probably didn't promise much there, except a view across the sea to Arran, a broad and sandy beach with a promenade and some boarding houses, which today look grimly out of season. Maybe the sunset conflagrations over the island made up for the lack of romance, maybe anything looked beautiful after the western front. Or perhaps you didn't see any of it, but just looked to her and your real lives to come.

The chattering websites warn us not to visit after dark, so far has this little town sunk into sadness and decline. Street after street of empty shops, charity shops, pound shops, fast food wrappers, polystyrene chip boxes that tumble in the wind like modern sagebrush at high noon. Perhaps behind those flickering curtains residents wait for the gunfight, or fist fight to erupt, shatter the peace and ebb away. The town is not alone in its post-industrial decline but it is surely one of the most deprived.

The church has lost its pretty garden, cherry trees felled, lawns and flowerbeds tarmacked over and marked into characterless parking spaces that no self-respecting bride would want to be photographed upon. The pretty Victorian Catholic church, its architecture echoed by so many of its time, now sprouts additions, porches, wings, no doubt utilitarian, but not what was originally planned. Worst of all, its name, its beautiful dedication changed. Stella Maris, Our Lady, Star of the Sea has become plain everyday St Mary's.

So from this inauspicious spot your married life began.

For Freedom and Honour

FRANK AND HILLIE ENJOYED SEVEN days of their new married life. Frank then returned to the 18th Battalion after his leave and found them still in the Frontline trenches around Ypres. Towards the end of September a draft of men and officers from the Lancashire Hussars joined the 18th to form a strengthened amalgamated battalion.

Letter 12

18th Battalion, The King's(Liverpool)Regiment   B.E.F France
October 25th
My Dearest Hillie,

 I feel simply ashamed of myself for not writing before, but I know you will forgive me when I tell you all my miserable excuses. I, of course, found the company without officers when I arrived in the line, and I have been in command ever since and it's rather a big job re-organizing on the move 'single-handed'. We are slowly getting back to rest billets but won't arrive until the day after tomorrow at the earliest. Goodness only knows in fact, when I'll be able to get this note away. So don't swear at me dearest Hillie, for not writing, will you? In fact I haven't written the letters of condolence yet for the men who have 'gone west'.

 It feels awfully important to be in charge of the company and make people fly around, but the circumstances under which I got this job are too painful to allow me to enjoy my new found dignity.

 Anyway I suppose a big draft of new officers will soon arrive and I will get the sack pretty quickly. I hope we get decent fellows; it makes all the difference out here.

 I think it is rather a record, the state of affairs in this battalion, at present — all the company commanders are 2nd Lieutenants, all joined the ranks in the 17th Kings and all were trained at the Inns of Court.

 I think the next leave is really going to come off, Hillie, isn't it…..

There are no further letters extant until Spring 1918.

For Freedom and Honour

THE PALS BATTALIONS SPENT SEVEN months in the Ypres Salient, with prolonged periods in the Front Line. In early January 1918 the 18th Battalion entrained for the south to relieve an area previously held by the French. The Brigades were being reorganised at this time and some leave came through for officers.

LIVERPOOL EARLY 1918

Lime Street Station was full of small family groups, meeters and greeters, tearful parting lovers, excited children, as Hillie, and Frank's parents, made their way to the central concourse to look at the arrivals. Screaming train whistles and ejected steam made conversation difficult but they watched as the times of the arriving trains and their respective platforms clicked and rolled into place. At last the London train was signalled.

'Platform 5,' Hillie called, and the group moved towards the barrier gate to watch as the mighty engine hauled in the carriages and the sounds of the steam engine slowing, brakes grinding and pressure dropping, filled all Hillie's senses.

She'd waited so many days and months for this moment, when her new husband finally escaped the battlefront and obtained some leave. At least five months and some of the worst fighting of this hellish war had passed, since they last saw each other. Some days Hillie couldn't believe that Frank had survived thus far unscathed. Until she saw him with her own eyes, held his hands and heard his voice again, only then would she trust in his survival. He asked her to come to Liverpool, so that he could see his parents too. Leave was limited and he didn't know when or if, it would come again. At first Hillie was a little angry at the request, she wanted him all to herself, but she realized the need, *his* need to see them, so travelled up to Liverpool. The group passed many anxious days together waiting for his telegram to say he was finally on the boat train, or had arrived in Folkestone, or London, or anywhere out of France.

The passengers slowly began to disembark the train and Mr and Mrs Lawless senior held back reluctantly, wanting to give Hillie and Frank those first private seconds of meeting. Hillie stood by the gate, eyes straining, watching as the uniformed men disembarked, sombre, with small kit bags slung, all of them weary and travel stained. Suddenly, coming through the gate she saw the figure she was searching for, half a head taller than most of the others, looking swarthy and unshaven but still, undeniably, her Frank. She called his name and hurtled forward like a bullet from a rifle, tumbling into him. Frank's arms opened in time to envelop her and sweep her from her feet and lift her up to his face, to kiss her over and over.

'Your Mum and Dad are here too,' Hillie said, as the intensity of the immediate greeting subsided. Frank looked her with pride as well as longing, for the sacrifice she had made. He took her hand and they stepped forward to meet his parents, but as they walked Hillie noticed that Frank's gait was slow, slightly painful.

'You've been wounded?' She asked in cold fear.

'No, nothing much -just my boots, they're a bit stiff.'

At the sight of his parents, Frank dropped her hand and reached towards his mother to hug her. He extended a hand towards his father and they concluded a manly greeting

'How are you? How are you?' His mother asked, over and over.

'I'm splendid, fine, well, the Hun hasn't got to me yet.'

As the family emerged from the station and into the afternoon sunlight it became clear to all that Frank was exaggerating his state of health. He was unkempt, unshaven and beneath several days growth of beard his skin was sallow and sunken. He had lost weight and definitely had difficulty walking briskly.

His father hailed a cab and they headed for home.

'How long have you got my boy, how long can you stay?'

'Four weeks if all goes well and no more great battles begin, what is left of the battalion has been moved back, the men are resting, regrouping, being reassigned. I have to wait for orders where to go next.'

Frank sank back into the corner of the cab, and his eyes closed momentarily. Hillie heard the great sigh of relief and comfort that he exhaled and squeezed his hand tightly. 'Home soon,' she said brightly, as the familiar streets of Liverpool began to flicker past, unchanged since his departure all those months ago.

They entered the house and Mrs Lawless put the kettle on, she and Hillie stared at Frank.

'You need a shave son,' his mother said gruffly, and then we can look at you and see how you really are.'

Hillie's face reflected her own unspoken anxiety.

'I'm just tired mother,' Frank said. 'And my feet hurt. I need a meal and a bath and a night's sleep. Tomorrow I'll be as right as rain.'

Hillie stood by his chair and took his cap and his gloves from him. She helped him with the jacket and saw blood on his shirt.

'It's not mine' he told them all quickly, 'It's from one of the men. We carried him to an ambulance.'

'How long have you been wearing these clothes?' Hillie asked.

'Six, maybe seven weeks, I don't really remember when I last had the chance to change.'

Frank began to apologise for arriving in this state. 'I was so desperate to get home I didn't bother to spend time seeking out fresh uniform,'

Frank's father stood up, 'I'll light the boiler, so you can have a proper bath, son, as soon as there is hot water.'

While they waited for the water to warm up the family sat around the fire, drinking tea, talking little common-place pleasantries about Frank's journey, but as they sat, Hillie noticed a smell which gradually overwhelmed her. It came from Frank's clothes and body. Every inch of his skin that she could see seemed ingrained with mud. He smelt of mud and shellfire and sweat and fear and another man's blood. His leather riding boots reached up to just under his knees, his twill britches tucked over, cemented with mud.

'I couldn't get the damn boots off.' Frank remarked casually. Hillie's response was immediate.

'What do mean you can't get your boots off?'

'I'm sorry, they will smell terrible, I have worn them day and night for weeks and weeks, when they get wet they shrink, I can't pull my feet free. My orderly did try but it hurt so much, he said it was a job for the doctors.'

Hillie and Frank's mother looked at each other and called a truce between themselves.

'I've been nursing for months, Frank, I can stand smelly feet, so can your mother. We can do this for you.' Hillie said.

She wanted to say, any part of you is precious to me, there is no part of your body I do not love, will not care for, cannot tend, but the presence of her mother–in–law forced her to be practical and keep her thoughts to herself until she and Frank were alone.

Frank's father busied himself organising the tin bath in front of the fire and filled it with jugs of steaming water. He collected towels, carbolic soap, razors and hair brushes.

Hillie made Frank lift his feet and rest them on a footstool. 'Can you still feel your toes, can you move them?' He nodded. Hillie carefully peeled back the fabric of the britches tucked over the boots. Even gentle tugging seemed to cause him pain,

'We need to cut these trousers off, then we can see how to move the rest,' she said. The thought of taking a sharp blade anywhere near Frank's skin chilled her, but necessity made things clear. His mother fetched scissors.

'We will be damaging army property here,' Hillie joked, as they cut away the britches up to his thighs and had a clear sight of the tops of his boots.

Hillie almost wept when she saw how the leather uppers appeared to have embedded themselves into the muscle of his legs. A lip of flesh over hung the stiff top of each boot. The skin was filthy.

'I'm pleased to see it still shows signs of pink beneath the dirt,' she reassured him.

She tried gently pushing a finger between the boot and the skin, easing it with a little liquid paraffin oil.

'We'll need to cut them off, slowly and gently, if we can make a space to get shears in,' she told him, 'can you bear it?'

'Get Dad to put a drop of whisky in my tea, that'll help and I'll be fine.'

Hillie held her breath, fearful of causing him further pain and then slowly, gently, began to enlarge the gap she had opened until it was wide and deep enough to take a blade and inch by inch she cut the leather downwards with a pair of poultry shears, trying all the time to avoid any pressure on his flesh. The leather was stiff and almost attached to the skin in many places.

By the time she reached the heel the strength in her hands had given out and Frank's mother took over. Hillie saw the sweat of pain running down and catching in his eyebrows, his breathing was controlled, deliberate and focussed.

When the women reached Frank's ankle they tried easing the first boot delicately from his foot and eventually, as he gripped the side of his chair to brace himself and deflect the pain, the boot came away.

Around his foot the sock had virtually rotted away and the stench was powerful. His father went to open the back door, throwing out the stinking boot and remnant of the first sock. The nails were blackened and misshapen or missing and the wrinkled skin a death- like grey in colour.

'Show me you can move your toes,' Hillie demanded.

Frank obliged and they immersed the first foot in a bowl of steaming water.

The women repeated the process for the second boot. In all, the whole operation took over two hours and when Hillie finally gazed down on the two freed limbs the potential for catastrophe overtook her. Frank's skin, from the calf, to the tips of his toes was wrinkled and blackened like an ageing walnut. At the top, where the stiff leather had cut in, there were deep weals, angry and sore; around his ankles callouses had formed where the leather had rubbed. The skin on the soles and between his toes was festering and peeling.

'You're lucky,' Hillie said, 'a few more days and these would have been trench feet, liable to gangrene, I think we have freed them in time.'

She leant over and kissed his brow, her hair rustling across his face like some St Veronica or Mary Magdalene. She would have dried those beloved feet with her hair if it could have helped him recover.

For Freedom and Honour

FRANK RETURNED TO THE BATTALION in February 1918. Due to a severe shortage of troops, there had been further reorganisation and the 18th had re-joined the 89th Brigade under Brigadier Stanley's command. The old French frontline, which the Pals battalions were deployed to hold, (and which had originally been thought of as quite a 'cushy' position) was long and the troops were thinly stretched opposite the town of St Quinten. By the end of February it was clear that the Germans, with their armies now released from the Russian front, intended a major assault. Everyone understood that this was likely to be imminent, before the arrival of American Forces to support the allies. However, nobody knew where along the front lines this attack would come.

Letter 13

Feb 12   1918   E.F.C. Officers Rest House And Mess
My darling Hillie

We aren't getting on our journey very quickly, are we, Hillie darling?

The boat left about half past nine this morning and didn't get in until after twelve. The train doesn't go until a quarter past ten tonight, and so I'll have to kill another day, you see. Ugh! A night journey!

That means arriving at the railhead somewhere about ten in the morning, I suppose. I shall feel like nothing on earth.

A simply horrid crossing, Hillie darling. A nasty fog, cold, and the waves… I wasn't out but my poor little …felt very queer at times, I do confess. I was made O/C Boat,◊ but a full Colonel turned up at the last moment, and I was promptly sacked again.

Here is your cheque Hillie darling, with all my love.

They made such a fuss about giving me a cheque here--- and hadn't any books. They made me cross it because it was going by post, so you'll have to cash it at Cox's, darling Angel. I'm awfully sorry my darling, to give you the trouble of trotting down there, but it can't be helped this time, can it?

A huge big extra kiss, my darling, to tell you not to be cross with me. I've only sent one cheque, 'cos I think the allowances will have been credited by now, and, in any case, they would only trust me with one here.

This is a big new club house, which has been opened. Pretty rough and ready and served by the WAACS – Ugly ones, Hillie darling.

I spent last night writing a long letter to your mummy. I hope it duly arrives.

I was thinking, darling, you ought to advise her to, in these uncertain days, to write her letters in pencil, and take a duplicate with carbon paper, posting the copy by a different mail to the original. You would then have a far better chance of getting each letter she writes, wouldn't you? (Good brainwave, eh?)

◊ O/C = Officer commanding

How are you Hillie darling? I did think a lot of you last night. I simply dreaded going to bed, so I tried to read after dinner, but it was no good. I felt my face must look so gloomy that people would get scared about me and so I bundled myself off to my room. Oh Hillie darling. How lonely I was without you, dear. How I longed for you to come in. It seemed terrible, too, to think that you would be lonely there in London, and that if only I could go back to you, you would be happy again.

Were you cold, Hillie dear? I was. Damnably. But it isn't any good being cold any more is it…not until I come again, eh? April you know my dear, can be awfully, awfully chilly if she likes. Truly. Sometimes it snows. Shall we wish for it to be, eh?

There was a girl having dinner last night at the Hotel, and she wore blue and a white furs and a flat hat, and, from the back, she reminded me of you dear. The elderly officer with her, her husband I supposed, didn't look the least little bit excited. A shore job, no doubt, and he has her there all the while, and does not know the awful desolation of that 'first day' of 'after leave' Oh Hillie dear!

Truly the war has done a bit of good for us in showing me how dear you are to me and how utterly, utterly, blank and purposeless would be a life apart from yours. You know tho,' darling Hillie, how deeply I do love you and you are my only aim and care. I may look decent enough, dear, at times, but truly, truly I can never look like the Home Services Officer and the lady with the white furs, I promise.

The day I am not thrilled through and through, dearest Hillie, at the sound of your voice and the touch of your tiny hand will be the day I do not love you any more –

So you know I shall never offer you half my heart, my darling, or a dutiful love, because you were brave enough to marry me.

Always, always will I be the same, Hillie darling, and adore you to the utmost… your lips and the hair which I love and did not brush; and your dear beautiful arms with their dimples which I grieve now for not having kissed enough; your dear tiny feet which delight my heart.

Every bit of my darling's fragrant lovely body and every bit of her brave and beautiful soul.

Tell me when you write Hillie dear, that you are better of your cold. Mine was very active yesterday, but the terrors of the channel crossing have entirely driven it away today, and I am very fit now. Yesterday, in the hotel, I felt simply rotten. The grief of leaving you darling, and my cold seemed to give me a bit of a temperature and I was 'weary' about it and slept all afternoon. It has quite gone today, thank goodness and I am cheery as cheery can be, truly, and feel quite well again.

Just fancy, my own Hillie! Two days gone already, why the time…

Letter 14

February 1918

...it is seven months now, since our marriage, on the 25ᵗʰ, dear Hillie, isn't it?

Only today I was looking at the piece of paper the Priest gave me about 'Hildam' and 'Franciscum' and I gave it a huge kiss, 'cos it brought all that lovely day to my mind again, dear, and I thought of all the wonderful things we did. It really was a precious, perfect day, wasn't it, Hillie, and I wouldn't change one tiny thing. No, I really mean it. Not even your tiny fright of me, my sweet angel—'cos I think that was rather beautiful too... and of course it was right you should be a tiny bit frightened, and of course, silly old thing, I understood and understand, and I loved you and adore you a thousand times more for it.

Darling! You have promised to tell me truly whenever you are seedy, even a tiny bit, or in trouble, or anxious or in need of anything – just as I know I may share all your successes and happiness's, Hillie dear.

Now, today, when I read and kiss your promise, I feel we are heaps, heaps...

For Freedom and Honour

BY MID-MARCH THE 18TH BATTALION was helping to protect what Stanley described as a 'lightly held outpost line.' The enemy were seen to be massing in the area around St Quinten and one raiding party had already been intercepted. It became clear that the expected attack was almost certain to take place in this lightly defended part of the line. Corporal G Williams of the 19th Battalion reported receiving orders such as 'You will go into your positions and you will not retreat. You will be either killed or be taken prisoner. There is to be no retreat, anyone retreating will be fired on as enemy.' The German plan was a simple one. To make a sudden, decisive breakthrough in a thinly defended area and then take their army through the gap and make for the Channel ports.

Letter 15

Mar 18th 18th B.E.F

Darling Hilda

A lovely letter today, sweet Angel... Yesterday a letter came from Dorothy, enclosing another photo of you, my darling, and so I have thanked you a tiny bit for today's letter by kissing my new photograph of you hundreds and hundreds of times. I like it oh so very, very much, darling Hillie. Why didn't you send it to me instead of waiting for Dorothy to steal a copy for me?

Dearest girl! I think you look a tiny bit sad in it ----- I hate it and I love it... hate it because it is dreadful, dreadful, for me to think of you as seedy, my angel... and I like it because it is a big reason why I should love you more – and I never can love you enough, can I?

Hilda! Can you know how I adore you? Oh, I do, do, want you to believe that all my life is yours, sweetest little angel, and I am worried sometimes because I think perhaps you can never know how utterly I have given over my heart to you–and how I want you to take it, Hillie dear. I shall try awfully hard again when I am home to tell you. How can I do it best I wonder. Cannot you give me one little hint?

Dear Hillie! Your hair, which I love so much, looks sick again and I am very troubled. Tell me truly, shall I come? To save even one, I will come. Tell me now, dearest Hillie, just what you wish me to do and I will do it and be happiest in doing what your tiny heart wishes. I would give my life for one single lovely hair, sweet angel wife and be oh so happy to be privileged to give it.

Don't let me always talk and write about my love only, dearest Hillie. Tell me if you want me to come and I will write an application for 'Home' that very day that I have your answer if it tells me to do that. What does...

For Freedom and Honour

BRIGADIER STANLEY TELLS US THAT the night before the Great German Push began, the senior commanders of the Brigade enjoyed a grand dinner party, followed by an entertainment given by their concert party, the Optimists, "in their best form." It was "a cheery evening and all of us laughed a great deal, being under no false illusions as to what we were all in for the next day."

Frank, as adjutant, was not invited and spent his evening writing what he must have known could potentially be his last letter to Hillie, dreaming of her, to keep his mind from the next day.

Letter 16

March 20th   18th KLR   B.E.F

My darling Hillie

    Two simply topping letters today, sweet angel, and I send you two very special kisses for them, my dearest old thing. It was topping for them to come today, Hillie dear 'cos the wind is 'eyebrows' (as the men say when it is very much 'up') and everyone is nervy and jumpy and impossible and I felt I would give the world for a breath from my angel to make me forget this crazy life here.

    It is simply glorious, my darling, to think of the flimsy black frock and let it make me forget the horrid ugly war and what the Hun is going to do. Hillie angel! Don't wear it for those awful neighbours, will you? Or if you wear that one, save the black velvet one for me dear, so I can have one of my very own, for our month.

    Even if we are just by ourselves, dearest Hilda, you will wear one for me won't you.... and I promise, if you will dear, to love...

For Freedom and Honour

ONE WEEK AT WAR 21ST -30TH MARCH 1918

ON THE 20TH MARCH THE weather changed to benefit the German attackers. Low cloud and rain prevented the British observing the German positions and movements from the air. At 4.30am on the 21st the order 'Man Battle Stations' was received and the assault began. The Germans used every weapon at their disposal, including gas.

Frank left a detailed handwritten account of the days that followed in his official Adjutants 'Narrative of Operations' written in the field. Frank's record is an unadorned military account, practical and modest of his own achievements.

Abbreviations used

Bg- Brigade

Rgt – Regiment

Inf –Infantry

Coy – Company

G.O.C –General Officer Commanding

R.A.M.C Royal Army Medical Corps

M.G Machine Gun

SAA Small arms and ammunition

FY…. Refers to trench numbers

Other numbers letters are map references

Btn – Battalion

K.L.R. Kings Liverpool Regiment

R.S.F Royal Scots Fusiliers

O/R –Other Ranks

O/C Officer Commanding

M.O. Medical Officer

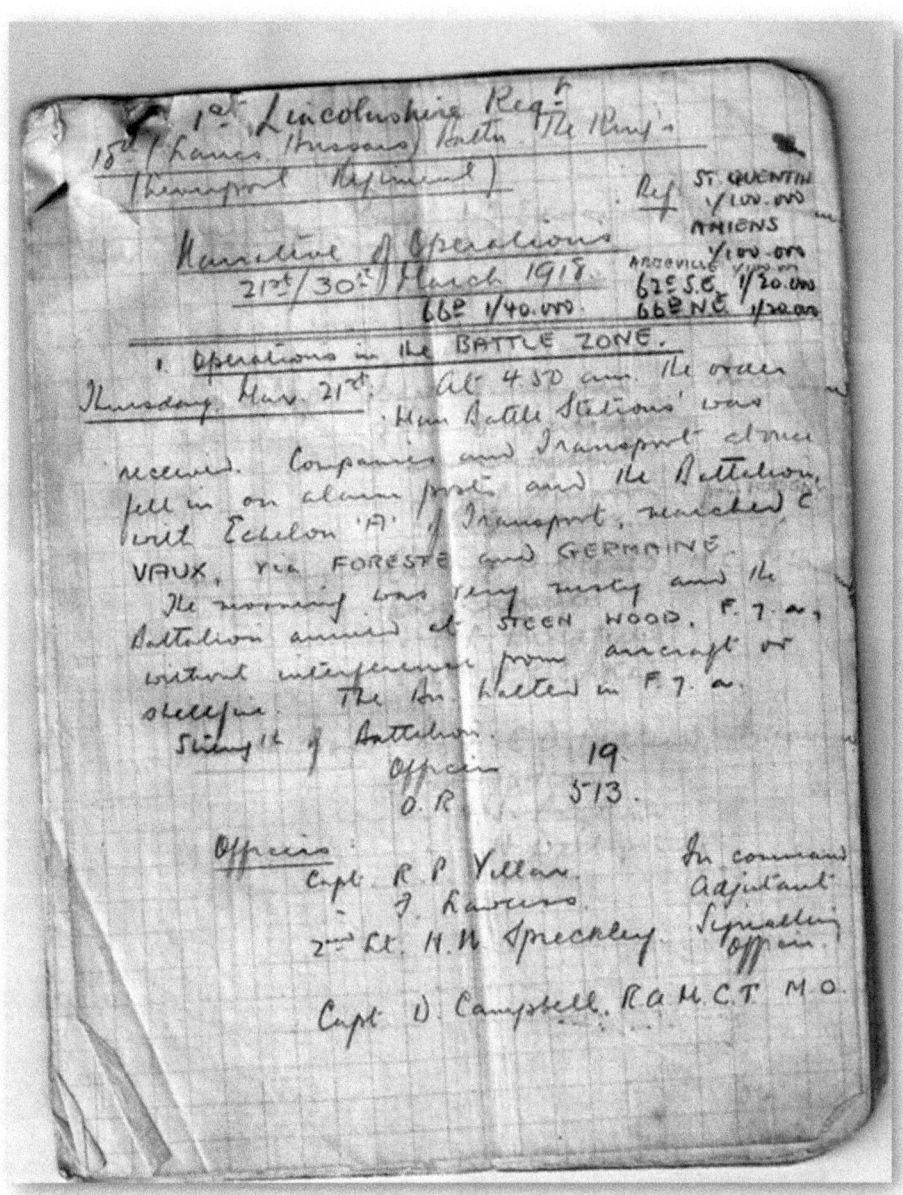

Adjutants Field Diary

18th (Lancs Hussars) Btn The King's
(Liverpool Regiment)

Narrative of Operations	**Ref St Quinten 1:100.000**
21st -30th March 1918	**Amiens 1:100.000**
	Abbeville 1/100.000
66d 1/40.000	**62 d S.E 1/20.000**
	66dN.E 1/20.000

Operations in the BATTLE ZONE

Thursday Mar 21st *at 4.30 am the order 'Man Battle Stations' was received. Companies and transport at once fell in on alarm posts and the battalion, with echelon 'A' of transport marched from HUGINEY to VAUX via FORESTE and GERMAINE.*

The morning was very misty and the Battalion arrived at STEEN WOOD, F.Y.a without interference from aircraft or shellfire. The Btn halted in F.Y.a.

Strength of Battalion.

Officers	*19*
O.R	*513*

Officers

Capt R.P Villar	*In command*
Capt F.H Lawless	*Adjutant*
2nd Lt H.N. Speckley	*Signalling Officer*
Capt D. Campbell	*R.A.M.C.T. M.O*

No1 Coy

Capt J.S Edwards   In Command
2nd Lt R.W Sparks
2nd Lt A.S Cox
2nd Lt A. E. Burlow

No 2 Coy

Capt . J. Lawson   In Command
2nd Lt D.Burbridge
2nd Lt C.W.P Simpson
2nd Lt R.J Turner

No 3 Coy

Capt F. M. Sheard MC   In Command
2nd Lt E.L Bradfield
2nd Lt H.H Cowley

No 4 Coy

Capt C.D. Redhead   In Command
2nd Lt J.A Fisher
2nd Lt H.J. Bayliss
2nd Lt H. Derbyshire

Btn H.Q was established at F.Y.a 8.9, close to battle H.Q of 90th infantry Bgd and billeting party was sent into VAUX.

They reported on their return that the village was clear of troops and they then guarded Companies and Transport to huts and standings lately occupied by the 17th Btn Manchester Regiment.

Btn H.Q was established about F.2.C. 2.2 with telephone communications to 90th Infantry Bgd.

About 11.30am a message was received from the 90th Inf Bdg to the effect that the enemy had penetrated the forward zone and that the redoubt had been put down by the artillery between MANCHESTER HILL and L'EPINE de DALLON, which positions were still holding out.

It was decided to move out of VAUX about 11.45am as the enemy has commenced to shell the village. Companies and transport reoccupied the positions they had previously taken up in F.Y.a and Btn H.Q moved back to F.Y.a 8.9

About 2.00pm, it was reported that the enemy had penetrated the BATTLE ZONEabout ROUPY and it was decided to dig in and defend the present position.

A line of trenches was dug from STEEN WOOD at F.Y.b 1.5 to F.I.d 3.1 with a defensive flank covering VAUX, running from F.I.d 3.1 to F.I.d 1.5.

Coys were disposed as follows:

Right ----------------- No1
Left --------------------No 3
Defensive flank------No 2
In reserve ------------No 4 in sunken road below STEEN WOOD

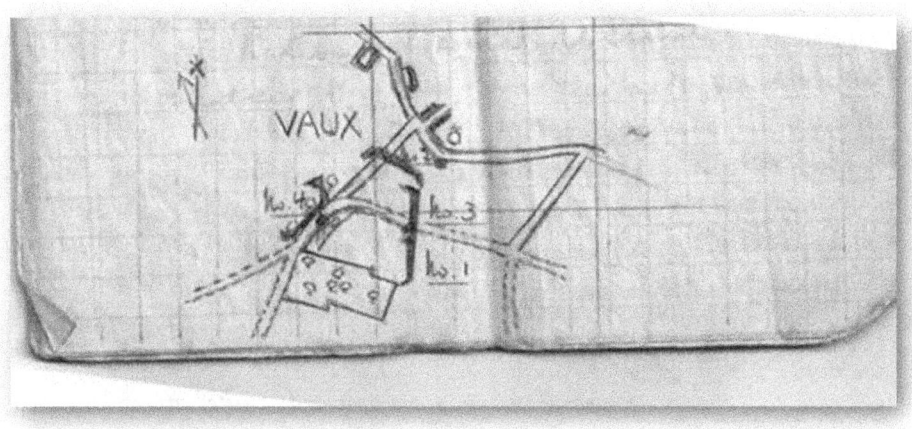

Hostile aeroplanes reconnoitred the position about 7pm, flying low and firing on the troops.

Shortly afterwards VAUX was heavily shelled, and some posts of No 2 coy on the left were withdrawn to the sunken road.

Close touch was kept with the situation in the Battle Zone, through the H.Q of the 90th Brigade, throughout the night.

The enemy was reported to be in possession of SAVY but had not succeeded in penetrating the defences of ETREILLERS, held by the 2nd Battalion Royal Scots Fusiliers.

About 10.00pm all transport was sent back to BEAUVOIS, to orders of G.O.C. 89th Inf Bdg, who gave further orders there for rearward moves.

Rations were received about midnight.

Sunday March 22nd

The G.O.C.. 90th Inf Bgd called on the Btn for carrying parties for the 2nd Btn Bedfordshire Regiment, holding the D.NORTH sector of the Battle Zone, and 50 men of No4 Coy under 2nd Lt J.A. Fisher were dispatched to STEVENS REDOUBT carrying S.A.A and grenades.

The party left about 9.00am and was retained at the Redoubt to assist in its defence.

About 10.00am the G.O.C. 90th Inf Bgd, reported that the enemy had succeeded in penetrating the left of the forward system in D NORTH Sector and he called for two companies to counter attack under the direction of the O/C 2nd Btn Bedfordshire Rgt.

Capt R.D. VILLAR left immediately for STEVENS REDOUBT to confer with the O/C 2nd Btn Bedfordshire regiment, leaving the adjutant, Capt F LAWLESS at Btn HQ to maintain liason with 90th Inf Bgd and control reserves.

About 10.30am Nos 2 and 3 Coys, under Capt J Lawson and Capt F. M SHEARD M.C. respectively, moved along the valley of the GERMAINE RIVER to STEVENS REDOUBT.

On their arrival there the situation in the forward system of D NORTH was so serious that it was decided to abandon the proposed counter attack and these companies were retained for the defence of the redoubt.

They remained there, fighting with the 2nd Btn Bedfordshire Regiment, until the garrison withdrew in the afternoon.

About 8.00am the G.O.C. 90th Inf Bgd; called on the Btn for reinforcement for the 2nd Btn Royal Scots Fusiliers, holding the village of ETREILLERS, and No 1 Coy, under Capt J.S Edwards, was dispatched immediately. This Coy fought under the command of the O/C 2nd Btn Royal Scots Fusiliers until their withdrawal from the Battle Zone later in the afternoon.

About 10.00am a second carrying party, of 50 men of No 4 Coy, was sent to STEVENS REDOUBT with S.A.A and grenades. This party, under 2nd Lt H. Derbyshire, returned to Btn H.Q about 2.00pm.

From 1.00pm onwards the enemy increased the pressure on the Battle Zone and he was reported to be in possession of ROUPY.

The O/C 2nd Btn Royal Scots Fusiliers at Etreillers, and the O/C 2nd Btn Bedfordshire Rgt at STEVENS REDOUBT, both reported, however, that their positions were satisfactory, for the moment at least.

News was received about 2.00pm that the Brigade on the left, about ATTILLY and the southern end of HULNON WOOD, was withdrawing to the line of trenches running from VAUX to VILLEVEQUE, and shortly afterwards the O/C 2nd Btn Royal Scots Fusiliers reported a rearward movement by the 21st Inf Bgd, from the D.SOUTH Sector.

About 3.00pm, the G.O.C..90th Inf Bgd, with his staff and Artillery Liason Officers left by motor car for AUROIR.

About 3.15pm Capt F. LAWLESS communicated with the O/C 2nd Btn Royal Scots Fusiliers and the O/C 2nd Btn Bedfordshire Rgt at ETREILLERS and STEVENS REDOUBT, respectively, and advised them of the situation. These officers asked for modifications in the British Artillery barrage – in the case of ETREILLIERS, to bring it closer to the village and in the case of the other positions to bring it round the flanks of the Redoubt. Barrage lines in accordance with their requirements orders were at once drawn up and communicated to the Artillery, who commenced to fire on them.

About 3.45pm the O/C 2nd Btn Royal Scots Fusiliers reported the 21st Brigade on his right were falling back, possibly in consequence of the retirement on the left to the VAUX- VILLEVEQUE line. Capt F. Lawless informed him the intention was to hold ETRELLIERS, upon which place the withdrawal on the left was pivoting, and the O/C 2nd Btn R. S. F. accordingly dispatched a runner to the Btn on his right, informing them of his intention of holding ETREILLERS and asking them to hold on. About 4.00pm a message was received from the 90th Inf Bgd to the effect that a withdrawal to HAM had been decided upon, and Battalion Commanders would hang on until dark or withdraw at once at their own discretion.

Capt F. LAWLESS communicated this message to the O/C 2nd Btn R.S.F. and 2nd Btn Bedfordshire Regiment and these officers decided, as the flanks had apparently given way, to withdraw at once.

Neither of these Btns had any further orders for the H.Q of the 18th K.L.R. and the order to withdraw to HAM was given to the details of the Battalion at VAUX.

Telephone instruments were then smashed and all documents and maps destroyed.

The shelling on VAUX and in K.7 was very heavy at this time but the withdrawal was made in good order and with little loss, via TETARD WOOD-AUROIR-BRITON COPSE.

At AUROIR report on the situation was made by Capt F. LAWLESS to the G.O.C. 90th Inf Bgd.

2 Operations about HAM

On arrival at HAM, about 7.30pm, Capt F. LAWLESS reported to the G.O.C. 89th Inf Bgd and was instructed to occupy a defensive position near the town, in support to the 21st Entrenching Battalion.

No news having been received of Capt R.P VILLAR, Capt F. LAWLESS assumed command of the Battalion.

Work was commenced at once with all available men, and positions dug on a line;

K.33.a.5.6 to K.b.6.8 - No4 Coy
K.34 a.6.1 and Btn H.Q

A line of posts along the HAM - FLAVY road, garrisoned by No 1 coy.
A defensive flank, from K.34a.y.1 to the road, garrisoned by No2 Coy.
Btn H.Q was established in a Brasserie, about K.33 central.

The companies at this time were very weak, but men staggered in throughout the night. Only about a dozen men of No 3 Coy had succeeded in getting away from STEVENS REDOUBT, and these were attached to No 1 Coy.

Rations were received about midnight.

Saturday 23rd March

About 1.00am orders were received to evacuate the position then occupied and move to a line running from about K.27.C.4.4 to K.So.a.5.0

Companies at once fell in and marched through HAM to the new position, which was occupied about 2.00am. The 17th Battalion, the K.L.R. was holding the line to the left and the 21st Entrenching Btn to the right across the canal.

Btn H.Q was established at 15.26.a.6.1.

Report was received that AUBIGNY had been occupied by the enemy and that his patrols were pushing forward from there. There was considerable rifle and M.G. fire from HAM on the left.

About 7.00am the O/C No 4 Coy reported that the troops on his left were falling back and that he was conforming, and immediately afterwards a message was received from the O/C 17th Btn K.L.R. to the effect that his Btn was withdrawing through HAM.

The order was then given for the Btn to withdraw through HAM, in the direction of ESMERY HALLON and this was done with few casualties.

Capt J.S EDWARDS, with a small party of the Battalion, withdrew along the HAM - NESLE road, and engaged the enemy throughout the morning, being reinforced by men of all regiments.

Later in the day this officer gained touch on his right with the O/C 17th Btn K.L.R.. and became engaged in operations under the command of that officer.

Capt F. LAWLESS, with a party of about 40 men of the Battalion withdrew in the direction of VERLAINES, and there took up a position on the right of the HAM- LIBERMONT road in line with the 17th Btn K.L.R.. This party was then placed under the command of Capt C.D REDHEAD and was engaged in operations under the direction of the O/C 17ᵗʰ Btn K.L.R.; who advanced the line east of VERLAINES in the direction of HAM about 2.30.pm.

Capt F. LAWLESS collected a mixed force of about 80 and placed them in a position at VERLAINES, as a reserve, under the orders of the O/C 17ᵗʰ Btn K.L.R..

In the evening this party was used to carry rations to the more forward troops.

The night passed quietly.

Sunday March 24ᵗʰ
3. Withdrawal through L' ESMERY HALLON

About 8am, in a thick ground mist, the enemy attacked strongly and a general withdrawal took place from the line east of VERLAINES.

A brisk rear guard action developed as the troops retired on ESMERY HALLON. Many attempts were made to rally the troops onto a new defensive line, but the enemy fire, for a time, was very heavy and the withdrawal was continued to the fringe of the village.

A line was made, facing North East, outside ESMERY HALLON, and patrols pushed through the woods in front. The enemy was not in sight in this direction and a promising advance in the direction of MESNIL when the right flank began to withdraw and the movement failed. Troops pressing through ESMERY HALLON were pushed out to the left flank in an effort to prolong the line in the direction of GRECOURT but the withdrawal from the right flank continued, and all troops fell back through the village.

A good orderly line was now made on both sides of the ESMERY HALLON-RAMECOURT road, in two waves, just east of a line GRECOURT–HOPITAL FARM, and a well conducted withdrawal to the canal was commenced.

Men of all regiments were mixed up in the line, but officers and NCOs quickly took the situation in hand, and the men were steadied and controlled.

There was little interference by the enemy's infantry, but his field artillery was quickly in action.

The French were already in position at the LANNOY FARM Bridgehead, and then a line of posts was reinforced by the withdrawing troops as they crossed the canal

Operations in the Vicinity of LANNOY FARM and MOYENCOURT

The 89th Brigade took up a line O.17.d - 23- b - 23d and the 90th Brigade took up a more northerly line through o.18.a - 12.c -11b

Battalions were reorganised during the afternoon and defensive positions in depth, towards ERCHEU and MOYENCOURT were taken up.

The 18th Btn KLR was allocated two tasks.

1. *A party, 30 strong, all companies, under Capt J.S Edwards, was attached as reinforcements, to the Royal Scots Fusiliers, and remained in a position in O.12.c until the withdrawal from the line of the canal the following day.*
2. *The remainder of the Battalion, about 80 strong, held the line of the canal in O.23.d until about midnight, when the whole of the 89th Infantry Brigade was allotted a fresh position immediately east of MOYENCOURT.*

RAMECOURT, LANNOY FARM, ERCHEU, and MOYENCOURT were all shelled during the afternoon.

Monday March 25th

About 10.00pm on the night of 24th/25th March, the Battalion moved from its position about o.23.d to MOYENCOURT, and dug–in on a line running from O.16.b.9.3 to O.11 .C.0.6. having the 17th Btn K.L.R. on the left and the 19th Btn K.L.R. on the right.

The line was prolonged to the right to RAMECOURT and LANNOY FARM by French troops.

French troops also held the village of ECHEU.

Btn H.Q was in a trench about O.16 .b.6.2.

Rations were received about midnight.

Digging continued throughout the night and by dawn the position appeared strong and defensible except on the right flank, where the French line appeared sketchy and thin. The night passed quietly.

During the morning of the 25th enemy aeroplanes reconnoitred the position and, about 1.00pm, the enemy commenced to shell the posts and the village of MOYENCOURT.

From 2.00pm there was heavy rifle and M.G gun fire in front and on both flanks and it was judged the enemy was pressing a strong attack on the crossings of the canal. About 3.30pm the French were seen withdrawing on both flanks and, shortly afterwards the order was received to withdraw to a line OMENCOURT–SOLENTE

This withdrawal took place in good order, through heavy shelling, via MOYENCOURT and the X roads in O.13.

   Heavy fighting appeared to be going on, on the right and the enemy was re-ported to be in possession of ERCHEU.

   On arrival at OMENCOURT an attempt was made to dig a line, but, with the few men in hand and the heavy shelling in O.23 and 24, the attempt did not promise success and a further withdrawal to a line between BALATRE and the BOIS de CHAMDIEN was decided upon.

   The men were put into old French trenches running through O.21 -28 -34, and digging of fire positions began at once.

   All men proceeding westwards were stopped and absorbed in the garrison of this line, and work on the trenches continued until orders were received from 30th division to withdraw all troops to ROIGLISE.

   The battalion was reorganised at ROIGLISE and officers and men fed and rested.

   About 10.00pm the Battalion enbussed and proceeded to PLESSIER, where men were billeted about 1.00am.

Tuesday 26th March
5. Operations about FOLIES

About 10.00am orders were received from the Battalion to occupy a line PARVILLERS–ROUVROY.

   Coys at once fell in and commenced the search, via HANGEST, and the O.C left by motor car to reconnoitre the position to be occupied.

   On arrival at BOUCHOIR, the enemy had made such progress that it was decided to hold the line BOUCHOIR-ROUVTOY.

   The O.C the Btn re-joined the Battalion at PETIT HANGEST and the advance to the new position was continued, in artillery formation via the wood in K.15 a- K16a- K.11.d- K12.d-K.13.b.

   At this stage units were disposed as follows by the G.O.C. 89th Inf Brigade

<u>*Front Line*</u>
from ROUVROY to BOUCHOIR
2 Coys 17ᵗʰ Btn KLR
11ᵗʰ Btn S Lancs Rgt
19ᵗʰ Btn KLR
Details of 89ᵗʰ T.H13 and M.G Btn
2ⁿᵈ Btn Bedfordshire Rgt

Two Coys of 17ᵗʰ Btn KLR were placed in support west of FOLIES and the 18ᵗʰ Btn K.L.R. was placed on the FOLIES-BOUCHOIR Road as a counter attack Battalion.

The position allotted to the Battalion was at once taken up and Btn H.Q established at K.17.d.9.4.

Coys were disposed as follows;

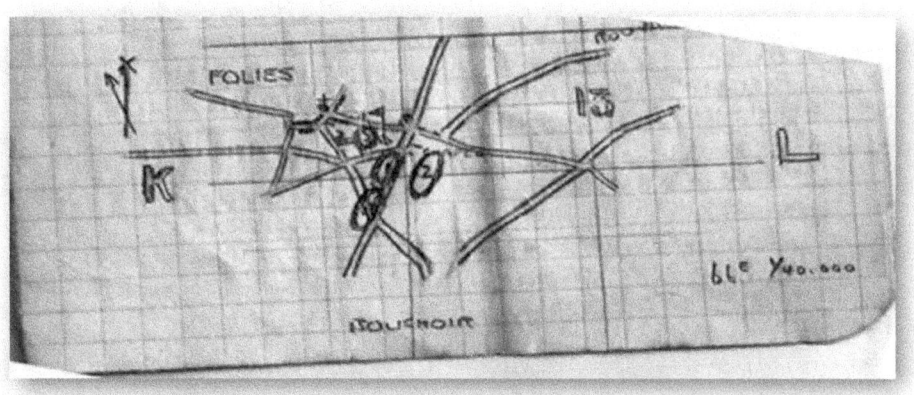

Liaison with Battalions was established, positions reconnoitred and arrangements for counter attack agreed upon.

The enemy was quiet during the night but appeared to make some progress in the night.

Rations were received during the night.

<u>**Wednesday March 27ᵗʰ**</u>
About 9.00 am orders were received that the Brigade would at once be relieved by the 59thInf Bgd then in support on a line through a line K. 1 a, b and c.

The O/C proceeded to H.Q 59th Inf Bgd and was conducting the O/C of the receiving Btn to FOLIES, to hand over the counter attack position, when a general withdrawal from the right flank commenced.

89th Inf Bgd was at once informed of the position and orders received to withdraw at once to HANGEST, in accordance with relief orders.

The Battalion accordingly withdrew, but was halted about K.1b central, as the withdrawal from the front line appeared to be continuing and the position generally was obscure.

The O/C despatched a message to 89th Bgd to the effect that the order to withdraw to HANGEST could not be carried out for the time being and reported to G.O.C. 59th Brigade for orders. After consulting with his divisional commander who was on the spot, the G.O.C. 59th Bgd decided to utilise the 89th KLR to restore the situation in front of FOLIES.

Two companies, Nos 3 and 4 counter attacked, about 12 noon, on the north of the village and Nos I and 3 Coys, counter attacked simultaneously on the south.

Btn HQ was established at K.16

The men of the Battalion went forward to these counter attacks with the greatest determination and steadiness, at a moment when the whole line appeared to be giving.

The morale effect on the retreating troops was very great and large numbers of men turned round and followed them back towards the enemy.

The advance of the Northern attack was checked by enemy fire about k.18 central and a line was dug from that point towards the CHAPEL and liaison established with two Coys of the 17th Btn K.L.R. on the left.

The advance of the Southern attack was checked by heavy enemy fire about the line of the road from the BEETROOT FACTORY to the CHAPEL. Liaison was established on the right with the 2nd Btn R.S.F. and on the left with the 59th Inf Bgd which had been pushed forward East of the Village, and the 7th Btn Manchester Rgt.

Digging was commenced at once on the new front line and patrols pushed forward.

An attempt was made, on the left, to push forward the line to the road running through L.13 central, but no progress could be made, and the enemy obtained possession of it during the afternoon.

About 8pm the enemy attacked on the left in some force but was repulsed by rifle and Lewis gun fire and left a prisoner in our hands.

French troops arrived during the night and pushed out small posts in advance of our line.

<u>*Thursday March 28th*</u>

About 6am the enemy commenced to shell heavily the whole of the forward line and brought French Mortars and Machine guns into action.

FOLIES was shelled and the area in rear of village as far back as LE QUESNEL.

Rations were received at dawn and parties were organised to carry them to the companies on the right. Owing to heavy fire however, it was not possible to get them up.

Heavy fighting was in progress on the right from soon after dawn, and at 8.00am the enemy was reported to be in possession of BOUCHOIR and progressing towards the BEETROOT FACTORY.

About 10.00am the 59th Inf Btn was notified that it was relieved by the French and the Btns of that Bgd were at once withdrawn in the direction of LE QUESNEL.

At noon the enemy was bombarding the village and vicinity heavily and reports were received that he was in occupation of WARVILLERS on the left and ARVILLERS on the right.

The front line east of FOLIES continued to resist until about 2.00pm, when the order was received from 89th Inf Bgd to the effect that the Btns were relieved by the French and would withdraw at once to MEZIERES, where men would be fed.

Companies withdrew, under some shelling and very heavy M.G and rifle fire from the left, through K.10-K.3 – North side of LE QUESNEL – to the main ROYE road, and reorganised about D 29.c.

The march from this point was conducted in good order, despite the congested roads.

At MEZIERES it was decided to continue a rearward movement and the march was resumed via VILLERS–MOREVIL–MORISEL to ROUVREL, which village was reached about 7.00pm and the Battalion billeted.

The men had marched 13 miles from the last position, in good order with practically no straggling. They were exhausted on arrival at ROUVREL, BUT IN GOOD HEART.

Echelon 'A' of the Transport joined the Battalion at this village and the men were fed immediately on arrival.

The night passed without incident.

Friday March 29th

At 10am, a composite Battalion was formed by the G.O.C. 89th Inf Bgd from the remaining officers, O.R and Transport of the 17th, 18th, 19th, K.L.R. under command of Lieut. Gen Rollo D.S.O.

The 18th K.L.R. formed one complete company and one half company for this composite Battalion, complete with officers and the following officers for H.Q

Second –in-Command	*Capt F. Lawless*
Transport Officer	*Capt W. Williams*
Intelligence Officer	*2nd Lt A.F Henry M.C*
Medical Officer	*Capt D. Campbell R.A.M.C*

At dusk Outposts were put out round the village and patrols were pushed out in the direction of MOREUIL throughout the night.

5. To End of Operation
Saturday March 30th

At 9.00am. The Composite Battalion left ROUVEL for SALEUX, via REMIENCOURT-ENTREES-HEBECOURT, and there entrained for ST VALERY-SUR-SOMME at 3pm.

Arrived at ST VALERY 9.30pm and Battalion billeted there for the night.

Sunday March 31st

At 9.30am the 89th Composite Battalion paraded and the men were reorganised into their various units.

The 18*th* Battalion K.L.R. left ST VALERY at 10am for BRUTELLES and billeted there about 1.pm

The following Officers re-joined the Battalion on March 24*th* during the Operations

Lt. J.C.Tinkler
2*nd* Lt H.L.Baker
2*nd* Lt W.H.Bailey
2*nd* Lt A.H.Rigby
2*nd* Lt E.D Bebb

About 100 O.R, ex Details, Courses, Leave etc joined the Battalion during the operations.

Casualties to Officers
March 21*st* Nil
March 22*nd*
Killed
Capt R.P Villar
2*nd* Lt (Acting Capt) J Lawson

Wounded
2*nd* Lt D.Burbidge

Wounded /Missing
Capt F.M Sheard M.C

March 23*rd*
Missing
2*nd* Lt A.G. Cox
2*nd* Lt A.E Barlow

March 24th
Killed
2nd Lt M. Derbyshire

Wounded
2^{nd}Lt H. Bayliss
2nd Lt W.H Bailey
Lieut E.L Bradfield

March 25th
Wounded
2nd Lt E.D Bebb
2nd Lt C.W.P Simpson

March 28th
Wounded
Lieut J.C.Tinkler
2nd Lt A.H.Rigby was accidently injured on March 24th and did not take part in the operation.

Estimated Casualties in O.R on 3rd April 1918
Killed   14
Wounded   76
Missing   <u>280</u>
            <u>370</u>

Signed_____**F Lawless**
(Cap't Commanding 18th Btn Kings Liverpool Rgt)
In the Field_____**April 3rd 1918**

For Freedom and Honour

THE FOLLOWING OFFICER LISTED AS wounded or missing is known to have subsequently died of wounds

Capt F.M Sheard M.C

The following officers mentioned by Frank in this action died later in the war;

2nd Lt R.W Sparks	**Killed in Action 20/04/1918**
Capt F Henry MC	**Killed in Action 08/05/1918**
Capt H.L Baker MC	**Killed in Action 01/11/1918**

In the ten days of this action, the three surviving Liverpool Pals battalions, 17th, 18th and 19th, lost 12 officers with 207 men killed and around 600 taken prisoner or wounded, many of whom later died.

Postcard

29ᵗʰ March On active Service

 Hillie Darling; I do hope you are alright my dearest Angel. I am and promise to be. I am a little part in the show, its nearly over now and I'll write.

 Just Chance.

 Have dashed into a house and written this- we are moving

A big kiss. Frankie

Letter 17

April 1st   18th B.E.F
My own darling
I hope to heaven you haven't been frightfully stuck-up through the non-arrival of your tiny cheque.
We've only just joined touch with the baggage which went missing off the coast when the attack came. I'm sending it off post-haste —with a huge big kiss darling Angel and a little violet the girl of the house has just presented to me. A big letter later today, Hillie darling. I do wish yours would begin to arrive again and a big, big kiss and one for my mum and Dorothy. Tell the Pater we will win the battle and he must not worry.
Frankie
Everyone says 'this is the end'. I do think so too, don't you?

Letter 18

Around April 3/4th   No opening pages
4.

...If you pray for me, and love me, all the while, as you are doing, then I know I shall always be safe – until I am back again with you. Darling – then we won't part any more, will we?

The French people are laughing at me for being such a 'jeune colo-nel.' It certainly is absurd to think of little me running the 18th. Stanley says he expects Clayton will come back soon, tho' it is just possible he has been grabbed at the Base on his way to us and rushed up to the Front in charge of some scratch battalion.

I have lost a lot of kit, of course, but one's life was the only thing that mattered really, wasn't it Hillie? I shall refit at Ordinance and get my hair cut in a day or two, when I can summon energy for a ride.

I am very pleased with myself today. I had a topping shave and pumiced stoned my hands almost clean again. Of course, the wretched Albert must abandon my new cap to the horrid Huns!

Little Devil! I was cross and told him it was a pity the Bosche didn't snaffle him too!

Write quickly, Hillie Darling, and tell me all the news. How you are, my own small angel wife, and how is Mummy and my dad and Dorothy and Alan and Bill? I am dying for news. Tell me you love and believe all this is ending now and that the last terrible trial for you, sweet Hillie, was the last.

Lord! We are lucky, we two, dear Hillie, I can never thank God enough for pulling me through that show, so our future plans would not go wrong.

Goodnight my own dear, dear Hillie - I love you a thousand million times more dearly than ever before and oh how I want you. Soon, soon now, sweet Angel. If there is a glimmer of leave I will be absolutely 'in' for it at once, 'cos Stanley is pleased with our show and is on my side now.

A big, big loving kiss, my own dear girl, to tell you I will come soon. Frankie

Letter 19

two sheets pencil on note book small paper page headed 3

April 5ᵗʰ

...from the battle. After that, when I know you are happy again and dear old Dorothy been able to go to William and Alan is having a good holiday... after that I shall be happy again too. Dear, dear Hillie! Don't worry any more my small angel–wife or let these happenings make you ill. Keep very strong and cheery, dear for our honeymoon in May. How splendid it is going to be.

Is peace near? They all seem to think it is. How weary the whole world seems of this fighting. It must finish through sheer weariness.

Tell Dorothy I think she is an angel for staying with you and I will write to her soon. She will understand, I know, how utterly impossible it is to write now, and tell my dad and mum, dear Hillie, with a big kiss, that I will write just as soon as I am able to. They must just trust me and not be cross and believe that it is impossible to write now.

Awfully wet today. Raining like blazes Hillie darling, which should put the lid on the old huns...

Field Service Post Card Dated 5th April

For Freedom and Honour

The Distinguished Service Order

FRANK IS EXCEPTIONALLY MODEST IN his field diary. For his work throughout that week and especially on Wednesday 27th March 1918, he was awarded the Distinguished Service Order.

Family history reports that he galloped out on Blackie, under heavy enemy fire and rallied his men to hold the position near Folies instead of withdrawing. So inspiring was his leadership that other soldiers in retreat turned back and joined his forces to hold the line.

From the London Gazette 16th September 1918

Lawless, Francis; Temporary Cap't Liverpool Regiment.

For Conspicuous Gallantry and Devotion to duty. When his commanding officer became a casualty he took command of the Battalion and remained as such during the whole of the ensuing week's operations. He fought his battalion magnificently, and his conduct was the admiration of the troops adjoining. His cheerfulness and coolness had a wonderful effect on his men and his efforts undoubtedly on several occasions caused heavy losses to be inflicted on the enemy and retard his progress.

◊ The Distinguished Service Order (D.S.O.) is out ranked only by the Victoria Cross and award-ed only to Officers. Family History reports that Frank was recommended for the Victoria Cross but was subsequently awarded the D.S.O as two VC's had already been given to others in the regiment. Other oral traditions say he was not awarded a VC because he was a Catholic. I have not found any evidence to support this, but there are many rumours that the Irish Catholic Liverpudlians were not promoted in the Army as fast as others.

LIVERPOOL COURIER

MAY 25, 1918.

LIVERPOOL OFFICER'S HONOUR.

Captain and Adjutant Francis R. Lawless, King's (Liverpool Regiment), has been awarded the D.S.O. for meritorious service during the recent heavy fighting on the Western front. The youngest son of Major and Mrs. Lawless, of 33, Harthill-avenue, Mossley Hill, Captain Lawless was educated at St. Francis Xavier's College, Liverpool, and entered the employment of the White Star Line in 1907, being transferred to the company's London office in 1913. When war broke out he was acting there as assistant private secretary to the chairman, and at once joined a Liverpool "Comrades" Battalion. In circles outside the commercial world Captain Lawless is known as a man of literary attainments, and the news of the distinction he has gained will be welcomed in many

For Freedom and Honour

LATER, WHEN FRANK HAD TIME, he wrote again to his brother Charley;

....The Battalion did wonderful deeds. Good men and true every one of 'em and it is only now, in the peace after the storm, that we are beginning to miss them. What a cost and yet what a name!

They have given me a D.S.O. because the men fought so splendidly (I was in command during the first phase of the show, as the C.O was killed on the second day!) and we have a huge list of Military Crosses and Honours for the men. It would be embarrassing to wear the Order under many circumstances, but I will always be very proud of it for the sake of those fine fellows who won it for me.

The Bosche can't ever beat the British army, no matter how hard he may try, because they never know when they are beaten. Day after day they fought to the point of exhaustion – and then fought again the next day. A wonderful and inspiring battle all through, and I thank god for showing me how fine men can be when they believe they have a fine ideal to struggle for.

For Freedom and Honour

FOLLOWING THE RETREAT THE SURVIVING men of the Pals battalions may have felt themselves entitled to a well-earned regrouping and rest. Instead on 4th April they found themselves once more entrained and returned to the Ypres Salient.

On 9th April a further determined German attack began, which attempted to break the line and reach the channel. General Haig issued his famous order;

'Every position must be held to the last man. With our backs to the wall and believing in the justice of our cause, each one of us must fight on to the end.'

The war became much more mobile and all the Pals battalions were moved around from place to place as needed, in and out of the line. Despite the thinly held lines the Battalions <u>did</u> hold on and the fierce actions, known as The Battle of the Lys ensured Flanders was saved by the British once again.

Letter 20

April 15th 18th B.E.F

My Darling Hillie,

No letter from you yesterday, Hillie darling, so I am hoping for two today. I wonder if my luck will be in and I will get them.

We haven't pulled out yet, but I expect to any time now as I hear Stanley has written saying he has heard the Training stint will take place immediately. I suppose it is just a question of someone coming along to relieve us and that always takes a little while - especially in days like these, when we run through troops so quickly. The news is better yesterday and I'm hoping the Hun is now firmly held here. Dirty dog, isn't he, to push us so far.

However his losses must be something frightful and I just wonder how much longer he can carry on. I should doubt very much if he can ever again launch such an attack as we got up against three weeks ago.

Just fancy, Hillie, the 15th - Three weeks longer and I shall be 3 months in and due for my leave again. Oh! I do want it to open again don't you? Your prayers for me have been so successful in every other way, my darling old thing that I am relying on you to get leave opened for me by the beginning of May so that I can put in my demand.

Of course if the training stint….Ends here

For Freedom and Honour

ON THE 2ND MAY THE surviving remnants of the three Pals battalions were once more merged into a single composite Battalion, the total number of troops considered fit for service consisting of 27 officers and 750 men. The composite battalion lasted for 10 days and was returned to the line where it came under intense attack. A further 4 officers and 47 men were lost.

The Pals battalions never fought together again and on the 11th May they were disbanded. On the 13th May the survivors of the 18th were redeployed training the newly arrived American troops out of the Front line.

Letter 21

May 7th   18th (KLR)   B.E.F
My Darling Hillie

So, so sorry, my darling Hillie….. I felt the meanest wretch on Earth when we got in and I found I had missed the post.

Geoff Clayton came along in the morning and insisted I should go into a big town about 12 kilo's off and have lunch with him. Poor old thing, I felt I must go, 'cos he's been so awfully decent to me lately and he needs a bit of bucking up after all his fighting. So off we trotted: had a priceless ride on dear old Blackie, a pretty disappointing lunch, a stroll around the town, a shampoo and some shopping. I sent you some pictures of the place. It's no good for feeding or shopping, but might be worth looking around from a 'buildings' point of view. However I don't think we will 'do' it on our Continental trip, Hillie darling, will we, 'cos I just loathe Flanders, and everything in it.

I am jolly fit, Hillie dear, tho' very worried about you, dear old girl, 'cos last night's letter told me you were very anxious about our going into the line again…. And since then you will have seen the papers about the big battle of the 29th of course.

However you will have read too, about how we gave it to the Hun bang in the eye and I know how it would cheer you a little bit to know how fine the 18th was in its very last fight.

No orders yet to go and pick up our Yanks, but everything is ready and we will go any time now. This is the most peaceful time here … the best I have ever had in the army.

I came back yesterday with a book of verse, 'La Cousine Bette' of Balzac and a resolution to tackle Italian again!

In the Coiffeurs yesterday I nearly made Geoff Clayton lose an ear by reading in 'La Telegramme' about the Huns scheme for an armistice this month. It was in huge headed type, via Holland', of course, but read splendidly and made us fearfully excited. Has it been in the English papers, I wonder! If only the Hun at home _would_ lose his nerve, eh!

I still think we are near the end, and a good end too. Things back here look much more rosy than when you are in the front trenches.

So old Alan has gone back. Hillie darling! I do wish I could have got home for his hols. It would have been alright I think if things had re-mained 'normal'. We'll give him a good time next chance, eh? I can well believe how lonely you are now, dearest girl, and how dull these long days are. Truly I feel a worm for writing so priggishly about you wanting to go back to town. You believe dear, that I don't mind a tiny bit if you decide to go, don't you dear.

I don't want to be an ogre, a tiny, tiny bit, and I shall believe it is all for the best if you tell me that Liverpool is too dull and unpleasant. You know I will understand.

But I believe, Hillie Darling, that this 'Yankee' business, is going to 'open the door' for a leave, and you certainly can hope that any old time now I will come…maybe only for a few days, dear Angel… But that would be splendid, wouldn't it?

I've written in to ask …Ends here

For Freedom and Honour

On 16th May the remnant of the 18th Battalion was sent to Woincourt to train an American infantry regiment.

Letter 22

May 24ᵗʰ   (1918)   18ᵗʰ B.E.F
My own darling Hillie

I would just love to have a flying kick at the man (or woman) who holds up my billet-doux. The filthy dog! And censors one too. Pish!

That's how I feel. My poor old girl! Why I am quite sure there was only one blank day during our move down here and I can't understand why you have had five kissless days. Dear Hillie! Although the letters did not arrive, I sent you the kisses just the same… I send you a simply topping one every single morning, to tell you that my world is just the loveliest possible since you came into it, and that I do most truly adore you and pray to come. Oh! If only it can be soon. Dear Angel! Thank you a thousand, thousand times for your communion. I am sure it will bring me to you dear. I am wondering how our next meeting will come about. Will it be that leave will open suddenly or will it be something quite unexpected? Every letter that comes in, and every telegram, I read eagerly, wondering if it is the miracle I want so badly. If only old Stanley would suddenly need someone to help him lay out lines and fences and think of little me! I'd go like a shot!

Anyway, by whichever way, by hook or by crook I feel a chance is coming now, of seeing you, darling Hillie. I will write to you immediately, my darling old thing, if ever there is a chance, would you come?

We have moved into a more wonderful place still. Another chateau, more modern with baths etc and only occupied in one or two rooms by caretakers. We have practically the whole place and it is quite fun but one can't help regretting the other place 'cos the people were so decent to me.

I sent you heaps and heaps of loving prayers at Mass this morning, Hillie darling, did you get them, I wonder? I do so want you to get them, my darling Hillie 'cos I adore you more than ever before and I do so want you. No! Don't threaten me with flannel nighties, dear girl, 'cos I want to give you, in that wonderful first night we are going to have, just the lovingest hug in the world. May I dear?

These changes make one jolly busy and tired, but things will settle down a lot later on, and I promise heaps and heaps of billets-doux then, dear Hillie.

There was a big bombardment last night and they say the new Push has started, but it has died down again today and we haven't heard anything about a new battle. Isn't it topping to think we are not in it, Hillie darling? You don't worry a tiny bit now, do you Angel? Good night my own darling! It will be soon, I know — Yes! There is even a chance for May even though it is nearly over. I can't give up hope, even re the 26th, 'cos I feel so strongly that a miracle will happen and I will find my own darling in my arms again.

Dear Hillie ! I will give you then such a very tender kiss to tell you how glad I am.
Frankie

Letter 23

May 25th   18th   B.E.F
My Darling Hillie

A big, big kiss for the topping letter of today, dear Hillie and an extra one because you say I am nasty and don't deserve my First Night Nightie any more.   Dear old girl! I am so sorry, tho' for the life of me, don't understand my sin. Why old man Cox is the most interesting fellow in the world and I think it is you, Hillie Darling, who is a bit mean for saying you don't care how many Francs he has saved up for us: Alright Hillie darling!.. and I tried to save such a lot too. I've just got the book and it's nearly £60.00 to May 13th.

Now, be an angel and say you are sorry for scolding me and threatening me with flannel nighties and send me a huge big kiss to tell me I've been rather clever to have saved so much for our Honeymoon in three months.

Oh! You owe me one kiss more, Hillie Darling. I stagger under a perfect shower of Military appreciation, for today my name is in Dispatches as 'mentioned' for last October/Nov period, for Good Work. Isn't it funny it should come just after the D.S.O?

I feel a bit of a pig because I shall get another 'mention' later on, for getting a D.S.O. as an 'immediate reward'.(D.S.O.'s for services in action 'carry' a 'mention' with them.)

Geoff Clayton is mentioned too – for which we are all rather glad, as the poor old thing has been left out in the cold overlong.

Yes darling Hillie, you can stick the letters on my envelopes if you like, as the award has already been mentioned in Haig's list.

I really can't help smiling at all this business, Hillie darling. It seems so funny, I think that this should have happened to little me, who always loathed soldiers so heartily. I wonder if I ought to tell them that I once laughed at the sentry at Chelsea! Do you think I ought, Hillie dear?

Why couldn't I have been a success in shipping I wonder or with the Theatre – instead of the army? What a funny old world it is, eh?

I think you are a dear little girl to say you are glad about the D.S.O. and I shall steal a tremendous big kiss from you, darling, to tell you I got it for you. Will you love it for that reason, dear Hillie… and never mind William and his views on Army Captains?

I just got in from the dentist. Rode over to the hospital town on the coast after breakfast on Blackie; had a rotten half hour; then a topping early lunch at a hotel on the Esplanade.

Oh I did miss you, Hillie darling. I only saw one man I knew, Douglas, the cricketer, and I dodged him and sat in a little corner by myself and watched the tide and the people strolling about and the fishing boats going out and all the rest of the life of this jolly little place – and I thought how simply glorious it would be if only I could hear the rustle of your skirt, Hillie and you would romp into the room and take the other chair. All sorts of other little girls did romp into the room and sit in empty chairs but my own little girl was so far off that not all my praying could bring her – so I finished my solitary lunch and hoisted myself on Blackie for home again. Hillie Darling, at times like these I feel I simply cannot bear the awful loneliness another moment. It seems too hard to bear… but then my heart hears you promise, darling, to love me for ever … and I think it can only be for a little while longer. This present pain will make the 'afterwards' more glorious still… But I do, do want my darling again.

Today, when I came home, tho', splendid news. The 'mention' and then a report that the Boche is getting on the defensive and won't risk any more attacks. Can it be true I wonder. 'Cos it means, if it is, Leave, darling Hillie…Just as soon as the glorious news that it is open again I shall put in for my month. May is getting near the end, I know. How wonderful if, after all, it was this month. Why not? It closed suddenly, by a little wire; it will open again just the same.…

Letter 24

May 30ᵗʰ   18ᵗʰ Kings   B.E. F
Hello Darling Hillie

Such a topping morning, dear and I feel just as optimistic and cheery as I can be, even tho' I didn't get my kiss yesterday. I have been reading through some of your recent letters, tho' my darling, at my office in the Chateau, and I have given each one of them a huge big kiss, to tell them that I think each one of them is beautiful and that I love them with all my heart for the kisses they bring me from my own small wife.

My dear, dear, Hillie! There isn't any chance of another three months mark, in our married life, passing without a real kiss, I am sure. I couldn't bear to think that possible. The 30ᵗʰ May today! How I did build my hopes on May. Now it must be June. It is all so cruel and unfair, my dear, and I am oh so sorry and so sad that I cannot come, I want you, to hold you more every single day, sweet Angel. The 11ᵗʰ of June will mark 4 months won't it Hillie.

Leave <u>has</u> actually reopened on a small scale, but one can't go under five months. That's not much good, is it, Hillie. I want to go now, now, this very day so we must hope that it will reopen properly and I can put in for my month.

This is a holiday with the Americans, so I have buzzed all my staff away to the sea, and am having a quiet day, trying to get rid of all my outstanding correspondence, I have a great stack of letters to answer. That medal has meant quite a lot of work in that line.

By the way, Hillie darling, you refer to a letter from Sanderson, but the Pater didn't send it on. I should like to read it sometime.

The newspaper rubbish was simply ridiculous. Shelley is an old fool and I shall tell him so when I see him. I got a dreadful fright in connection with it. The Mater wrote and said 'I hear there is something about your D.S.O. in the 'London Mail'. Good God, me thinks, why not 'Comic Cuts' or the 'Police News'!! She meant the 'Daily Mail' I hope.

My dear old Hillie! Why of course I do promise that big, big hug! If it could only be tonight. It is going to be more wonderful, I know, because it can't be tonight, but oh this awful, awful waiting. Never mind, dear old girl, it <u>can't</u> be long now. Can it, at most, be more than a month I wonder. Hardly, dear, I feel. These Yankee's will be going off, I suppose, in a week or two, and they could spare us while we are waiting for the next batch I should think.

I'm going to see the Yanks play Basketball this afternoon. I believe it is a weird sight and there are many casualties. I am a good deal more reconciled to the job now, Hillie darling. We are working with a far more interesting crowd from St Louis. The other people, the Kansas crowd, were remarkably dull and devoid of any personality whatever.

The Hun still progresses, I hear, in the Arras sector. I have been thinking a lot about our poor fellows down there, fighting all day in the dust and heat. These retreats are terrible shows. If only it would all end now. Surely enough men have been killed to show everyone in the world that War is too horrible to be tolerated.

Hillie darling, how is your hair now? Is it quite, quite well, dear? Tell me truly, then, if it is sick again. I promise to send heaps and heaps of extra prayers and kisses to make it better. When I come this time and we go away by ourselves, I really can brush it can't I Angel, if I promise to be very good?

Last time we used to stay up so late that I'm afraid we were very unkind to that lovely hair, weren't we? We must make up for it, tho' and show that we do love, love it.

Hillie dear, I do want some of the stuff you make for lunch, please, and I promise to say ...

Letter 25

Starts on page 2   no opening pages   Early June 1918

I've been doing a bit of reading again, these last few days. The first time for ages and I love settling down to a book. Do you have any time for a novel now, Hillie? My poor old thing, you won't work too hard will you my dearest, at the old Comrades place?

I do think five days a week is a bit too much, don't you think four would do, Hillie? I do.

Do you remember our train journey from Ardrossan to Glasgow, Hillie Darling?

Wasn't it exciting?... and the arrival at that Hotel when the awful man stood at your elbow as you signed the book. I often think over that afternoon, dear, and I still think it is one of the very loveliest of all. But I promise that our next honeymoon will be lovelier still, Hillie dear. How I have missed you since then…Those awful, awful days of March when I really did imagine sometimes that it was 'all up'… How I have learned what you meant to me.

Send me a huge big kiss, Hillie darling, to tell me you love, love me as much as you did that Saturday, and that you want our next honeymoon to come quickly too. What have you done with the frock you wore for our wedding, Hilda darling? Are you ever going to wear it again for me? … Or aren't wedding frocks ever worn again? (I've a suspicion that I've heard somewhere that they always put away and kept as souvenirs!) If I am very, very good, you could put it on one night, when we were all alone, just you and I, dearest, and then we will think over our marriage and how lovely and wonderful it all is. Can we, Hillie dear? And I will be really, really wicked again and buy you some more black stockings to wear with it, and another pair of wedding shoes….. and I will give you the D.S.O. which cost your dear, dear, trembling heart such anxious hours and I'll give you a loving kiss as I take you to my heart to promise that I will never, never make you anxious again.

Will you agree, Hillie dear? Say 'yes' and I will send you a huge big extra kiss for spoiling me.

I send you your cheque Angel, to take you all my heart, and a tiny loving kiss. Frankie

Letter 26

June 15th   18th K.L.R   B.E.F
My Darling Hillie

   Such a horrid blank day, my darling, because the mail came in and did not bring me a kiss.

   I said a big Damn and a big prayer for two to come tomorrow, and I sent my darling the lovingest kiss in the world, 'cos my disappointment reminded me a tiny bit more how I miss her and want her. Dear old Hillie! I can't ever, ever live without your kisses now. Do you realize just what it means, I wonder! That in the 'afterwards' you will have to put up with me, and my funny ways simply always. I shall try ever so hard, my angel wife, to be good, but I can't help thinking sometimes how tired of me you may become. You won't be tired of me during the three months at Aldershot, tho' will you, Hillie darling? Please, my dear small wife, may I have heaps and heaps of kisses then, eh?

   Do say 'yes, you may… if you are good' 'cos I have been so lonely all this long time since February, and there have been such horrid moments sometimes, during the nights of fighting, when you seemed so far away, dear Hillie, and I realised so clearly then, that if it was to be my fate to 'go West', the only thing I would ask for before my hurried departure, would be to take you once more in my arms and kiss your dear face, my darling.

   A topping letter today Hillie, from our dad in Hong Kong, and I send it to you to read. Will you send it back, Angel please, so I may answer it? I have done rather well lately, in my letters from the East, haven't I?

   I am just off to tea and then a bath and a change and at six o'clock I set off on Blackie for the farm of La Madelaine, in the forest, where Billie Williams is standing a Military Cross dinner for six of his pals. It will be my third dinner there and I simply love 'em. One day Hillie darling, when we 'do' France, I promise that you and I will dine there, eh?

   It is most gorgeous; right in the heart of the forest, the dinner and wine perfection, and one eats on a table spread under the apple trees. You must ride of course, 'cos the Forest track is up a hill and La Madelaine stands high, but we'll get you a very well behaved pony, Hillie darling. Will you come?

The lovingest kiss to make you promise – and to tell you I adore you. Frankie.

Letter 27

June 24th   18th   BEF
My Darling Hillie

    A simply lovely letter today, my own darling girl, and I send you a huge big kiss for it. The kiss is to tell you some good news too.

    Morrell, late of ... And now of the army, dropped in for a cup of tea and told me that leave is bucking up from the 1st of July if there is no battle by then. Isn't that topping, Hillie darling, 'cos I am due on the 11th and I'll try for my month. So go ahead with the Welsh cottage Hillie dear and I promise faithfully to come soon. He also said there was quite a chance of us all going home to train a new British Battalion – probably these old men who have been called up – but if that falls through, we are likely to get more Americans and go back to our old comfy billet, near the countess's chateau. That would be pretty good, wouldn't it dear, 'cos that was a topping neighbourhood. This is quite good, but I love to be near the coast.

    The lady who owns the house is the wife of a French artillery colonel– about 50!

    We are great pals and she asked me this morning, if I could possibly get to Le Havre, to bring her daughter along. This is a triumph, isn't it Hillie? I suppose she thought I looked pretty safe, particularly as I confessed to a small wife! Havre is 130 miles, it'd be a difficult journey even if I did manage to borrow a car so I suggested telegraphing and am motorbiking to G.H.Q in the morning to try if it can be done.

    It's fantastic sort of business, isn't it, dearest, but Geoff Clayton says I'd better do what I can as we may be in her house for some time and it's always well to keep well in. It is a perfectly charming house, simply stuffed with books and music and pretty curtains and flowers and things. I do wish all the while that you were here Hillie darling, perched on that funny old piano-stool, or (am I very wicked), perched on my knee, my own small wife, so that I could give you just the biggest huggle and the tenderest kiss in all the world to say how much I love you.

Letter 28

Starts at page 2   early July 1918

...the Marne; the Hun should be held there and it is even on the cards that he is 'through' our line on too narrow a front to be healthy for him. I am praying hard that we can manage to get 'one in' on him in return for all this fright he has given us. If we hold him until winter, he has precious little to encourage him in the prospects for next year, when France will be stiff with Yankees. They are pouring over now at a great rate.

G.H.Q asked for our names today. I wonder if it means we are going to be put on this job permanently. No! Hillie darling! There is no chance, truly, of our being sent up to the line to push the Hun back from the Marne. They've got lots of Yanks now and our little few didn't count as a fighting force.

How are you Hillie dear? Send me a very cheery kiss and tell me you are top hole...

By the way, have you decided where we are to go on our leave, Hillie darling? Let us spend at least a week, if it is only a fourteen day leave, right away from anybody at all we know, who could steal one moment from our honeymoon. I do want you all for myself Hillie darling, is it so very wicked, eh?

Shall it be Broddick, or new ground? The Lakes or Wales or Ireland or Yorkshire, or where? Isn't it fascinating to think we have the whole British Isles to ourselves and we can go where we like and do what we like and not one single person can interfere?

I do, do think our marriage is wonderful, darling and I love, love that 25th of August which gave you to me. Dear Hillie!

I send you the hugest kiss in the world for the silly thing you did when you promised to love me and take care of me – and I adore you dear old girl because you trusted yourself to me.

Goodnight sweet Angel. Every bit of my love and one extra loving kiss tonight for the lovely letter I got today.

Frankie

Letter 29

July 19ᵗʰ   18th BEF
My own darling Hillie

Out all day on a tactical ride with the Yankees. A most dreadfully boring show, hot as ... and a lot of flies.

I dashed home on old Blackie, thirsting for a cup of tea and found my kiss, my own sweet girl, waiting for me...and lots of news.

First of all dearest girl, a big, big kiss, right here for sending me that special Communion last Sunday. Oh yes, dear Hillie, I do always get your lovely Communions, I promise. Aren't they the secret of my wonderful luck out here? I think they are, you know.

Angel darling, I often wonder if I should still be in the land of the living if it wasn't that my own small wife had looked after me so well. You'd agree, old girl, I know, if you knew the many 'squeaks' I'd had.

Is the shirt for Dyserth a success, Hillie darling? Even if it is a scream I promise to love it dear. I wonder if you know what a real love I have for your frocks and shoes and hankies, my angel wife... and I am such a bad, bad man that I love, love your pink-ones and your green-ones and other wonderful little odds and ends of clothing too.

It is very wicked, I know, dearest but it is all a big lovely secret between you and I isn't it eh? and no one else need care.

I still have the hankie you wore near your heart for me on our last night together and I often give it a sly kiss when I feel blue and wonder if I can possibly bear this separation any longer.

If you wear the Dyserth shirt, Hillie and it becomes identified with you, then I shall love it and it will be like no other shirt on earth, I promise.

You won't forget that you have promised, one night, when we are all alone, that you will wear your wedding frock for me. Oh Hillie darling! Won't it be just splendid if that can be on the 25th?

I shall pray extra hard for that. I cannot imagine anything more lovely, can you, dear old girl?- and please Hillie darling you have promised to wear the black velvet one night for me.

I think it would be lovely if we could have a topping little dinner one night and you could wear it then. We could have a private room, olives, a cold chicken, a salad, a jelly and a bottle of something fizzy couldn't we Hillie, darling. I owe you a dinner for...

For Freedom and Honour

A DAY OR TWO AFTER that letter Frank was unexpectedly redeployed as Adjutant to the 1st Battalion Lincolnshire Regiment and returned to the Front line. The posting to Aldershot, with his original Battalion, 17th K.L.R, which he had been hoping for did not materialise.

Hillie was grateful afterwards, that the move with the 17th did not happen. After three months in England they were sent to Archangel in Russia, where they remained until September 1919.

Frank wrote once again to his brother Charlie;

July 28th 1st Battalion Lincolnshire Regiment
B.E.F France
My Dear Charlie
Yes! Isn't it horrid to have to write 'Lincolns' instead of the dear old 18th King's! I was sitting at dinner just a week ago tonight, when a wire arrived from G.C.H.Q. telling me to report at once to this regular Battalion as adjutant. Ugh! You can't imagine what a shock and a disappointment it was to me. I felt utterly miserable to break with the Battalion I have served with all my time in France, and all the dear old things who were left in it.
However our end was drawing near. It only meant that I was the first to go. By this time I suppose they will all be scattered all over France in different jobs and our old Battalion will have passed from human ken. We aren't likely to forget tho'.

It was difficult to come here at first. Regulars, I found, are an insular crowd, and it was plain I wasn't wanted. There was a Regular adjutant functioning, and he didn't agree at all with the idea of Higher Command, that I should relieve him. I had to be pretty firm with 'em and a detached air and the Brigadier on my side smoothed things a little after the first bad start.

Now things are going swimmingly and I am determined to be a Happy Lincolnshire, until the beastly war is all over; and the 18th can foregather over a little dinner occasionally and be together again...

Letter 30

July 25ᵗʰ   (1918)   1ˢᵗ Lincolns   B.E.F
Hello Hillie darling

    A very busy day my darling Angel and I have just snatched a few minutes before the ration train leaves to send my darling small wife a tiny line of love and send you a huge big kiss. You are in my thoughts so much my darling and I have prayed so jolly hard today to be in your arms. Things, thank the Lord, are going along very smoothly now and everyone is quite friendly and decent. The line (touching wood) is quite cushy.

    By the time this arrives, darling Hillie, we'll be nearly due to come out again, won't we?

    I heard today that officers leave has been increased after being in the line. Isn't that splendid Hillie darling, eh? With a bit of luck that wretched order about officers having to wait 7 months will be rescinded?

    I suppose my case isn't a tiny bit as hard or cruel as that of some poor chaps. The sacked adjutant is next to go. His last was in November. Nine months!

    I have written to Geoff Clayton telling him to send me Blackie. I do hope to heaven he is able to manage it. The horse I rode last night in the line was a tiresome beast after my fat old mare of the 18ᵗʰ…

Letter 31

August 13th   1st Lincolns
My darling Hillie

A horrid day because it did not bring me my kiss. I have solemnly cursed France and the packet boat and Wipers, and my rotten luck and everything else I could think of my darling. And I have wound up by sending you the biggest lovingest kiss in all the world to tell you I do miss you and how I love you and how I am never, never, never going to be happy again until I am with you. At last a leave for an officer has come through. I hope it's the first of a decent batch. At any rate it will clear my way won't it, Hillie darling?

I've just been playing in a cricket match – I made 10! Don't you think that was rather clever of me eh? I do.

I wonder if you remember the game of cricket we played one Sunday afternoon at '29' in the backyard, when I gave you a tremendous whack and thought you were a great brick for not making a fuss. I was really dreadfully frightened of course… oh that funny river of fates. At Hindhead we played again, we played against Gates (much to his disgust) and again I gave you a most frightful crack on the shins.

What funny methods I did employ to be sure, to win you, my own darling.

I often laugh sometimes when I think what an extraordinary person you must have thought me.

If you had hated me, my dearest angel, it would have been more natural wouldn't it? But you do love me instead don't you my darling, and I adore you too. And we will have just the wonderfullest life that ever was in a little while now, when this beastly war is finished.

Everyone firmly believes now that it is going to end this year, darling, truly, the old hun has nothing to hope for by hanging out 'til next year – except a big whipping and the idea is that he will howl loud for peace very soon.

My own darling, another leave for an officer has come in since I started my letter and that means there are only 4 ahead of me now. How topping as that makes the 25th still look possible doesn't it Hilda? I hope you will let us make believe one night, when we are alone, that we are keeping our anniversary, will you darling? I should love us to have a very special dinner a deux, when I can give you a very, very, very loving kiss, darling, and tell you all the great secrets of my heart. I think it would be simply topping dear, if you wore your black frock for me. Will you Hillie darling?

Do you know Hilda, my dearest small wife that I could never, be so silly as to worry you...

Letter 32

No opening page   August 1918

…places and we can be quiet and fear nobody bursting in on our honeymoon.

Why, of course sweet Hillie, if Aldershot had been on I would have lived all the while with you, and there wouldn't ever have been any question of sleeping in camp. Dull! ah you cruel, wicked little girl! I don't know how your heart could let your fingers write that! To show how dull I was and how badly I had regretted having come, I would have spent every single precious moment with you, my darling. No, I don't think you need fear, dear Hillie that I will 'miss' anything else, after our real life starts, – the excitement of the front, or ones pals, or Blackie, or any other blessed thing. Everything, everything, will be forgotten, I promise, in the happiness of finding you again, my own darling. I promise because you are all my life, you wicked old thing. How dare you say I would find Aldershot dull!

Hillie dear!

Will you be an angel and send me a book called 'The First Seven Divisions.' You can get it at Phillips in Church Street or Young's. It costs 6 shillings, I think… If you've cashed already the other blank cheque, tell me dear, and I will send another. I don't send one now so as not to have a lot of blank ones floating about. They are hardly worth stealing but we mustn't squander our small fortune, must we?

Poor old Lawson! I'll send you full details tomorrow, Hillie darling, so you can give his fiancée my sympathy and all the particulars I have about his end.

Did you get a package from Padre Roche? Get 'em developed, old thing and tell me if any of the snaps are any good.

Good day my own dear girl, until tomorrow. I adore you. I want, want you, oh so much darling.

The lovingest kiss

Frankie.

ps I have written to our Mummy in Hong Kong today.

Letters 33 and 34

August /September 1918

Frank is beginning to think about employment opportunities after the war.

2

.. Government office in London which runs the recruiting and ask for particulars. My shipping experience, my darling old thing, would be useful, wouldn't it Hillie darling, and it would give us a wonderful chance to fly round. Consul at Biarritz or Le Touquet would suit us wondrous well for a year or two my darling, wouldn't it eh, and we'd do some kind of writing so we'd maybe be able to drop it in a little while. What do you think of the scheme my darling old thing?

If it looks 'on' I could write to Sanderson and say I intend to apply to be put on the list and that I could force him to say, one way or the other, if he proposes to give me a job, après La Guerre.

The company gas officer, a fellow named Jessop, who used to be in the 18th, drove in today and said he heard that the 18th had been entirely smashed up.

I wonder if it's true? He said Lush had written to him to ask him to give him a job as a gas officer, so it looks as if it true. Poor old things. I wonder where Geoff Clayton and Billie Williams have got to. They'll both be completely at sea amongst strangers I'm afraid.

By Jove but its hot as h......

Poor old fritz is getting a rotten time from our heavies. He must be sweating.

His lines are marked by a huge cloud of dust going thousands of yards up.

We're in an awfully interesting place, in a road, on a ridge, overlooking his country for miles. It's awfully fascinating, on a fine day, to watch the war...

And it would be a fine thing if I could have an appointment wouldn't it. They asked what countries I would prefer if I was sent abroad and so I said China, Italy or France.

That's all right Hillie darling.

Its rather exciting isn't it and I'm going to try hard to pull it off. The pay seems jolly good. They say we must have heaps of shipping experience and so I laid all that on thick.

What will Sanderson say? I don't think he can get annoyed about it, can he? If he wants me he can always say so and I'll stay provided he pays!

Well Hillie darling, I must get some sleep now. I send you the lovingest kiss in all the world to say I love my small angel wife with all my heart and I am oh so glad I am coming to her soon. A huge hug dearest.

One extra loving kiss to tell you to tell you not to worry about this battle, we will be out of it when you get this dear.

Frankie

Post Card postmarked   22nd August 1918

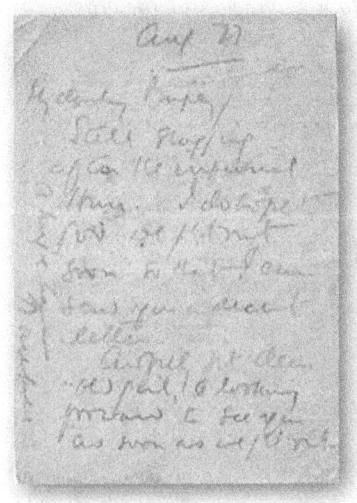

My darling Hillie

Still slogging after the infernal Hun. I do hope to God that we can rest up soon so that I can send you a decent letter.

Awfully fit, dear old girl, and looking forward to seeing you as soon as we get done. A hug and kiss

Frankie.

For Freedom and Honour

THERE ARE NO FURTHER EXTANT letters between the end of August and the beginning of November 1918. Towards the end of September Frank's leave finally came through and he returned to England for several weeks.

SHROPSHIRE HILLS AUTUMN 1918

Hillie sat, quietly, almost demurely, but all the while gazing across the carriage at Frank's face. He was looking out of the window at the passing countryside and she watched the outline of his face, the tilt of his eyelashes and the angle of his nose. She wondered what he was thinking, what he saw as he looked, dreamily, beyond the passing clouds of steam and flecks of soot. Did the fields full of cattle and sheep make him long to return permanently to the English countryside, or did they remind him of the serried ranks of soldiers he had left behind in France, if only for a few weeks leave? Her married life had had the strangest of beginnings. They had been married for 14 months. That's sixty one weeks, she thought, or four hundred and twenty seven days, ten thousand hours. And how much of that time had they been able to be together? About eight weeks, forty two days. The only advantage she could see to the arrangement was that every meeting was like another honeymoon, long awaited, exciting and deeply romantic. But every time they came together, Frank had to go again; there was still no clear end in sight for this disgusting war.

But now they had a whole month of leave to be together. To reassure his mother and family that he was still alive they had spent a couple of days in Liverpool but now the time was all their own. She knew that all that Frank wanted was to be alone with her, undisturbed, somewhere quiet and peaceful, away from the flat, mud soaked, battle riven landscapes of Belgium and France, to be somewhere high, British and beautiful. Somewhere they could explore, or walk, see the sky or small farms and villages, somewhere that reminded him of why he risked his life on a daily basis. So for this reunion she had chosen a cottage in a remote corner of Shropshire, and here they were on the train, leaving Liverpool behind and heading first for Shrewsbury. There were no local trains out to the village that evening so they had planned to spend the night here and move on to the countryside the next day. At Shrewsbury they followed the porter who lifted their bags from the train and took them down the steps to the front of the station, where cabs, motor driven and horse drawn were waiting. Frank asked for the Lion Hotel and tipped the porter. The driver opened the rear door of his car for them and loaded the bags onto the luggage rack at the back.

'Not far sir, just a few minutes up the hill and down again to the hotel.'

Looking back they gazed on the massive red sandstone walls of Shrewsbury Castle, as it towered over them, its garrison silent, no need to guard its walls, the enemy now further away than Wales. The little car heaved itself up Castle Hill and turned past the ancient Church of St Mary's and then down the Wyle Cop. They were entranced by the medieval buildings and over hanging streets, so different to the brash Victorian splendour of Liverpool. The Lion looked almost modern in comparison, with its fine Georgian façade adorned by the gilded statue of a lion on its pediment. A fine, if faded coaching inn still welcoming travellers.

Frank squeezed her hand, 'We can explore later,' he assured her.

Hillie reluctantly let go of Frank's hand and moved to warm herself by a huge log fire whilst he signed them in. She still loved to hear those words, Captain and Mrs Frank Lawless, but sighed as his gave his address as the Ist Lincolns Regiment, B.E.F. France. She heard him order dinner for 8pm and ask if they had a small private dining room where they might eat. She saw the old man who served as porter and desk keeper, raise a knowing eyebrow in her direction and chose to hide her smile by gazing around at the ancient oak panelling and faded hunting prints that dotted the walls.

Hillie and Frank followed the old man as he shuffled up the broad sweeping staircase, its faded carpet blood red and looking dangerously threadbare in places, along a landing, to the threshold of a their room. He put down their bags and left them to themselves. Frank hugged her as they sat on the edge of the bed.

'Did you know Charles Dickens stayed here once? It's a great place for a writer, maybe we can find some of his inspiration.'

Hillie was more prosaic, 'I hope they have changed the sheets since his day, they certainly don't look as if they've changed the curtains or the carpet.'

Frank lifted her off her feet in one great hug, and Hillie knew he was considering whether to check out the quality of the sheets and bedsprings or to take her for a walk. He opted for the walk, on the principle that the light would fade but the bed would still be there later. Hand in hand they set off to lose themselves in the maze of small wynds and side streets that bisected the hills of Shrewsbury, and led up and down to the loop of the River Severn as it encircled the town.

Dinner, in their little private dining room, was a romantic affair. The yellow flickering gas light hid the stains on the table cloth and the pleasure of sipping the chilly wine, naturally cool from musty cellars, overcame the blandness of the dinner. Maybe the old man had roasted the mutton and over boiled the cabbage as well as run the hotel. But the sense of privacy was exciting and Hillie had changed for dinner into one of her best dresses, one she had worn on their first honeymoon. The velveteen brocade clung around her figure and then floated out into a wider swishing skirt as it fell away from her hips towards her calves. Frank could not take his gaze from her and they lingered slightly over the dinner, as if to heighten the enchantment and remind themselves that for once, they had the luxury of time.

Frank pondered, 'I wonder what Dickens was working on when he stayed here; maybe he ate in this very room, or was giving a reading to his admiring fans. *Bleak House*, perhaps or even *A Tale of Two Cities*, stories of pointless conflict or heroic self-sacrifice.' Hillie prayed that any dark reflections on war were chased from Frank's mind as they climbed the stairs. She sensed his eyes penetrating through to the outline of her form beneath the carefully chosen velveteen frock. By the time they reached their door she hoped he had only one thought in his mind.

Next morning they walked back up to the station, with their bags following in the hotel hand cart and took the tiny, two carriage train that served the little branch line out towards Minsterley and the hills. Sitting amongst farmer's wives and milk churns, bicycles and baskets of hens, their shared smiles and enjoyment must have been evident to all the other passengers, but neither cared who knew they were in love. The landlord of the cottage greeted them off the train, showed them the little village, pointing out butchers and bakers, church and chapel and gave them the key to their temporary home. The cottage was everything that Hillie had hoped for. Snug and clean with a tidy grate already laid with a fire for the evening, oil lamps and candles against the darkness and a bunch of late roses to bring cheerfulness to the days. A scrubbed wooden kitchen table and a pair of faded floral armchairs completed the homely look.

They could rest here; play at being a little family unit, a normal couple who would be together always. Hillie visualised them sitting by a little fire like this in their old age, she darning his socks as he read the paper, or wrote, getting up to make a cup of tea or stoke the fire or let the cat out. Or maybe she would have a piano and could play and sing for him if her voice still held. Her mother could still sing, so maybe she would be fine too.

The time passed gently, nights as close together as it is possible for two humans to be, evenings spent talking and singing, reading and writing and days walking the hills. And always they made plans for the future, what they would do, where they would travel, how they would earn a living, after the war.

Pontesbury Hill towered to the east, steep and tall, like the extinct volcano it probably was and known locally as the Sleeping Dragon. Frank was keen to climb it and asked locals for the best route. He worried that the climb might be too much for Hillie but she was cross at being thought unequal to any physical activity.

'I've got stout shoes and we need not rush, we can take all day if we want to.'

The lower reaches of the hill were not too strenuous and they made a steady pace through beech woods, stopping to admire carpets of golden leaves, the first fallers of autumn, and the squirrels skittering along the ground or up the trunks of trees secreting the ripening nuts. As the gradient increased and they climbed above the treeline, they spoke less and concentrated on the climb. The path wound round the hill, increasing the length but avoiding the need for a vertical ascent. The grassy banks were closely cropped and Hillie always wondered how the grazing sheep that they passed from time to time, managed to keep their balance. Perhaps, if you saw them on flat ground, they would have legs shorter on one side than the other. Loose animals, even sheep, made her nervous and she held out her hand to Frank for protection.

As they neared the summit the path passed through a maze like structure, the double blind gateway to the hillfort that occupied the hilltop. They passed into the ditches and Frank described how in the Iron Age the hill was encircled by deep ditches and banks, dug by the villagers to protect themselves and their animals from invaders and wild animals. He looked at her affectionately, but with a wry smile.

'You wouldn't have liked it here then, if you don't like the sheep now, Hillie, with wolves and bears wandering the forests, picking off the herds and occasional shepherd boys.' Her reply was to poke him in the ribs with a sharp finger.

At the top they rested, looking out across Shropshire, the flat plains to the north, the Wrekin, Caer Caradoc and the Clees to south and to the west the Stiperstones with their rocky outcrops and mine workings. In the blue above a late skylark circled and called and a lapwing rose from the grass, startled into her familiar peewit call, ready to defend her territory. It was warm, peaceful and far removed from war, Hillie thought, hoping Frank would be revived by the sun and fresh air.

They walked across the flat top of the hill, counting the little circular platforms that Frank said were the ruins of huts built by the tribe who lived here, safely enclosed by their massive banks and ditches, palisades and trenches and snake like entrances. Frank stood quietly on the top of the bank, looking down into the ditch.

'Funny, how nothing changes in two thousand years. Men still dig ditches to protect themselves or hide their armies, make complex entrances to fool the enemy and expect men to die to protect the line. How many men lie dead in the ditches here, do you think? Did the Romans attack or just a neighbouring tribe, was the settlement sacked and burned, did the enemy have gas to blow over and drive the defenders from their trenches, emerging like rats from a sewer gasping for air?'

Hillie hated to hear him speak so, and he rarely vocalised his thoughts on the war to her. How hard it must be, to walk away from your men and the battle and the loss and arrive home a few hours later and try to act as if you are normal, as if fighting a war is the most everyday job in the world, that seeing your friends and comrades die is an ordinary, everyday thing.

She saw the shadows that had crossed his face and the shiver of his shoulders. She put her small hand into his and tugged him towards her, seeking a kiss to deflect the train of his thoughts. She was successful. Frank put the trenches into the compartment of his brain labelled 'war' and opened instead the one labelled 'love'. He willingly accepted her invitation and instead of seeing trenches, saw soft inviting turf and a landscape which they alone occupied. He pulled her down, gently, gently to the grass, spread out his jacket and then responded to her kiss.

The lark rose again above them, soaring, calling his last call of the year, and then left them to themselves.

—⟆

A couple of days later, whilst the weather still held, Frank and Hillie set out to the hills again. They got a lift in the back of a farmers cart up to Snailbeach where Frank wanted to see the lead mines.

'They're very quiet at the moment,' the farmer told them, 'most of the miners have joined up, they make great tunnellers I've been told.' Frank agreed and praised the work the tunnellers had achieved at the Front, laying charges deep under the enemy and then blowing them sky high.

The Stiperstones were a wilder landscape, less green, strewn with rocky outcrops and erratic boulders, a broader ascent towards the highest outcrop, massive grey, raw rock, sharp edged and savage, called the Devil's Chair.

They walked hand in hand, over the stony surface, ankles turning every now and then, towards the summit and this time Hillie let Frank climb the scarp alone and seat himself on the Chair. 'There's no devil here today. Old Nick has been driven away by your beauty,' he told her when he came down, hands and knees grazed from his climb. They set off to find the little pub the farmer had told them of, hoping to find a bite to eat.

Comfortable and secure against the hillside, the inn lay protective and welcoming, a resting place for miners and farmers, and the occasional visitor to the hills. Beer and sandwiches ordered, Frank looked out from the doorway to take in the view. On one side the open moorland they had crossed, on the other, mine workings, small pit heads, tall chimney stacks and low tunnels, many yards long that cooled the smoke from the smelters. A desolate landscape, dotted with slag heaps, poisoned by the precious lead it yielded.

An old man hailed them from the corner of the bar, passing the time of day, seeking news of the war, wanting to know where Frank was serving, if he had met any Shropshire men. Frank told him that many had joined the King's Regiment and they chatted amiably. They asked him about the local walks, and he described routes over the hills to the next valley or towards the Stretton hills.

'Round here you must be careful of the old mine workings, holes appear, ventilation shafts, sheep disappear, people lose their way and are never seen again. We say Wild Edric has taken them.'

Frank loved a good story, whatever its source, and encouraged the old man with further questions. Hillie shivered slightly and wasn't at all sure she liked ghost stories or local folklore.

'Wild Edric was the King of these parts,' the old man recounted, 'in the days after the Romans. He fought battle after battle and was admired for his bravery, leading his army from the front, galloping over miles of country, a pack of hounds at his heels, driving his enemies from his lands. Close to death he led his faithful army and his hounds to the mine workings and there they all live to this day, waiting for the time when their people have need of them again. Sometimes Edric and his army emerge and are seen, galloping at full tilt across the Stiperstones, hounds baying, horns calling, red hair flying out behind.'

'When do they appear,' Frank wanted to know, 'have you ever seen them?'

The old man nodded. 'The legend is that he comes when the country is in danger, he is a warning sign. The miners are a superstitious lot, they say Wild Edric last crossed the moors at the beginning of August 1914.'

Hillie sighed again, even when it was over, this war would linger and linger in people's minds, in Frank's mind. It might take more than a few acts of love to put the past behind them.

For Freedom and Honour

TOWARDS THE END OF THEIR leave Frank and Hillie returned to London where they attended an investiture at Buckingham Palace and Frank received his D.S.O. from King George V. A wooden platform had been erected in the courtyard of the Palace where the King received officers and handed out awards for gallantry.

Letter 35

Nov 2nd   1918   B--

My own darling Hillie

I have thought about you every single moment of this dark day, dear and I have just said a tiny prayer for you, that you will not be too sad a little girl during this separation and that it may quickly end. I felt optimistic when I left you, my own sweet Angel, far more cheery than ever before, but, never the less, the old pain and longing came with my heart before I had taken many steps from your door and all my love for you cried for me to run back to your arms. These first days after our happy leaves are so dreadfully, dreadfully cruel my angel. I would have given the world to have spared you this last parting, or to have been able to make it easier. Thank God, tho', this is the last. Soon we will be together again, my darling, darling Hilda and then never to part again.

I was too overcome by grief to talk to a group on the train, but everyone seems to be excited at the prospect of an early finish and most of the gossipers seemed to think, with me, that a fortnight will see us at peace. So, Hillie darling, prepare to come to me right away, sweet angel, 'cos I am going to send for you the very first moment I can. I cannot bear to be away from you one single hour when I might be with you.

Such a happy, happy month it has been, sweet Hillie, full of your love and sweetness and I shall never forget one single one of the precious hours. I have just found one of your hairs, my darling, as I was brushing my hair. Will you think it very silly of me, I wonder, but I kissed it, dear, before I threw it away and a tiny tear fell down my face 'cos I felt so lonely here, so far from you. Last night you were so near to me and tonight I will be all alone. I will always be quite, quite alone without you, Hillie, 'cos you have all my thoughts, and no business or friend can ever take your place or satisfy my longing for your love.

A veil over my crossing this morning!

It was very rough, I was very ill and I felt dreadful when I landed here.

My cold wasn't so bad but my head was splitting and so I went straight to bed.

Its seven 'o'clock and I've just got up and washed and feel a good deal better. I start up country at seven in the morning and will be quite right by then. I'll go to bed again after dinner.

A dreadful rumour reached me in Boulogne, from a man I met out of the 19ᵗʰ Kings, that Billie Williams was killed a fortnight ago: I didn't believe it. Surely I would have heard in Liverpool or from Geoff. I am writing off at once to find out. Do pray it isn't true, Hillie darling,'cos I wanted old Billie to come through with the rest of our little band who have stuck it out.◊

I felt too ill to do the shops for the camera, old girl and I know you will understand, dear. I'll get it very first chance. Who knows, maybe I'll bring it to England to you myself in a week or two, or perhaps we can choose together here.

Don't worry sweet Angel, there are swarms of our troops making to the boats as I am writing, singing and shouting as if they were mad. I wonder if they are going home. They must be 'cos they've got all their kits. So cheer up sweet Hillie. The Infantry won't be long now, will it?

I see in the paper that Austria has downed arms. Everything is going swimmingly, dear

Ends here

◊ I have not been able to trace any evidence of Billy Williams' fate. He is not listed as 'killed' in Maddocks' list.

Letter 36

Nov 7   Ist Lincolns   B.E.F
My own darling Hillie

So very sorry, my angel wife, that I haven't been able to write to you. Utterly impossible, truly, sweet Hillie!

It was early on the morning of the 4ᵗʰ when I got the train at the base and I didn't land up at the Battalion until about 10.00 o'clock last night. Everything is O.K. They have been fighting hard but we're not in the front line now and no one expects that we ever will be again as a wire has come from G.H.Q. to say that the German delegation left Berlin yesterday for Paris to receive Foch's terms of armistice. Everyone expects the war to end either tonight at Midnight or tomorrow. Isn't it all too wonderful Hilda, my own darling. It means that tomorrow perhaps, I shall write for you to come to me. I know you will dearest Angel and oh! I shall want and give you a huge kiss of welcome when I see you again. Oh how, how I have missed you. I am so happy and excited today tho' 'cos I feel that in a few hours' time your tiny heart will at last have peace and you will not be anxious about me anymore. A fellow is just going down on leave and is waiting to take this, so I can only write a few lines. Another letter later on if it is humanly possible, my own small angel, but we are moving every few hours, keeping up with the advance.

The Hun is falling back rapidly and we are advancing thro' villages full of civilians, who welcome us with open arms. Poor wretches! They have had a bad time and it is a splendid privilege to see their joy at the end of their long exile. The end of arms is at hand now, my own darling and if my love can be any reward to my brave darling, then she will soon be truly happy at last.

All news tonight, when I write, dear Hillie, and by this little chit, just the lovingest kiss in the world to tell you I will see you soon, in a few days I hope ---and that I adore you more, more, more than ever I did before.

Dear old Hilda! I did so love our month. You are a darling to have spoiled me as you did, but please, I like being spoiled, and I want you to promise to do it all over again next time.

Good day, little Hillie and every bit of my love and life. Frankie.

Letter 37

1st Lincolnshires   BEF
Nov 7th
My darling Hillie
    It is quite true my own sweet angel, about the armistice.

    We've just had a wire to say the Hun delegates left Berlin yesterday and we are all expecting to hear any time now, that the armistice has been signed. How wonderful isn't it my small angel wife. <u>Now</u> are you optimistic at last? My darling little doubter. When this is in your adorable little fingers I expect that all your doubts will be ended for good and all and you will begin to look out for my letter to say that I am coming or that you can come to me. I am dreadfully excited Hillie darling, 'cos this isn't rumour any more but solid reality and it means the very, very end of your anxieties and fears, my own brave Angel. I am oh so glad, glad, glad and we can never thank God enough for having kept we two and our love so safe during these dreadful, dreadful years.

    I have been talking to the curé of this village this afternoon. (The Huns were here the day before yesterday). They are all so thankful to see the British at last. The battalion has done extraordinarily fine work during our leave Hillie, and we are about thirty miles nearer Germany than when I left 'em. The C.O has got his third D.S.O. as I forecasted, clever lad isn't he? I'm sure no honours were better deserved than his are.

    My tunics haven't turned up yet, dear old girl. Rather a nuisance to have to come up to the line in my old clothes, but no matter with the war over, eh?

    I've had no time to write to Mummy yet, or anybody. There is quite a lot of 'settling in' to do, of course, after being away a month.

    How is Alan? I expect he is back at school today, poor old thing. I captured some more ammunition today for his gun, in a house, yesterday, so he'll be able to have a splendid time on Peace Day, when he blazes it all away.

I'm looking forward to the mail tonight my darling, 'cos I want the little message you promised to send me on Saturday.

Dear Hillie, it did hurt, hurt me to have to kiss my darling good bye again. Oh dear, oh dear! Those dreadful last mornings! We've had too many, my angel, I know. I promise, very faithfully, that Saturday was the last and we will never part again---
I love, love my small wife
Frankie

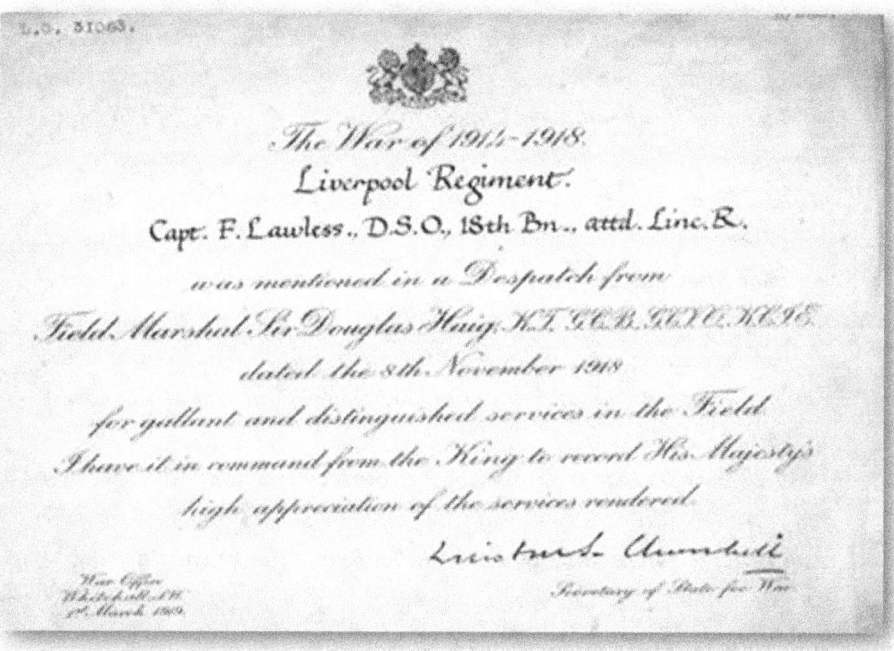

Letter 38

December 10th 1918   1st Lincolns B.E.F
My Darling Hillie

Such a very topping letter today my own angel, and I send you a huge big kiss for it. I am so glad that the Uncle Willie problem is solved so satisfactorily, and that he is going to go off to his brother's to get over the worst of his convalescence. Poor old chap! How rotten he must feel to be so helpless and such a nuisance to everyone and I do think it is too bad of his brothers' people to rub it in by making a song and dance about taking care of him for a time.

I wonder if you will be at Nazareth House for Christmas Hillie darling. Anyway whether you are or not they will send on my message to you on the 23rd won't they my sweet girl, and so I will send it there. How I do long to spend a birthday with you, Hillie dearest. I am so happy that you have made all the nuns pray that I can come quickly to you, 'cos I have such tremendous faith in their prayers and I will look forward now to another miracle, over and above the others which have been worked for you and me, Angel, and this one is to bring you into my arms on your birthday, dear old girl.

Tell Dorothy that if I cannot come, she is to love you that day extra and extra specially, 'cos I am wanting you to be loved so much. I wonder if she can love you as much as I can Hillie, I don't think your sister can? I am just jealous of old Dorothy I may say. Fancy having you all to herself in that big lonely convent. Oh the luck some people do have!

I wish I was at the guest house, Hillie,- I'd love you and spoil you all the day long—if you would let me...

London December 1918

Flocks of starlings were swooping and calling before they settled to roost on the ledges of the shops and hotels as Hillie emerged from the station. She hated the starlings, their massed numbers seemed like an army in the sky to her, dark and threatening, the rising and falling, coiling and spreading of the flock, calling to itself, making ancient but ever changing patterns in the dusky pink, fading sky before reaching their final resting place. She hated the way they darkened the sky without leaving a shadow, the rancid smell they left behind, the greedy way they fought the pigeons for food in the London squares. Vermin her mother called them, filthy vermin and Hillie agreed, she thought of the image of death as the Grim Reaper and felt he would be preceded by a flock of starlings, screeching to announce his arrival.

Even by 3.00pm the daylight was fading and the air of central London was frosty, plumes of breath rising from each passer-by and the acrid, sulphurous smell of coal fires being lit all over town was beginning to taint the atmosphere.

Hillie had finished her shift on the ward and wished the men a Happy Christmas. She had said goodbye to the other nurses in Cleve Hall, packed a small bag of necessities for the few days she would be away and headed for the train. It was such an odd feeling, to be married, but to be alone at this time of year with the war now finally over. She had not seen Frank since his leave in October but they corresponded daily, sometimes twice a day now things were quiet at the Front and the high point of each day was waiting for the letters then finding a peaceful place to read and enjoy the love and kisses that he sent. Sometimes she found it hard to believe that the war was actually over, after so many months and years of anxiety and fear of loss. She had three days leave over Christmas and today, the 23rd of December, was her birthday. She knew Frank hated the idea of her spending it alone or working on the wards, so she was delighted when Dorothy suggested they meet and go for tea. She headed towards Piccadilly, glad of the great fox fur stole that enveloped her neck and shoulders and protected her from the chilly afternoon

Trying to shake off such bleak thoughts Hillie walked briskly down Piccadilly, past the Ritz and crossed carefully between the buses and hackney cabs near the Royal Academy. She turned down towards Berkeley Square and the hotel where she was meeting Dorothy for tea.

London seemed full of men in uniform and sometimes she imagined she caught a glimpse of Frank's tall figure striding towards her, surprising her for her birthday, but each time, as she got closer, her heart felt the disappointment of unreasonable expectation. It surprised her that London should not be more excited, more joyful and reverberant, in this first Christmas since the armistice. But somehow joy was repressed, too many men had died, too many were still serving, too much suffering altogether. Now it was just relief that it was finally over.

She was glad to see the braided doorman at the hotel entrance who greeted her and pointed her towards the warmth of a collection of sofas before a great log fire. She vaguely wondered why the man wasn't in the forces, surely being a doorman was no reason not to serve but as he turned to take away her coat she realized one leg was dragging. A wounded veteran, discharged, she gave him a tip and her warmest smile of thanks.

Hillie was delighted to see her sister waiting for her in the tearoom and greeted her with a hug. It was their first meeting since the armistice had been declared and miraculously, both their husbands had survived. They had shared their fears and today was an opportunity to share their relief. For a while conversation was commonplace, Hillie enquiring about Dorothy's journey up from Portsmouth, news of mutual acquaintances, letters from Hong Kong, but finally Hillie asked;

'How's William, where is he, do you have any news of when he might be home?'

'I've very little news' replied Dorothy, 'except a short chit to say how wonderful that the armistice has come and that the ship is safe. What about you, do you have any news when Frank may be demobbed?'

A waiter brought hot scones, dripping with butter and delicate cups of highly scented China tea which were a rare luxury after the food of the wards and nurses home, a rare Christmas treat.

'I know he is pretty well, except for a cough which troubles him in the damp weather. I pray he has a dry billet. But he has no new physical wounds and he is beginning to talk of what kind of jobs might be available once he gets home. There is so much about the world now that is unknown, what the men will come back to.'

Dorothy dug around into her handbag and brought out two small parcels, a birthday present and a Christmas gift.

'I am sorry you won't come back to Portsmouth for the holiday with me.' she said.

Hillie explained that she wanted to be in London, just in case, even if there was the slightest chance, that Frank might make it over, if only for a few days.

'I need to be here. I'll be staying with Aunt Margaret and the other nuns at Nazareth House for Christmas. It's infinitely preferable to spending the holiday in Liverpool without Frank. His parents have invited me but I've used the excuse of distance and train timetables for staying in London.' Tea over, Hillie said farewell to her sister, collected up her bags and the extra presents and set off for Hammersmith and the convent. A regular visitor to Nazareth House she often stayed in the guest house there. The Sister Porteress greeted her as a friend and showed her to the warm but simple room in the guest house she usually occupied. Her aunt, Sister Margaret Mary joined her for supper and they exchanged news of Frank and all the family in Hong Kong and Scotland too.

'We're pleased you're here,' Sr Margaret said, 'you can help fill stockings for the children and decorate the hall and serve lunch. There are hundreds of jobs that need doing.'

Hillie was glad to be kept so occupied and distracted from her own thoughts. On Christmas Eve she and one of the lay sisters went into the gardens to cut holly and ivy and other evergreens to decorate the hall and chapel. The grounds were winter bleak. The empty beds, dug over by diligent gardeners and residents, neat lines of frosted muddied furrow, immediately sent her thoughts back to the Front. She became angry with herself, the way everything she saw, looked at or touched reminded her of Frank and the dangers he had faced.

She helped the nuns fill great brass vases with the greenery and place them on the sanctuary steps in the chapel. Small vases of funereal white

chrysanthemums graced the altar and several of the pensioners were building a miniature stable, filling it with straw and a manger ready for the plaster
animals and statuary to be placed in the nativity scene at night. In the hall the
children were helping to decorate a tree with the small angels and gingerbread
biscuits they had made. She helped the little ones as they teetered on chairs,
each eager to place their decoration in a place of honour.

Hillie joined the nuns and able bodied older residents at Midnight Mass
on Christmas Eve. Carols reverberated around the chapel as the infant Jesus
was laid in the manger, guarded by the guiding angel and the loving parents.
The sight of the baby reminded Hillie how glad she had been to find there was
no after-leave pregnancy to cope with without Frank by her side. She thought
constantly of him and his men in the bleak midwinter of northern France.
Were they in a warm billet? Had they left behind the icy trench, silent now,
with no further shell fire? Perhaps Frank was at Mass somewhere, listening
to French villagers and his men, instead of nuns, singing Christmas carols
around a crib?

The next morning Mass was less reflective. The chapel filled with thirty
or forty of the orphan children and elderly destitute that called Nazareth
House home and the nuns their family. The children were excited at the day
ahead, the sense of occasion and the sight of the nativity at the bottom of the
altar steps. They giggled and fidgeted and nudged one another as hymn books
slipped and clattered and old folk coughed. The sense of excitement and an-
ticipation was infectious and Hillie found herself glad that she had come to
this place. She joined in the Mass with deep reverence. Tears welled as she
watched the little ones file past the crib, genuflecting, making silent prayers
for the lost or missing, for families and friends.

Christmas lunch was a lively affair, with special treats provided by local
donors. Afterwards one of the older residents dressed as Father Christmas,
gave each child a tiny stocking containing a candied fruit, a prayer card and a
new pair of socks. There were communal presents too, of toys outgrown and
donated by local families, washed and given a lick of paint by the older men.
When the excitement died down the children sang for the old people and an
impromptu concert party began. Hillie was much in demand for popular

songs and Irish airs. Charades and party games followed and it seemed the nuns had done their utmost to help everyone forget the war for an hour or two. In the end the whole day had passed more quickly and pleasantly than Hillie could have hoped for.

Sr Margaret had repeated her offer, that Hillie should come and live in the guest house and help with the children, until Frank returned, feeling children might do more to raise her niece's spirits than nursing injured soldiers. But Hillie had refused again. She always felt, especially as many of the soldiers she cared for were French or Belgian, that if she couldn't look after Frank, she would do her best for his allies and comrades in arms. Her silent prayer had always been that if he had ever been injured some wife or mother in France would have returned the favour and taken good care of him. Her final request to Reverend Mother, as she left the next morning, was that the community should keep Frank and his comrades in their prayers until they were finally discharged and arrived safely home. She was reassured and told that they had prayed for him by name every single day.

For Freedom and Honour

FRANK, STILL SERVING WITH THE 1st Lincolns, had one final short leave in early January 1919, part of which he used to explore job opportunities both with the Foreign Office and his former employer, Mr Sanderson, Chairman of the White Star Line.

Letter 39

Jan 21ˢᵗ   1919   1ˢᵗ Lincolnshires   B.E.F.
My Darling Hillie

*Such a very lovely letter from you today, my angel Hillie and I send
you a huge kiss for it, to take you every tiny bit of my love. Such exciting
news from the Foreign Office, too, Hillie! A letter saying how Curzon
has looked into the question of my sitting the Foreign Office exam on Feb
4th and has seen the consular People at the Home Office about me, and
they have decided that it's no use my sitting, 'cos the Consuls have already
decided to offer me a job and were only waiting until they knew I had
reached England again. Hurrah! Hurrah! Fifty thousand cheers because
my scheme has worked. I only put in for the Foreign Office, of course, in
the hope of bucking up the Consuls, and it has worked splendidly. How
simply topping isn't it, Hillie. It means an additional reason why I shall
get home in a few days now, and the splendidest handle in the world with
which to wind up Sanderson to the pitch of a good screw for Paris. If the
Consuls job looks particularly tempting, of course, The White Star can go
hang, eh!*

*Hillie, my own dearest Angel, see what luck you have brought me,
dear...*

*That half hour when you were shopping and I was at Burlington
House was rather a successful one, wasn't it, eh? You must send me a huge
big kiss to tell me you are pleased that things are working out just as we
planned in October. Hillie darling! Can we ever, ever lose hope over anything after this, my darling, eh? You see every blessed thing comes right in
the end, doesn't it, little angel wife?*

*I'll get home first chance and we'll put our small heads together and
decide on Paris or the Consuls, eh? How splendid if the Consuls is a good
screw and in France and not in Africa or Timbuktu, my angel.*

We'll soon see now.

*It will want a bit of stage managing I'm afraid, this playing off one
against the other, and Sanderson mustn't, on any account, have any*

inkling of my double-faced game, must he, or he'll just put me to the right-about.

I expect I've to thank old Stanley for putting me right with the Home Office. Dammed good of the old bird, isn't it my Darling.

I enclose your tiny cheque, angel Hillie, with a huge kiss and a huggle to make you like it and to tell you I adore you and would give you just all the world were only it were mine. We'll have lots of treasure later on tho' won't we, Hillie angel, 'cos I've been coming to the conclusion lately, that you and I are rather a lucky pair of coves. Don't you think so too?

Good night my own sweet bride. Just every tiny bit of my heart with this kiss I send you dear, 'cos I love, love you so dearly and want you so much.

Frankie

Letter 40

Jan 22nd 1919   1st Lincolns   B.E.F

My own Darling Hillie

    So sorry my angel Hillie, 'cos I forgot the cheque yesterday. My own book was finished and I had to borrow one and that was why I forgot to put it in. A big kiss to ask you to forgive me, my angel, for being so forgetful. Another big kiss too, sweet Hillie for two very lovely letters I got today.

    Dear old girl! Indeed, indeed I thought again of your seedy days and sent you oh ever so many kisses to try to tell you how glad, glad, glad I am that I have you now to love always, and to take care of on every single one of your days, the good ones and the bad ones, so that we make the good ones really toppers, eh and the bad ones not so very bad, not nearly so bad anyway, as they would be if we had not one another to love and keep thro' them.

    Dear Hillie! Perhaps next month I shall be with you dear, and then I can really try to show you, by love, loving you and spoiling you rather specially, how truly I do adore you and want to share every tiny moment of your life. I pray hard I shall be with you then Angel, and I feel I will be.

    It just rests with the C.O. to approve de Bussy, the fellow who is taking on the job and I don't think he will be unreasonable. I'll tackle him again tomorrow and tell him I must go now because of the Consuls.

    Vickers wants to go before the end of the month too, in order to get back to Oxford. He's got no job of course, when the C.O. is present and so there's no particular difficulty about him.

    Hillie darling! Fancy old Halacinda turning up again. I'm so glad to have written him tonight to tell us his plans. Bocher and I were talking about him in Paris and wondering where on earth he had got to. It'll be rather fun to meet him again, won't it dear?

    Such frosty weather. I'm wondering, if it keeps on, if we'll get any skating. These Somme marshes would be rather fine I think.

    I picture you in that new blue jumper, Hillie darling. I think it must be rather fine, but I'll reserve judgement until I see it, eh?

Have you got your hat yet Angel? What a gorgeous time you will have in Paris, with hat shops, little girl, won't you eh? I saw some wonderful hats in the shops.

Good bye for tonight, my own darling, I send you just the biggest, lovingest kiss in the world, to tell you I adore you and that I will come any day now to you and then never leave you anymore.

Frankie

Letter 41

Jan 23ʳᵈ 1919   1ˢᵗ Lincolns,   B.E.F
My darling Hillie,

A tiny line, after a Regimental Dinner (one of the biggest, Hillie, I've ever seen!) to tell you I love you, my angel, and that I will be with you, <u>quite, quite</u> definitely before the 6ᵗʰ February - probably on the 4ᵗʰ.

I have to be at the Foreign Office on the 6ᵗʰ, in connection with the consuls, and so they have got to let me go and the C. O. says I can go. Hurrah! Only a few days longer, my angel Hillie, and we will be together again. Will you please get that Merchant Shipping Act book up from Liverpool, my angel, if you haven't it already in London.

What about rooms, sweet Hillie? Is Miss Evering available, I wonder? Anyway dear old girl, I'll have to leave that to you, won't I eh?

I'll have to go to Liverpool to '33' I suppose to dump all my kit and also get my clothes and odd things, eh, and I expect you too have got lots of things there you'll want for Paris or wherever we go. Anyway the Mater is just bombarding me with letters saying we must go, so I suppose she is trying to make up for all the Paters' rudeness at Xmas to you and me. Have you got my blue suit in London, Hillie darling? If not I wonder if you'd mind getting it and keeping it until I come, dear -also a couple of white shirts.

It's possible we may be able to go to Liverpool immediately after the 6ᵗʰ, do our business there and then go straight off to Paris, or wherever else we may be bound for. On the other hand, Dear old girl, they may want me to wait in London after the 6ᵗʰ for further interviews, either with the White Star or the Consuls -hence my wanting the suit. I can buy some more clothes in Town, eh?

I must try to fix up the Consuls job without White Star knowing I am coming home, until after I've been to the Consuls.

A big letter tomorrow, Hillie darling. I am so excited to think I am coming home at last my angel. Our life is really going to begin now, isn't it?

The biggest huggle and kiss in the world to tell you I adore you, dearest old girl.
Frankie

This is the final letter

For Freedom and Honour

FRANK RELINQUISHED HIS COMMISSION IN the army on 6th February 1919. He retained the rank of Captain. There was no glorious homecoming parade for the Pals Battalions past St Georges Hall, no band or march past down Lime Street. The surviving troops of the 18th Battalion arrived home in May 1919. The 17th Battalion remained at Archangel in Russia, finally leaving in August and September 1919. Between 1914 and 1919 2,800 men from the Liverpool City Battalions died in the service of their country. Many more were wounded and suffered disabilities which affected them for the rest of their lives.

LONDON AND LIVERPOOL FEBRUARY 1919

The boat train slipped slowly into Victoria station and Hillie, imprisoned behind the barrier and unable to see over the heads of all the other wives and family members, could only vent her impatience by stamping her frozen feet, trying to put life back into icy toes on the bitter February afternoon. She was still trying to get to grips with the reality of Peace and homecoming. So often she had waited to greet him, enjoyed their days together and then lost him again to danger and war. But now it was over, Frank was coming back. He was alive, relatively uninjured, and he would never have to return to the Front again.

Hillie ran through, once again, all the urgent preparations she had made when that letter had arrived last week. *'The Brigadier says I can go, I have an interview on the 6th, I could be in London by the 4th'.* So she had taken rooms in a boarding house where they had stayed once before, a large bedroom, sitting room, shared bathroom, meals provided. It was warm and the landlady was pleasant, it would be fine until they knew exactly what the next steps were, which part of Frank's schemes for future employment had come to fruition. She had gone out and bought him a basic set of new clothes, underwear, shirt, socks trousers. She had no idea what he kept with him and there was only one set of his clothes that she took with her wherever she went so as to always have a reminder of his physical presence. But now she wanted him out of uniform as swiftly as possible. Hillie had also done as Frank had asked, contacted his mother and requested that his blue suit be dispatched. She had collected it herself from the Post Office, hung it to air, brushed it, rubbed away any marks, each rub a tiny act of love in preparation for his return.

The pressing crowd thinned as men disembarked the train and families surged forward to reclaim their loved ones from the war. Frank saw her first and she heard her name called above the heads of the crowd and she burrowed her way through, towards the voice, the beloved voice. Within seconds she was enfolded in his arms, kissed over and over, clasped so tightly to him she could barely breathe. She buried her face into his neck, longing, hungry, for the feel, the scent of him. Her hat went flying and they broke apart to retrieve it before it was trampled underfoot. Placing it back on her head, Frank looked down into her eyes. 'I will never, never, ever leave you again, not even for a single night, this is when our real life begins.'

Hillie led them both home to the boarding house, listening to details of his demobilisation, his farewell to his fellow officers, to Blackie and his remaining men.

'It will take weeks, maybe months to unpick the war,' he told her, 'to be certain the armistice will hold, to agree all terms, to retrieve men and equipment. The men might not get home until late spring. Only those with jobs and urgent family reasons are being released.'

The landlady welcomed them, congratulating the returning hero, pointing out the way to a hot bath after his journey and then withdrawing discreetly to her own part of the house. Hillie encouraged him into the bath.

'You look frozen, a bath will warm you through, are you well, have you another of your colds?' She had heard the ruttle of his chest and the rasping cough when she had laid her head against him in the cab. He dismissed her concerns.

'It's just another rotten cold, from sleeping in vile billets.'

She gazed at him as he lay in the steaming bath, offering to scrub his back or help wash his hair. She mentally checked him over for any scars she had missed before. The scar on his chest from the Givenchy bullet showed white and granular against the surrounding flesh, but his muscles looked strong. Maybe he looked older, more drawn than the young man she had fallen in love with, but he was still her beloved Frank.

Hillie was eager to see his uniform discarded. He was handsome in uniform, there was no denying that, but now it was over, the khaki could go, a fresh white shirt was needed for the first day of the new life.

For the next few days the pair were physically inseparable, hands always clasped, or she sitting perched on his knee or elbow to elbow at the table, gazing, always gazing into each other's eyes. It was as if they believed that if they stopped touching or stopped looking the other would disappear, evaporate, was only some kind of ethereal spirit or phantom waiting to be sucked back into the maws of wartime once again.

When Frank went up to town for his interview at the Foreign Office, Hillie went with him and paced the streets around Whitehall, waiting for news.

'How did it go, how did it go?' She asked breathlessly.

'Well I think a job offer definitely looks on the cards.'

'Did they say where or when or how much they would pay?'

'No, all the details are unconfirmed. I don't think they know themselves how long it will take to change everything over from the war footing. It's very hard for them to be specific.'

On the following day Frank returned to his old office at Oceanic House to talk his former boss, the man whose personal assistant he had been before enlisting, Mr Sanderson manager of the White Star Line, to discuss re -employment opportunities. Frank and Hillie were adamant between themselves that they wanted to travel, to work abroad if at all possible.

Frank had a long discussion with Sanderson, who was keen to have him back. The company had lost many good employees to the war and many ships too. Several of its liners had been requisitioned as hospital ships or troop carriers. White Star had been pleased to do their bit for the war effort but several ships had been sunk and others were all over the place in no state to carry passengers. Business was highly unpredictable. The potential passengers were still feeling nervous about travelling and needed their confidence restored. The Government had assured the company there would be German ships made available in reparation, but these would need refitting and it would all take time. So Sanderson felt he needed good people that he trusted about him and for the first few months, at the very least, that would have to be in London. Frank went home excited.

'It's London and Liverpool to begin with Hillie, maybe for six months, maybe a year. He has offered a very generous 'screw' then an overseas posting as soon as he can, when things have returned to normal.' Frank flung his arms around Hillie's waist and twirled her round the room, breathless with excitement.

'I could start next week. What do you think? Shall we take his offer, and leave the F.O to their uncertainty?'

Frank and Hillie discussed their options during the journey north to Liverpool. By the time they had reached Lime Street Mr Sanderson and the

White Star Line had won the argument, a definite offer being better than a vague one and the prospect of a posting to New York or Paris or Italy in the longer term was very tempting.

'No band to greet us Hillie, no standing on the steps of St Georges' Hall to watch me march by in glory,' said Frank, as they came out of the station and looked across the road.

'Too many won't be coming home for there to be any glory. It seems in-appropriate to celebrate a home coming, when so many others are grieving'. Hillie responded.

Hillie approached Frank's family home again with her usual trepidation. There had been more unpleasantness when she had declined their invitation at Christmas and further recriminations in their letters to Frank when he spent his short January leave solely in London.

Frank's mother was overwhelmed by joy at his survival and hugged him over and over, tears streaming. But whilst so many of her neighbours would never welcome home their sons, her joy was personal and muted.

'I've listened to the sounds of wives and mothers weeping, asking God why their sons have fallen. Sometimes I have felt guilty that mine has been spared whilst others were taken,' she said.

'It's over Mother, over. We must try to forget, and have some belief in the future. Don't think for one moment that I don't feel the same way, not thought about what have I done to be a survivor when so many of my friends are dead. It was all luck, the war was a lottery and just being in the wrong place at the wrong moment was all it took to die.'

Hillie sensed that the familiar arguments about them staying in Liverpool were about to be raised. Frank's father was delighted about the job offer and tried to sooth his wife.

'Jobs are scarce, the country is in turmoil, this is a great offer and Frank must take it, where ever it is. There is no point dwelling on the fact that he may not be here in Liverpool long, Frank and Hillie will visit us whenever they can.'

Frank's mother turned her concerns towards his health, 'I hope this young woman can look after you decently. You still have a cough. You look thin. Is she feeding you properly?'

Hillie turned away in disgust. She knew whatever she said or did would never be enough to satisfy her mother–in -law. If Frank had been killed at the Front, somehow that would have been her fault too. His mother seemed to forget that Frank was as keen as she was to travel, to explore the world. She was not some siren voice dragging him away. She tried to find sympathy for this mother, whose other children had all left her, one way or another, but Hillie struggled, she really struggled to warm to her and left it to Frank to reassure her that the cough was clearing and as he had only been home a few days she must blame army rations, not his wife, for any apparent loss of weight.

Three days in Liverpool were enough. The air of sadness, the pervasive grief was stultifying, everyone was taking time to adjust to peace, to the new order of life, life with so many sons missing. For Frank the loss of so many friends and comrades made the city unbearable and they headed back to London to restart their lives together.

White Star were as good as their word. The salary was good and Frank and Hillie were able to take a decent flat of their own. Hillie delighted in learning to cook meals for him, to spoil him and generally care for him as she felt a wife should, despite his mother's worst prognostications, and so, gradually they re-built life in London with family and friends. Alan, now nearly sixteen was able to spend his last school holidays with them before leaving school and heading back to Hong Kong and a job with his father's firm. Jean was a regular visitor and Dorothy and William, living in married quarters in Portsmouth were frequent callers too. William, a naval man long before the war, continued in his career.

Regular, if short, visits to Liverpool were improved slightly for Hillie, as her aunt, Sister Margaret Mary, had been sent to Nazareth House in Formby and Hillie could always escape there when tensions rose too high in Harthill Street.

The only cloud on their horizon was Frank's health. He suffered frequent colds, which always ended in coughs, and intermittent bouts of gastritis, which he knew he had caught first in the trenches. They both hoped and prayed that time, decent housing and an excellent diet would resolve the issues. During the summer of 1919 Spanish Flu' swept through the country and Hillie was terrified that after all he had experienced in the War, flu' would capture him. But Frank's luck held and they both escaped.

As the passenger shipping industry rebuilt itself, new opportunities opened up. Mr Sanderson did not forget his promise and somewhat reluctantly, when a post became available at their office in Naples, he let Frank go.

Frank opted to take Hillie to Naples by train. That way they could do their own Grand Tour as they had always planned. They stopped en-route in Paris, Geneva, Milan and Rome, arriving in southern Italy late in 1919.

Finding Frank

WHY IT TOOK US 40 years to come to Naples to follow your trail I am not quite certain. In the early days it was the fear of Southern Italy that I could never quite conquer.

I often wonder how Hilda fared among the Italian men of the early 1920s. Was she able to go out alone, a young and beautiful foreign woman? My earliest forays in Italy as a student were ruined by leering, bottom pinching men, who followed in an intimidating fashion, persistent, insinuating and not at all attractive. We got as far as Rome, intending to visit Pompeii and Naples after, but the aggravation was too much and we headed north to safety.

I tried again, ten years later with a husband and small children in tow, hoping for better success. There was less unwanted attention, but Naples' reputation for crime, reports of cholera and lack of clear information on where to search meant once again I pulled back.

So finally, in 2012, aided by middle age, low cost airlines and willing companions, I tried again, looking for traces of your ghosts flitting around the city.

I knew the name of the house where you had lived, but nothing more, and no internet search bore fruit. But Lo! The guiding Angels were with us. Emerging from a station of the wonderful funicular railway that connects areas of Naples, we saw a map of bus routes and one stop labelled 'Villa Rocco Romana' in Posillipo.

We took the bus to Posillipo and the Villa Rocca Romana was easy to find, but the high stone walls ensured the occupant's privacy and restricted our view. A man emerged from the gate and noting our interest, asked our business. We told him of Frank and Hilda and with extraordinary trust, he called his grandson, Lorenzo, who showed us around the grounds.

POSILLIPO THE BAY OF NAPLES 1919

Hillie stood on the terrace, in awe of the sheer beauty of the Bay of Naples and Frank's skill at finding them this utterly glorious place to live. The Villa Rocco Romana was built, as its name suggested, on the ruins of a palatial Roman villa, which in its turn had chosen the site for its beauty and setting.

Posillipo was the prettiest suburb of Naples, approached up a steep, pine covered hill, with a series of villas facing out towards the sea. From their terrace Hillie could lookout southward and see Vesuvius, smoking gently, brooding over the city, her slopes encased in fertile black soil decked in vines and olives. Beneath the volcano, the port and city of Naples spread out before them like an opened map, wider streets contracting in to a denser mass as the came closer to the medieval and roman heart. Hillie could see the domes and campaniles of a dozen churches and hear their answering bells each midday as the angelus rang out all over the city. 'The angel of the Lord declared unto Mary...'

She thought the hand of the angel of the lord had been guiding them to this spot.

From the terrace too, she and Frank could watch the comings and goings of a dozen or more ships a day using the busy harbour. The passenger steamers, Frank's livelihood, belched their smutty fumes into the bluest of skies, ferries and fishing boats, cargo tubs, coalers and local traffic. Some ships announced their every move by blasts on their horns, others slipped silently under sail, in and out of the harbour. Ships of all nationalities used Naples and sometimes they amused themselves looking for flags or noticing a new ship, previously unknown to them. The harbour by day or by night was a scene of endless movement played out in front of the city.

Up in Posillipo, among the pines, it was peaceful, restful -a haven for Frank after the years of mud and filth of all kinds at the Front.

Hillie thought back to the day, about a week after they had arrived in Naples and were still staying in the hotel.

'Hillie come, come and see,' Frank grabbed her arm and pulled her towards the door. 'I've found the perfect place for us to live.' And he had rushed her out into the waiting cab, away from the offices of the shipping lines, the hotels shops and cafes and up the hill above the city.

Villa Rocco Romana was a substantial neo-classical mansion surrounded by a high wall that hid it from the road. Frank teased her when she asked in shocked tones, how they could afford all this.

'Not all' he laughed, violet eyes dancing, 'just some, its apartments now.' He picked up her hand and kissed it, 'come and see.'

He guided her to the first floor, whose landings and corridors were dark after the brightness of the day. The pervasive smell of polish reminded her of convent days and she wondered if all nuns ordered their floor polish from Italy. Frank unlocked the great mahogany double door and as it sighed open into the salon, the sunlight tumbled in and filled the space around.

'How splendid, how glorious is this Hillie, look. See where we can sit outside on summer evenings, watching the stars. We can see the hills near Sorrento, I can sit here and write and we can listen to music and you can sing for me.' Frank was breathless with excitement. Hillie drifted towards the windows that opened onto the terrace and took in the pine fringed view over the bay. She ran her fingers over the heavy brown furniture, old- fashioned but spotless and comfortable. She took in the elegant proportions of the room, the mouldings on the ceilings, the polished wooden floors, the faded rugs.

'It's beautiful' she said.

They wandered like children, hand in hand, exploring. As well as the salon and terrace they found a modern bathroom with excellent fitting, a dining room, kitchen and maids room.

'We can have a cook or a maid to help you,' Frank told her, 'we can afford that.'

The final room they opened was the bedroom. Hillie was almost overcome. The room was delightful, dark wooden windows framed a view of the sea. There was cornicing and panelling and a carved marble fireplace, where interlacing cherubs played hide and seek amongst vines and acanthus. There were floating drapes, gilded mirrors and carved closets. But above all there was the bed, high, huge and beautiful. Mahogany framed with corner posts and embroidered silk hangings behind the head and floating lace to the sides. There were piles of pillows and crisp white sheets and coverlets. She saw Frank looking at her for approval and she threw open her arms.

'You clever, clever, man. How did you find this place?' Frank bent down and kissed the tip of her nose. 'It's absolutely splendid,' Hillie continued. 'We will be so happy here for ever and ever. When can we move in?'

Later that week Frank signed the lease for a year, renewable and their life as a couple moved out of hotels and rented holiday cottages and parents' spare rooms and sleeper trains from Paris, to the apartment in the Villa Rocco Romana. A real home for the two of them, in the warmth and colour of Italy. It was the perfect contrast to the mud and horrors of the Front, the fogs of London and Liverpool and the sweaty tropics of Hong Kong.

Italy would be theirs, their new life, made together on new ground. Frank would be well, all would be well.

POSILLIPO 1920

Hillie's days in Naples developed a gentle rhythm to them which she grew to love. On weekdays Frank rose early after his morning kiss, and left her to rest a little longer on her mountain of pillows. She could hear him in the bathroom, his daily ritual of washing and shaving never ceasing to fascinate her. The maid would leave a jug of hot water and he would pour it in to the bowl before the mirror and she would hear him humming some aria or recently acquired Neapolitan song. She would listen for the swishing of his shaving brush in the water as he began to lather his finely boned cheeks and handsome neck and then the singing would die away as he concentrated on drawing the cold steel of the cut throat razor across his face and upwards from his throat to his chin. Hillie loved that rasping sound of blade against stubble. She knew almost exactly how many strokes of the razor he took to shave. Then he always gave a cheerful little whistle, rinsed his face and cleaned his teeth. He would present himself to her again - clean shaven and demanding further kisses before leaving.

On workdays Frank had his breakfast and coffee in the office, leaving Hillie to enjoy hers alone on the sunlit terrace. The terrace was overhung with a bougainvillea on one side, festooned in season with pink and purple blossoms, and in spring was filled with the smell of jasmine and roses. She loved to gaze over the pine filled garden where the scents grew headier as the days became warmer. By midsummer the cicadas were in full voice from dawn to dusk, their gentle incessant chirping a constant but unobtrusive background to all other sounds.

Of all the breakfasts in her much travelled life these Neapolitan ones were Hillie's favourites. Memories of salty, lumpen porridge in Scotland or tacky glutinous Congee, rice soup, in Hong Kong, not to mention the boarding school menu of fatty, gristly bacon, cooked in water and eggs boiled for so long they would bounce down convent corridors if you threw them. No, Hillie loved the fresh fruit, cold meats and sandy textured cake served with fragrant Italian coffee. Small cups of coffee, strong and stimulating, that set you up for the day. Then she *really* felt her Italian heritage stirring.

Each day after breakfast Hillie and the cook would confer to plan Frank's lunch and dinner. Frank did not like Hillie wandering through Naples alone. If he could not be with her he insisted she was safer in the company of the maid or cook, experts in dealing with the local menfolk's unwanted attentions. So the ladies would visit the local meat and vegetable markets and look over the tantalising piles of vegetables and fruit, choosing the finest, the freshest, and the most interesting cuts for Signor Frank.

She was conscious not only of his growing love of Italian food but also of nurturing him, feeding him only the best to support his recovery from the increasingly frequent colds or coughs which still plagued him despite the better climate of Naples. Hillie watched in awe as the cook gave her order, haggled successfully over the price, insisted upon the time of delivery and assigned that job to some poor lad, who had to struggle up the hills on a tricycle, hauling a cartload of vegetables behind him.

When Frank was free and their time was their own they explored Naples and the surrounding area. Within the city they discovered ancient, narrow streets, laid out upon a timeless grid in antiquity. Some streets so narrow you could stretch out your hands and touch either side, others wide enough for a passing cart or overburdened donkey to trundle by. Some streets were deeply shaded, overhung by balconies decorated with washing, draped like bunting for a festival. These tiny streets criss-crossed one another, sometimes opening unexpectedly onto a sunlight piazza or courtyard decorated with a baroque fountain or great church. Every walk, every day, was a series of new discoveries.

They found a tiny shop selling sheet music, displayed in racks in the street, to flick through. Frank chose new songs for Hillie to learn, and other compositions, some ancient, some modern, to add to their collection. Going inside to pay was like entering a cave of spider-filled darkness and Hillie half expected an elderly troll to emerge to take their money. They visited shops and museums and galleries buying items to fill the apartment with objects of their own taste and choosing. There was a splendid Majolica plate, green and yellow, featuring a semi naked god, Neptune maybe or Hercules. Frank teased Hillie when they chose it saying she preferred the rolling fat of the figure's stomach and his long white beard, to his own rather thin physique. She denied it with giggles and the plate was hung in their dining room.

From the city gallery came a print of a renaissance cartoon, a Madonna and Child. Frank placed this picture in their bedroom and Hillie wondered if it was a hint, a polite way to try and open a conversation about babies. She wasn't sure why there had been no pregnancy, after all these months together. It had been understandable when she and Frank had been apart so much during the war days, but now she was puzzled. It was all in the lap of the gods she supposed. She was indifferent herself, not being that fond of babies, but she knew Frank would love children and for his sake wanted to bear them. But there was so much to do together that neither of them dwelt on anything that might be lacking.

There was a vibrancy, a life about Naples that Hillie loved. It reminded her of Hong Kong, overcrowded, jostling, people yelling and everywhere the smell of food. The scents of cooking wafted from homes and balconies, from open air pizza ovens, from trattorias and from smart restaurants. You could hardly escape the smell wherever you went, the rich inviting smells of home baked pasta dishes, frying fish, oregano laden pizza, deep fried doughnuts, a speciality from roadside stalls on certain festivals.

Naples had a great tradition of theatres, of music and of galleries and the couple grew to know many writers, artists and intellectuals. Many evenings were spent in the café society of the great glazed Galleria's de Umberto 1, discussing the latest productions, political happenings, new showings at galleries and social gossip amongst the protagonists. Slow gentle evenings, after dinner, sipping coffee or lingering over a glass of wine.

On one such evening Frank and Hillie visited the opera. Hillie loved the Opera House, in all its gilded baroque glory. Sometimes they attended with groups of friends, but on this night they had gone alone. Frank took a box and they drew their chairs close, alone in the darkness. Frank had watched her dress and chosen one of his favourite frocks for her to wear. She had seen him resplendent in his white tie and tails and they had made a striking couple entering the theatre.

Auditoriums such as this always reminded Hillie of churches, the gilt, the carved angels over the proscenium arch, the hush and reverence of the audience, the solemn raising of the curtain, but there the resemblance ended. The acoustics here were famous for their purity and she relaxed back in her seat to enjoy the music. As the opening bars began Hillie felt Frank draw closer and closer to her, his hand reaching for her in the darkness, enveloping her fingers with his own. She felt the pressure tighten and loosen as he became more and more engrossed in the performance. As the curtain descended for the first interval, but before the lights came up, Frank leant over and claimed a small kiss. Hillie never tired of these reaffirmations of their love.

Later, as the theatre emptied into the balmy Neapolitan night, Frank led her to one of their favourite cafes for a final nightcap. They settled outside on the small piazza, gas lights glowing in the street, small candles lighting each table, the occasional gleam of a cigarette burning in the darkness. Hillie took the first sips from her glass of cognac and watched idly as a car drew up outside an office across the square. Two men got out, almost invisible in their black clothing, more perceptible as shadows in the darkness than human forms. As they walked towards the office, one drew out a machine gun and sprayed the front of the building with bullets. The other pulled something that looked like a rock or stone, from his pocket and hurled it through the window.

Hillie, bewildered by the unexpected noise sat frozen, staring, but Frank, recognising the sound from the moment the first spray of gunfire hit the wall, jumped instantly to his feet, knocked over the table they were sitting at and dragged Hillie and himself down behind it. The evening erupted in terror. Further gunfire echoed across the piazza and the boom and splinter of an exploding glass frontage sent smoke and shattered fragments into the air.

'Stay down, stay down, keep low, don't move,' Frank ordered her.

From across the square screams were emanating from the offices of a local newspaper. As Hillie felt her face touch the unyielding stone of the pavement, she shrank into Frank and felt, not just his arms, but his whole body tensed over her, a protective shield to deflect any danger.

'What is it Frank, what is it? '

'Black shirts, Fascists, they are burning out the newspaper offices.'

The couple remained rooted to the pavement, behind their table, listening to the sounds of conflagration, explosion and terror for several minutes more, until, over the noise of the developing blaze, a vehicle was heard to drive away. As Frank helped Hillie clamber slowly to her feet, she realized he was shaking uncontrollably and about to be sick. Recognizing that he was overcome by the all too familiar noise, sound and smells of battle, she took charge of their situation and led him gently out of the piazza into quiet and darkness again. It was many nights before Frank could sleep without recurring nightmares haunting him.

POMPEII 1920

Shafts of early morning sunlight fell across the bed, motes of dust trapped like a gentle snowstorm in its beams and details in the fine lace drapery highlighted like a spider's web in autumn. Frank was luxuriating, his face nestling in the tresses of Hillie's almost black hair. He found a sensuous joy every night as he watched her loosen it, shake it out over her shoulders and brush it over and over in that rhythmic way of hers. He loved the way the hair spilt across the pillow as she slept, allowing him to kiss the locks without waking her and gently run them through his fingertips. Her hair was precious to him, a part of her that he had taken with him to the Front, folded close to his heart always, no matter how terrifying the battle. He marvelled now, that each morning he could wake up beside her, immersed in the scent of her skin, washed over by that hair. He left their bed reluctantly every morning to work but today was Saturday and the hours ahead belonged to them.

Over tea in bed they made their plans for the day and decided upon the excavations below Mt Vesuvius. Frank borrowed the office car and brought it to the front of the villa,

'Bring a cushion Hillie, the roads are rocky, full of holes'

Vesuvius rose up in front of them, majestic, coronal, and they imagined they could see the faintest wisps of smoke emerging from the cone as they headed down the coast road. Frank was adamant they should enjoy the view,

'Let's keep the roof down Hillie, Its more fun when we can feel the wind.' Hillie was more anxious about the sun and dust.

'But my hair...' She protested. Knowing argument was useless she gave in to his laughing eyes, as she always did and tied her sun hat more firmly on her head.

They stopped at a roadside stall to buy water, peaches and bread then drove on, between the vineyards that covered the volcano's lower slopes and the glorious blue shimmer that was the sea. Frank had tried to awaken Hillie's enthusiasm for ruins by reading snippets from the local papers to her. He told her about the excavations, revealing the great Roman city, buried by the volcano and just now beginning to be revealed.

' Do you know, my Darling, that even the cellars of our Villa Rocco Romano have ancient walls within them, the concierge told me, and all the farmers round here and all around the Bay of Naples are forever digging up statues and coins, and bits of old houses. You see them for sale in the markets, but I guess quite a few are fakes.'

Frank loved the idea of all these ancient Romans beneath his feet. His Jesuit education in Liverpool had taught him Latin and classical literature and he told Hillie the story of the eruption, documented by Pliny the Younger. Hillie found the idea of digging up the remains of those long gone less fascinating. She loved the art, the statues and paintings she had seen, but found the idea of poking around inside other people's lives slightly distasteful, disconcerting even. She had the absurd idea that the owner might suddenly return and ask 'why are you scraping through the rubbish of my life, what right have you to be here?' It was an almost ghostly foreboding, but she kept her reservations to herself and tried to match Frank's keenness.

The couple knew they were approaching the site when the roads began to be lined by small impromptu stalls, manned by small boys. The boys ran out, barefooted, into the roadway, forcing approaching traffic to slow or stop and then jumping on the running boards, fists filled with ancient coins or marble statuettes for sale. Frank parked the car beside the dusty roadway and paid a smart looking boy a handful of lira to mind it. Taking the picnic basket in one hand and Hillie's arm in the other he led them away from the raucous market and up the hill towards the ruins. They followed a cleared roadway paved in great blocks of tufa, clearly showing rut marks where ancient carts had passed, through a narrow arched gate and up, as if to a plateau where they stopped and gazed around them.

The walk up was steep and hard going over the paving stones. The sun was high and warm, but there was no sign of the cough or breathlessness that often troubled Frank when he exerted himself too much in the heat of the day. Today he was too excited to feel breathless and spent a few moments just gazing around, to get his bearings.

'We are standing in the middle of a Temple or Forum, Hillie, see, those colonnades look like they were shaken down yesterday.' He pointed to a sea of fallen column drums, lying haphazard, shaken from their bases.

Frank walked about, inspecting a raised altar in the middle of the pavement and ranges of smaller ruined buildings all around. From this plateau they could see a pattern, a grid, of narrow paved streets radiating out. There were doorways and shops and then suddenly streets came to a dead end, blocked by the dark mass of the lava flow and solidified ash that had choked the byways and alleys and not yet cleared by the excavators.

Hillie caught Frank's enthusiasm as he tried to explain to her what he thought each building was. They explored cleared streets and peered into the shadowy entrances of houses, marvelling at statues and columns, lying still, just as they had fallen. Frank held her hands and jumped her over stepping stones and drains or put his hands around her tiny waist and lifted her up to gaze through glassless windows into long abandoned courtyards.

They settled for lunch in a corner shop, complete with counter, wine jars and pots for serving food. Behind them was an oven, looking for the entire world like the brick pizza ovens they saw each day in Naples.

'How old did you say it was Frankie?'

'Nearly two thousand years,' Frank said and lifted her up onto the counter and gave her a lengthy kiss. A fly had the temerity to entangle itself in her hair and he spent a few happy moments gently teasing apart some strands and releasing the intruder. Climbing down they sat silently, backs against a sun warmed wall, watching the lizards that darted out and jittered between the bricks and listening to the cicadas humming through the heat of the day. Leaning back against the wall they sank into their private world again. He kissed her over and over, covering her sun toasted face in gentle tiny kisses that she lovingly returned. Each and every day Frank thought of his life now, and how impossible it must be for any love to be greater than theirs, for any two people to feel so entwined, so complete when they were together and so desolate when they were apart. Hillie stopped and looked up to draw breath, and hearing voices in the distance pulled back from him. 'We must show more decorum 'she laughed. Frank was unconcerned 'These walls have seen it all before, there are paintings here no one will allow the ladies to see, the Romans were very open about things of the body, they saw no shame in love.'

Collecting up the bags they moved on, following the cleared streets wherever they led them. Two- storied houses opened above and shops with wooden shuttering, fossilised by the lava and covered with ancient graffiti, intrigued them and Frank amused himself trying to translate the Latin script. The scrawled handwriting defeated him but on the floor of a porch which opened into a courtyard garden they found a mosaic pavement inlaid with a dog and the words *Cave Canem.* 'Beware of the Dog' he told her triumphantly.

In one area they found a group of workmen clearing and scraping at the walls of a large house. The professor in charge was eager to display his newly uncovered paintings. On the walls, slowly emerging into the light of day for the first time in nearly two thousand years were deep red panels with golden frames.

'We call the colour Pompeian red,' their guide explained, 'it was their favourite colour, we find it all over the town.'

Because Hillie's Italian was fluent the Professor was happy to chat and show off his knowledge and his discoveries. He led them to an adjoining house, where a gate had been erected over the porch. Unlocking it he ushered them into a sunny courtyard with buildings cleared on all sides.

'There is much here waiting to go to the museum, but come see the paintings in the great hall.' Hillie and Frank followed where he indicated.

Inside the sunless hall, once their eyes grew accustomed to the dark, they saw a landscape emerging from the wall, a gentle green hillside in the distance with the Cypress trees forming a backdrop, and in the foreground a tall and gentle lady, in flowing robes with a small angel-like baby on her shoulder. Frank wanted to know who she was.

'We don't really know but we believe she may be a priestess of Dionysus waiting to undergo some trial or sacred ritual. There are other paintings similar around here.' For all their beauty the wall paintings, with their unknown pagan rituals, were sinister and Frank felt Hillie shiver and clutch his arm for reassurance.

'You should look in our store rooms before you go,' the archaeologist said, 'just to the left of the gate where you came in.'

It took time for the couple to find their way back through the streets, the regularity of the grid had a maze like quality. By keeping Vesuvius behind them they gradually worked their way back to the city gate and saw the stores. The doors were open and they wandered in, glad of a little more respite from the glaring sun and hot stone streets outside. They gazed at statues and fountains and carved stone capitals admiring the artistry and skill, until they came to a line of tables down the centre of the store. On the tables lay grey rock like masses, which neither of them recognised until they came up close. Then they saw human figures, turned to stone, petrified by the power of the volcano. Faces that still showed the terror of suffocation. Hands scraping at doors, or clutching at each other in desperate attempts to escape. A mother nursing a baby, a dog chained to a wall.

For Frank it was suddenly overwhelming. These ancient people of Pompeii, felled in the prime of their lives, brought back to him the lines of his soldiers trapped on barbed wire, left where they had fallen or buried forever in the mud of no man's land or the flooded trenches. Two thousand years or three years ago the suffering and the fear, the smell of death and the struggle to escape were all the same.

'Let's go, 'he said, grabbing Hillie's hand, and they fled out into the sunshine.

Posillipo September 1921

Frank prowled around the garden, anxious, restless and as acutely nervous as any man about to become a father might be. He wanted to stay with Hillie throughout her labour and for several of the early hours he refused to leave her side. It seemed incredible to him that he should be banished from her at the very time she might need him the most, when she was in pain, frightened and quite possibly in danger. But he had been ejected from her room as things progressed and finally accepting that he had no role, had headed for the garden.

Although delighted at the prospect of a child, Frank was fearful and did not want Hillie to endanger her life. He knew pregnancy and childbirth were risky. He had heard his mother relate it, time after time, throughout his childhood.

The refrain 'I nearly died having you. It took me weeks to recover and this is how you behave now,' had been a frequent response to any misdemeanour or minor act of rebellion.

The doctor tried to reassure him when they had the pregnancy confirmed.

'Yes the Signora is a little old, at thirty, to be having a first child. Yes, she is small, only just five foot but that does not necessarily mean a difficult or dangerous labour.'

The doctor promised the best of care, great watchfulness and the most skilful midwives. Frank was not to worry and must not transfer his anxieties to his wife.

So here he was in the garden of the Villa Rocco Romana, wandering the gravel paths, flicking dead heads off the roses and listening as the cicadas sang their crazy little hearts out as the heat of the afternoon reached its climax. Frank settled on a low stone wall and stared out over the bay towards Vesuvius. He saw small trails of smoke. Passing wisps of small clouds appeared to trickle out of the volcano, their hot deep breaths emerging from the fiery lungs of the earth. His own chest felt like that sometimes, as if it were burning inside when his exhalations came slowly and with pain. Now too, there was always a cough that he never seemed able to shake off. He had not told Hillie about the pain, not wanting to worry her. But he had consulted the doctor.

'It is the gas, Captain Lawless, the effect of the gas. We do not know the long term damage even the slightest exposure to these chemicals may have caused, nor how to treat it. We can only recommend warm sunshine, fresh air, good fresh food and avoidance of over exertion when the cough is troublesome or the pain severe.'

Frank had declined morphine for the pain and to help him sleep and put his trust in God and the climate of Italy.

Sitting there on his sun-baked wall, Frank thought back over their two years in Italy, the wonderful early days, the novelty of their marriage, their delight in each other, the fulfilment of all their dreams. He thought of this delightful home and all the friends they had made amongst the musicians and artists who thrived on the Neapolitan light and southern European atmosphere. And they had been productive years for him too. As well as working for White Star he had completed two more plays. He had tried to leave all memories of the war behind him, feeling it was too painful and unhelpful to dwell on the horrors. Instead he had tried to put his loathing of all things German into one of his plays, *'The Enemy'* making the central character the embodiment of Teutonic unpleasantness.

Frank loved their home on this pine clad hillside. Someone had told him the name Posillipo had meant *'a stop to pain'* or *'where sadness ends'* in ancient times. It had certainly been both those things to them. He rejoiced that their baby was to be born here. The singing of the cicadas was lost suddenly as he heard Hillie's call,

'Where is Frank, where is he, I want him now!' followed by groaning, the agonising groan of a mother in deep labour. Frank heard the soothing tones of doctor and midwife reassuring her,

'He is close by, hush Signora, keep your energy for the work ahead.'

Frank heard the clatter as the balcony doors were shut against him and knew he must wait until called. He thought back to one of his greatest pleasures, his daily return home from his office in the city. On fine days he would open the great iron gates and approach through the garden along the gravel walks, almost on tiptoe, in case Hillie became aware of his presence. He held his breath as he listened to her accompanying herself on the piano as she sang. The balcony doors were open to the sunlight and the view, and her voice, her sweet delightful voice, tumbled across the air as light and lovely as thistle-down on a summer breeze to greet him.

From their very first arrival in Naples Frank had encouraged Hillie to keep up her singing and had arranged lessons for her at the music conservatoire with one of the best singing masters in Naples. He had never felt jealous of Maestro Tecchio, her teacher. Hillie, he knew, would never, ever give him cause for concern. Never the less, the singing lessons involved a close and intimate encounter between pupil and master, and Frank felt happier staying close by. Usually they arranged her lesson for late in the morning, just before lunch and Frank could leave his office and head to the conservatoire to meet her. If he got there in good time he liked to stand in the courtyard, sometimes sheltered beneath an archway, sometimes wandering quietly along its cloister. It was a quiet, shady, ancient building, just set back from a bustling street. The windows of the practice rooms and studios were often open and listening to some student practising a scale on the piano or attempting a piece of some difficult work, repeating it over and over until it was right, made him smile. And above these medleys of musicians at practice, Frank strained to hear Hillie's voice, repeating a phrase or reaching a note. He knew Maestro Tecchio thought highly of her voice, and believed she had the capacity to become a professional singer but Hillie was happy as she was, singing for him, or at the parties and impromptu concerts they gave or attended. She was not interested in large audiences or greater adulation. Besides, her singing had taken a secondary role now that their baby was expected.

Poor Hillie, she had been so seedy, so sick those first few weeks that she had lost interest in most things, but as spring had opened she had blossomed, feeling well, glowing and optimistic and with a gently expanding waistline that he teased her about endlessly. Frank thought back to how much he had loved that swelling stomach, stroked and kissed it and felt their child's movements. Those first gentle flutters that had grown stronger as summer progressed and become the hefty kicks and squirms of later pregnancy.

That summer had taken a toll on Hillie. To be seven, eight, nine months pregnant in the full heat of a Neapolitan summer had been draining and she had given up nearly all her usual activities. They would walk together in the early morning before sunrise, enjoying the clear light as they explored the gardens, or in the cool of evening, watching the setting sun over the sea. Frank had felt so protective of her then, her figure so changed, her neat waistline gone, hidden under a voluminous dress that seemed to trap the heat. He was proud of her too. She had never complained of the hot days, the weight of the child, the discomfort that kept her awake at night. He loved her and their baby with the same fierceness and tenacity that he had felt for her when he was in the trenches, the time when staying alive to be with his small angel wife again was all that mattered.

And now, when she needed him most he was excluded, left to pace the garden alone and in limbo. As the evening gathered in he could see lights come on in their bedroom and shadows flit across the window gauzes. No further sounds of labour were audible, no clues as to how things were progressing. For four more hours, well into the darkness of the night, Frank waited. The cicadas had fallen silent and moths the size of sparrows had inhabited their nocturnal space. He had watched the moon rise and the city below light up and he had heard the church bells measure the passing hours. Once he turned, excited, heart pounding as he heard a door open nearby and a figure come towards him, but it was only the cook, come to offer him an unwanted dinner. Finally, just before midnight, he heard the balcony door open above him and the doctor's voice call down.

'Come, come now Signor Captain, all is well'

Frank raced up the stairs his breath catching, burning in his throat as he ran, and burst into the apartment. The midwife opened the bedroom door and smiled,

'Congratulations Signor! '

Leaning back against a mountain of pillows was his Hillie, his small angel, pale, exhausted but smiling. Sleeping in a crib beside her bed was their tiny child, swaddled tight but with a seraphic expression and a mop of damp black hair showing.

'Hillie, my darling Hillie, my brave, brave girl' Frank buried his face in her sweat soaked hair, her beautiful neck and sobbed. His relief was palpable. When he was able to speak again he asked her, 'How are you, my darling?'

'I am tired and sore but fine' Hillie looked down at the tightly swaddled bundle in her arms. 'But Frankie look, we have a daughter.'

Frank looked down at the child and stroked her face with his finger. The baby stirred, rooting towards his touch.

'She has your hair Hillie. And your little chin.'

They both stared at their baby for several minutes in silent awe, taking in the monumental nature of the change to both their lives.

'I think she is the image of you Frankie, look at the tiny nose and dip between her nose and mouth, they are just like yours.' They both giggled,

'We never thought of having a little girl Hillie, did we? We always thought it would be a boy. I am overjoyed and proud to have another young lady to call my own, to love and protect. What shall we call her?'

'We do not want old family names from the past, no maiden aunts or aged grandmothers. She must have a new name of her own.' Hillie said decidedly.

Frank laughed again,

'We will start our own new dynasty. There were famous queens of Naples once, called Giovanna. We will call her Giovanna Maria, and if all that is too much of a mouthful for such a little girl, she can be Janna to us at home.'

Finding Frank

GIOVANNA MARIA WAS BAPTISED IN the Church of Santa Maria della Consolatzione around Christmas 1921. She wore a handmade, cream silk Christening gown, trimmed with lace and satin rosettes, made for her by local nuns. Frank held her over the font with great pride and care.

The gown that Frank held that day has since been worn by his grandchildren, great- grandchildren and great-great- grandchildren at their baptisms, a tangible and fragile link over five generations.

Posillipo April 1922

The early April sun warmed Hillie through as she sat, exhausted, on the terrace. Amelia had brought the baby out to her, in the hope that Janna's chubby smiles and coo's would cheer her. But tiredness enveloped her like a chilly mist and she had waved the child away, wanting only to close her eyes for a few minutes.

There had been no sleep last night, as she lay beside Frank, listening to the rasping of his breathing, the feverish restlessness and the outbursts of a deep choking cough. Hillie had risen numerous times to refresh a cool flannel and wiping down his fevered face. She had turned down the blankets to try and cool his sweating neck and chest as the doctor had instructed. When he was conscious she offered sips of water but there was little else she could do for him. This time his chest was worse, the cough deeper, more strangled, each breath seemed more effortful as Frank drifted in and out of a delirious consciousness. Sometimes he knew her, held her hand, told his small angel all would be well by morning. But at other times she could hear him call out to his invisible men, 'Shoot', 'hold your fire' 'fire to the right' 'halt!' All was jumbled, nonsensical to her but meaningful to his confused and overheated memories.

It hurt him to breathe. Hillie could tell that from the effort, the struggle he made to keep each breath going, to move forward to the next. And she whispered to him constantly, 'For me Frank, for us, for Janna, take that next breath.' She could not even bear to think that the effort might become too much.

This morning the nursing nuns had come, two of them from the hospital of Santa Maria. There was no point taking him to hospital the doctor had told Hillie, he was better off at home, in his own bed.

'Let the sun in upon him and the good fresh air, I have no other medicines to offer him. The nuns will wash him, feed him if they can, help him to stay cool, pray for him and allow you to rest.'

Hillie had left the nuns, wimples bent low over her beloved man, sponges in hand, calm, professional and detached. And she had come out and sat on the terrace and listened to the spring chirruping of the flurries of sparrows in the hedges, to blackbirds marking territory, building nests, preparing for new life.

Collared doves were cooing softly amongst the almond blossom and finally Hillie's eyes closed as she prayed and prayed that the fever would reach its crisis soon and the inflamed and gas damaged lungs would recover as they had each time before. Her fingers closed tightly around the silver cap badge, the Eagle and Child, which she had worn around her neck every single day since Frank gave it to her, a talisman for his survival. How often she had clasped it, rubbed it, pressed it against her chest. As she did so now, she felt it snap in two.

Hillie slept fitfully for an hour or so then awakened suddenly. Realizing how long she had been absent from his side, she rushed back to the bedroom.

Frank was dozing, propped up on a heap of pillows, eyes closed and his cheeks drawn. His breathing was soft, low and rasping and the interval between each gasp seemed longer to Hillie, than when she had left him. She stood, counting the seconds between each rise and fall of his chest, trying to judge the length of the pauses. The nuns were kneeling now, one each side of the bed, rosary beads slipping through their fingers, counting off their prayers as Hillie counted the laboured heavings.

'We should call Father Paulo, Signora' said one of the sisters, 'Signor Lawless needs his blessing, the sacrament of the sick.'

Hillie's brain collapsed for a few moments in terror. All those awful words flew past her, Extreme Unction, the Sacrament of the sick, the dying, Fortified by the Rites of our Holy Mother the Church. Where were God's holy angels now? She wrested back control of her thoughts again. What would Frank want? What would help him, give him strength?

She nodded to the sister, 'Si, Padre Paulo' and silently the nun rose and left the room.

'Can he still hear me?' she asked the remaining nun.

'I believe so, come, talk to him, hold his hand, encourage him.'

'Please, call the doctor back and ask Amelia to bring the baby.'

Hillie sat down beside Frank, leaning back on the pillows. Amelia crept in with the sleeping child. Hillie lifted Frank's arm and placed the baby in the crook.

'Listen Frank, Janna is here, she's waking, feel her wriggling in your arms.'

She leant over and raised his other hand, making it stroke the baby's face. She placed the baby's fist close to his finger and instinctively the little hand unfurled and clasped it.

Hillie was sure Frank stirred in response to the child's grasp. A wisp of a smile crossed his face then faded slowly as if the effort was too much for him.

'She has a tooth now Frank, it came through two days ago, Amelia has her eating real food, cereal, mashed fruit, she has a splendid appetite. She makes us laugh, her face all covered with food. You will see her in a day or two, when you are feeling stronger. She is longing to show her daddy all her new skills. She is looking more like you every day.'

When the doctor arrived he stood quietly at the door as Hillie lifted the baby and placed her little rosy cheeks, one by one against Frank's lips. She saw him make a tiny stirring of movement, the merest effort, and then returned the baby to the nursemaid. The doctor crossed the room and took a stethoscope from his bag.

'Does he seem worse?' he asked.

'The breathing is slower, I wondered if he was in pain. Last night it seemed painful and the coughing harsh, but now it is more peaceful, just slower, each breath seems slower than the last.' Hillie brushed her fingers over Frank's brow.

The doctor opened Frank's nightshirt and listened to the front side of his chest, then Hillie held Frank propped against her shoulders, whilst the stethoscope was placed, slowly, deliberately across his back. Frank seemed insensible as Hillie and the doctor laid him back against the pillows, the examination completed. She waited expectantly for the doctor's verdict.

'I do not think he is in pain Signora Lawless. His lungs have filled with patches of fluid, the bronchitis has turned to pneumonia. It is painless. We will just have to wait, to see if he has the strength left in those lungs to fight it off. I will come back this evening'

'Is there nothing more you can do?' Hillie heard the crack of despair in her own voice.

'You must continue to keep him cool, I will leave more aspirin for the fever, if he is conscious enough to swallow it but I have nothing to treat the infection, he must fight that battle for himself. I will ask the sisters to remain with you to assist.'

Hillie opened wide the balcony doors to let the April breeze, which blew gently in from the Bay of Naples, fan over Frank's face. She unpinned the restraining chignon on her head and lay down beside him, burying his hand within her hair. A sunbeam fell into the room and as she lay, minute after minute, hour after hour, it tracked time like a sundial across the floor, marking out his final moments.

Hillie was unsure when she first realized his breathing had ended, maybe as the priest quietly opened the door and stood at the foot of the bed, unwilling to disturb her but anxious to offer the sacrament. She looked down at Frank and bent to kiss him, holding her lips close, hoping, hoping to feel the slightest turbulence of air, but there was none.

She stood up and indicated to Fr Paulo to begin his anointing and commendation of a departing soul.

As he invoked the Holy Angels Hillie returned once more to the balcony and the wail of anguish from her heart reverberated over the bay, past every ship, every mountain and was echoed back by every building, every cliff, every person. Her sobs, a receding tide of sadness, took many hours to stem.

Finding Frank

WITH THE POWER OF THE internet and the help of the Consul, The British Cemetery proved easy to find. And there you were, unvisited for ninety years, lying on a pine clad hillside above the city.

A grave, framed in white marble, with your D.S.O. and regimental badge carved out in pride on the top.

Captain Francis Lawless DSO
Beloved husband of Hilda
Died at Naples 9th April 1922
Age 31 Years
Till we your loving wife and little daughter meet you again

And as we laid flowers, the red roses that Hilda loved, we cried for her loss, picturing her standing there, inconsolable, bewildered.

We cried too for our loss, that we had never known you, except by repute. We cried for the waste of your young life, a life of so much promise and for the pain you must have felt in leaving.

Naples May 1922

Hillie's diminutive figure, as she was helped out of the cab, appeared shrunken and diminished. She was encased in black, with a cloche hat and demi veil that obscured her face and a calf length linen coat that wrapped the rest of her. There was no mistaking her widowhood. Amelia, nursing the baby, clambered from the back of the cab and a bevy of porters emerged from the noisy crowd on the dockside to pick up the cabin baggage and take it on board.

Hillie looked over the baggage to check all was there and clutched tightly at the only piece she carried herself, refusing to relinquish it to an over eager porter. It was a soft brown leather attaché case, scuffed and worn but containing every letter Frank her written to her from the Front, his plays and his diaries, the love poems and silly rhymes he made up for her, his medals and citations, their marriage certificate, his death certificate and a drawing of the marble headstone that marked his grave. Everything that proved to her their life together had once existed, nestled inside that bag. Hillie sighed and started to move towards the boarding gangway.

As she reached the foot of the walkway her escort touched her arm.

'Is there nothing we can say to persuade you stay in Naples,' her singing master asked, 'no sunshine, no future, and no chance for your beautiful voice to join our Opera? We would all care for you here.'

Hillie looked at him with a grave smile. 'I am honoured Signor, by your kindness towards myself and my daughter, and I thank you for all your recent help and support but there is nothing to keep me in Italy any longer.'

He kissed her hand in a reluctant farewell and she began the long walk up to the first class deck, heading the small, sad procession of nurse, baby and shore porters. As Hillie reached the deck the Captain came forward to offer his personal greeting and welcome her on board.

'The company offers you our deepest condolences, Mrs Lawless, all of us who knew Frank, valued him. Please just ask if there is anything you need that my crew can provide for you.'

Everything however, even a bassinet for the baby, had already been provided. Amelia put the baby down and began to unpack and Hillie sat at the walnut dressing table, musing as she lifted off her hat and veil and loosened one or two of the pins that held up her long black hair into its painful and overly severe bun.

She gazed about the cabin, but nothing held her attention for long. She opened her case and took out the envelope that Frank's manager in the White Star office had handed her. It contained a copy of the eulogy he had given at the funeral, intended for Frank's parents, so that they would know again and again, how much he had been valued and respected. She did not need such reminders herself, but nevertheless opened it and read again the words first heard in that sad oration.

Captain Francis Henry Lawless (Frank) D.S.O.
It is with great sadness that we gather today to mourn the untimely death of Frank Lawless here in Naples at the age of 31.

Frank was born in Liverpool and had worked for the White Star Line since leaving school, in a variety of shore based roles. His skills as an administrator were highly regarded and he was a loyal and trustworthy employee of the company.

Frank served his country with great bravery during the recent war, enlisting in the City Battalions of the King's Liverpool Regiment at its outbreak and rising through the ranks to Captain and finally Acting Major. He was three times mentioned in despatches and twice wounded and was awarded the Distinguished Service Order for conspicuous gallantry.

Frank's health suffered from the effects of his military service on the Front and on his return to civilian life he was promoted by the company to assist in the management the new office here in Naples. He was a man with many friends and a wide range of interests outside the company including music and particularly a great love of literature. He was man of great faith and spirituality and many of us here today will remember his pride and delight as he and Hilda presented their baby daughter Giovanna Maria for Baptism only four months ago.

Sadly his health never fully recovered from his war service and he died on the 9th April.

Frank will always be remembered as a dear friend and colleague, a cheerful and stimulating companion and a brave man.

The company would like to extend their sincere condolences to his widow Hilda and baby daughter.

The air in the cabin grew oppressive and Hillie bolted for the deck, struggling with the grief that threatened her.

Naples was basking, unconcerned, in May sunshine as Hillie leaned against the rails and watched the purposeful activity of the Port and her own ship's departure. They were moored alongside the *SS Adriatic*, a White Star Liner heading for New York. Proudly emblazoned in company livery, its two buff funnels with their distinctive black stripe, the red flag with the bright white star and *SS Adriatic Liverpool* painted on the side. The last of the luggage was being loaded into her holds, and the third class passengers poured up their own gangway to steerage. Hundreds of bright, eager, young Italians, all leaving their homeland for a better life in America. Hillie envied them; they had optimism, a future, something to look forward too, whilst she had nothing. She was leaving the only thing she had ever wanted, here in Naples. Perhaps one of Frank's last jobs had been to organize these emigrants' passage to their promised lands.

Hillie felt the vibrations as the *Arcadia's* turbines started up and the steam from the funnels obscured the blue Neapolitan sky. Frank could have told her exactly how many hours a Welsh miner needed to work to produce the coal that drove those turbines for a single minute, or powered the solitary blast of the ship's horn as she began to pull away from the dock and move out into the bay. He would have known every detail of the ships manifest, how many passengers and crew, from laundrymen to surgeons. It was his job to know what cargo she carried and what supplies she needed, from drinking water to fresh flowers, for the final leg of her voyage from Naples.

Hillie remained on deck all the afternoon and into the evening, gazing always towards the shore, seeking the final sight of the rocky hillside where she had left Frank, in a grave she knew she might never be able to afford to visit again. She had left instructions with the consulate to have the grave tended, and money for Masses with the cathedral, but she would never take flowers there again, as she had done every day for the last month, nor be able to show her daughter where her father lay.

Only now did she fully realize what the immensity of Frank's being gone meant.

She was angry with him then. How could he have left her alone like this, how could he not be there to hold her hand, to guide her, to love her every moment of every day. When he was at the Front he had promised her he would come home and he had kept that promise, he *had* come back, when so many others had not, he had been wounded and damaged but stayed alive. He had no right to die now, when the war was over, when they had a future, a child to care for.

She thought back to the days in London and Liverpool, when he had come home wounded or on leave, to their wedding day in Scotland, and then all their hopes and plans for the future.

For three years, after the war had finally ended, she had lain beside him, listening each night to the coughing from his gas-damaged lungs. She heard and felt his terrible distress as recurrent nightmares forced him to recall the sights and sounds and smells of battle. Together, they had prayed so hard for healing, hoping that time and the warmth and colour of Italy would soothe away the hurts inflicted by his war. And they had laughed and sung and made a baby. Frank started to write again, plays and poetry, with grand plans for their life together. But in the end the Kaiser's gas and the filth of the trenches had completed the work they had begun at the Front, taking his strength and youth and finally his life.

Hillie found it impossible to visualise a future for herself and had no idea how she would even live. The company had offered a passage home and a month's salary but after that what was there? They would return to England, to join half a million other young widows and fatherless children. This ship would take her to Liverpool and the comparison between the brightness of Italy and the grey rain of Lancashire overwhelmed her. She might meet Frank's parents there, show them the baby, but she could not live there. She had no idea what to do with a baby. How would she manage after Amelia left? She supposed she would go to London and stay with mother. Even though it made her feel like a child again, dependent when she had been free.

Dusk began to fall over the bay of Naples as the ship steamed gently north and the setting sun was replaced by the lights of the city and glow of Vesuvius behind. As long as she could see that warming light Hillie felt in touch with the land where Frank lay.

For a while the light of the volcano glowed strongly but as the distance between ship and shore grew greater the light dimmed and finally faded to nothing.

With no tears left Hillie turned to the other side of the ship, facing England.

EPILOGUE

HILLIE PAID ONE SHORT VISIT to Frank's family as she passed through Liverpool. After that his parents never saw her or their granddaughter again and Janna grew up with no memory of her paternal grandparents.

Hillie returned to London to live with her recently widowed mother. She sank into deep sadness and Janna was primarily raised by her maternal grandmother and her Uncle and Aunt, William and Dorothy, alongside their only child John. John and Janna grew up very close as brother and sister. John followed his father into the Royal Navy in 1944 on leaving school. He served as Sub Lieutenant on a motor torpedo boat in the North Sea. He died on active service there aged 19 years, shot in the back by a sniper on a surfacing German U Boat.

Hillie died suddenly in 1946, aged 57, after 24 years of widowhood and ten days before the birth of her first grandchild. Frank's D.S.O. and photograph had stood proudly at her bedside throughout those years. After her death the medal was stolen by her younger brother Alan, and sold. Its whereabouts today are unknown.

In December 1922   Hillie wrote a final letter to the war office;

Finchley Road London
Sir
I have the honour to make application for 'The King's In Memoriam Scroll' and for the 'National Plaque' in respect of my late husband Captain Francis Henry Lawless, D.S.O. 18th Battalion, King's Liverpool Regiment and 1st Lincolnshire Regiment.

My husband died at Naples on 9th April 1922 and the House of Lords Pension Appeal tribunal allowed my appeal for a pension 'on the grounds that the disease from which my husband suffered was attributable to his war service'

I have subsequently been awarded a pension by the Ministry of Pensions.

My husband was awarded the Distinguished Service Order for services during the great German offensive in March 1918 and was three times mentioned in despatches.

I am, sir
Your Obedient Servant
Hilda Lawless

Hillie received her scroll and plaque. The plaque is inscribed;

FRANCIS HENRY LAWLESS
HE DIED FOR FREEDOM AND HONOUR

We will remember them

J. C. ALEXANDER HAS ALWAYS been fascinated by tales of her grandfather's heroism during World War I. She was saddened by the fact that she never had the chance to meet the extraordinary man. When she discovered his letters, Alexander drew on her creative writing studies at Edinburgh and dedicated herself to researching his story and sharing it with the world.

Alexander was born in Kent and grew up Shropshire, England. She studied archaeology at Newcastle University and spent many years working as a field archaeologist in the north of England. She still lives in the north with her husband. They have five children and five grandchildren.

SOURCES

⟶ᕰ

The Letters of Captain F H Lawless D.S.O. 1916-1919
The Field Diary   25th March – 1st April 1918   Cap't F H Lawless D.S.O.
Adjutant 18th Battalion   The Kings Liverpool Regiment
Military Service Records   Francis Henry Lawless 1914-1919
The History of the 89th Brigade 1914-18   Brigadier-General F C Stanley
Liverpool 1919
The V.C. and D.S.O. Year Book Vol 3   Facsimile reprinted by Navel and
Military Press
The History of the Kings Liverpool Regiment Vol 3 1918-1919   Everard
Wyrall   facsimile reprinted by the Naval and Military Press
The History of the Inns of Court OTC   General Errington
Liverpool Pals   Graham Maddocks Pen and Sword 1991

Music
Faith of our Fathers Hymn F W Faber
Moon Goddess from *Madam Butterfly* G Puccini
Aria from *Roedelinda* G F Handel /Haym
Angels from the Realms of Glory Carol James Montgomery